DARIUS THE GREAT
DESERVES BETTER

DARIUS THE GREAT DESERVES BETTER

ADIB KHORRAM

DIAL BOOKS

DIAL BOOKS
An imprint of Penguin Random House LLC, New York

First published in the United States of America by Dial Books, an imprint of Penguin Random House LLC, 2020

Visit us online at penguinrandomhouse.com.

Library of Congress Cataloging-in-Publication Data

Names: Khorram, Adib, author.
Title: Darius the Great deserves better / Adib Khorram.
Description: New York : Dial Books, [2020] | Audience: Ages 12 and up. |
  Audience: Grades 7-9. | Summary: "Darius Kellner has everything he
  thought he wanted—a new boyfriend, a new internship, and a spot on the
  soccer team—but growing up makes him question everything"— Provided by
  publisher.
Identifiers: LCCN 2020008231 (print) | LCCN 2020008232 (ebook) | ISBN
  9780593108239 (hardcover) | ISBN 9780593108253 (trade paperback) | ISBN
  9780593108246 (epub)
Subjects: CYAC: Family life—Fiction. | Dating (Social customs)—Fiction. |
  Gays--Fiction. | High schools--Fiction. | Schools—Fiction. | Iranian
  Americans—Fiction.
Classification: LCC PZ7.1.K5362 Dal 2020 (print) | LCC PZ7.1.K5362
  (ebook) | DDC [Fic]—dc23
LC record available at https://lccn.loc.gov/2020008231
LC ebook record available at https://lccn.loc.gov/2020008232

Printed in the United States of America

10 9 8 7 6 5 4 3 2 1

Design by Cerise Steel
Text set in Chaparral Pro

FOR MY FRIENDS, FOR KEEPING ME GOING

THE HISTORY
OF CREATION

The first cut is always the hardest.

"You ready?"

I met Mikaela's eyes in the mirror.

"Yeah."

The clippers buzzed to life and growled in my ear as she pushed the teeth through the back of my hair. The curls tickled my neck as they fell to the floor.

It was tradition among the student athletes on Chapel Hill High School's varsity men's soccer team (Go Chargers!) to get their hair cut before the first game of the season. It was supposed to promote team unity.

Except I had my internship at Rose City Teas on Sunday when everyone else got their haircuts, so I had to make a separate appointment.

It was my first haircut in two years.

"How high do you want this fade?" Mikaela asked as she neared my ears.

I'd never met Mikaela before, but Landon recommended her. She was beautiful, with brown skin, impeccable box braids, and the brightest smile I'd ever seen.

I shrugged, but I wasn't sure she could tell from under the plastic cover. "I don't know," I said. "What do you think would look best?"

She turned off the clippers and looked at me in the mirror for a second. "Probably something higher for you. Show off these beautiful curls up top."

"Okay."

I relaxed and let her turn my head this way and that as she worked, first with clippers and then with a pair of scissors. When she was done, Mikaela took me to the hair-washing station. I guess it wasn't designed for tall people: I had to scoot my butt to the edge of the chair to fit my head in the basin. But she washed my hair and massaged my scalp (which was just about the nicest thing I had ever felt) and got all the itchy bits off, and then it was back to the chair for styling.

"You use product?"

I shook my head.

She pulled at one of my curls—she hadn't touched the top, except for a little trimming—and twisted it around her finger.

"Landon said you're . . . Indian?"

"Iranian. Half."

"Sorry." She let the curl fall. "Lucky boy."

My cheeks warmed.

"Thanks."

Mikaela squeezed something that smelled like coconuts into her hands and massaged it into my hair. It made it a little shinier but kept it soft. She took one last lock from the very front and pulled it down into my forehead, so it dangled like a little question mark.

"All set."

I studied myself in the mirror. Instead of my usual messy

halo, I had a huge pile of curls up top, but the sides and back of my head faded from super short black hair down to my skin.

I hadn't seen the sides of my head in years.

I'd never noticed how much my ears stuck out.

"It looks great," I said, even though I was kind of anxious about my ears. "Really."

"Yeah it does," Mikaela said. "Let's go ring you up."

Landon was waiting for me up front. He got this big goofy smile on his face when he saw me.

"Wow."

I smiled and looked down to open the Velcro on my wallet.

"You like it?"

"I really do."

Landon's hand brushed mine, and I curled my thumb to trap it. He wove our fingers together and led me out the sliding glass doors.

It was one of Portland's perfect fall days, where it was warm enough that you didn't have to wear your hoodie, but cool enough that it was cozy if you did.

(I had on my hoodie.)

"Isn't Mikaela the best?"

"Yeah." I pressed my ear flat against the side of my head with my left hand. "I didn't realize I had such huge Ferengi ears."

"Your ears are cute." He pulled me to a stop and stood on his toes to give me a kiss on the cheek. "But what's a Ferengi?"

The first time Landon kissed me, we had eaten at Northwest Dumplings after closing up shop at Rose City, and I'd been nervous, because I'd never kissed anyone before. And at the time, we were still just hanging out. I didn't go in expecting to kiss him, which is why I made the extremely unfortunate choice of having too many onions at dinner.

When Landon leaned in close, I thought maybe I had something in my teeth. Because I never thought someone like him would want to kiss someone like me.

But then he took my hand. And he said, "Hey. Can I kiss you?"

And I was kind of surprised and amazed, because I really liked Landon, and I really did want him to kiss me.

I wanted my first kiss to be with Landon Edwards.

His lips were warm and soft, and he let them linger against mine. But then I made the mistake of sighing, which blew a noxious cloud of onion breath into his mouth.

He broke the kiss and giggled.

I panicked at first—I thought I had messed everything up—but he smiled at me. He squeezed my hand and said, "That was good. Even with the onions. Can we do it again?"

So we did, and the kissing got even better once we started using our tongues.

But my favorite part was the way Landon looked at me after and said, "You're beautiful, you know."

No one had ever called me beautiful before.

"You're beautiful too."

I'd gotten better about food choices since then. And keeping breath mints in my messenger bag.

"Come on. The streetcar should be here."

But then, as we turned the corner, my stomach dropped.

Chip Cusumano and Trent Bolger were walking down the street, jostling each other and laughing about something.

Cyprian Cusumano was the strangest guy I knew. He used to be kind of mean to me, but ever since the end of sophomore year, he'd turned around and been nicer.

We'd actually become friends.

I mean, it helped that we both played on the Chapel Hill High School varsity men's soccer team (Go Chargers!). It was the first year on the team for both of us—Chip used to play football in the fall—but we'd both managed to get spots on the varsity squad.

Trent Bolger, on the other hand, was the meanest guy I knew. He'd been picking on me since elementary school.

And yet for some strange reason—some Byzantine logic that defied explanation—Chip and Trent were best friends.

Landon must have noticed it when my shoulders hunched up, because his step faltered. Which is exactly when Chip looked up from his phone and caught my eye.

He looked from me to Landon, and then down at our linked hands, and then back to me.

Chip already knew I was gay—the whole team knew, since I told them at one of our team-building things when training started over the summer—but I was pretty sure Trent did not.

In fact, I was certain Trent did not, because when he saw me and Landon, he looked like Christmas had come early.

"You know those guys?" Landon asked.

"Yeah. From school. I play with the taller one."

Chip had grown at least an inch over the summer. He was almost as tall as me now, and I had plateaued at six three over the summer.

I kind of hoped I would hit six four eventually.

"Hey, Darius." Chip grinned at me. Cyprian Cusumano was one of those guys who always seemed to be grinning. He wore a pair of black Adidas joggers—the same kind I wore, with the white stripes down the sides and the tapered calves—and a plain white V-neck T-shirt.

"Hey, Chip."

"Nice haircut."

"Thanks. You too."

Chip always had nice haircuts. He was a Level Eight Influencer at Chapel Hill High School: Whatever haircut he got, about half the guys in our class ended up doing some variation of it. Now that he was doing the Standard Soccer Team Fade, though, I wasn't sure what everyone else would do.

"Oh. Chip, this is my—"

The thing is, Landon and I hadn't talked about whether we were officially boyfriends. Even if it felt like we kind of were.

How did you ask a guy if you were officially boyfriends?

"This is Landon. Landon, Chip. And that's Trent."

Trent was hanging back, playing with his phone. He wore a crimson sweatshirt that read PROPERTY OF CHHS VARSITY FOOTBALL—he'd finally made the varsity team this year, as a something-back—and a pair of black swishy shorts.

Chip was still grinning, but he looked Landon up and down. Almost like he was judging him. "Nice to meet you." He held out his fist.

Landon blinked for a second and then bumped his own with Chip's.

It was the most awkward fist bump in the history of creation.

"Well," I squeaked. I cleared my throat. "We've gotta catch the streetcar. See you later?"

Chip bumped fists with me too. "Yeah. See you."

I stepped to the side so he and Trent could make it past us and tightened my grip on Landon's hand.

"Later, Dairy Queen," Trent said.

Great.

ZERO POINT
SIX EIGHT SECONDS

Rose City Teas was in the Northwest District, a couple stops down the streetcar line from Mikaela's salon. It was a brick building with ivy growing up one side, and a little wooden sign hanging over the door. Big windows made up one wall, with the shades half-drawn against the afternoon sun. In the corner, shelves of tea tins lined one wall, and opposite it, the tasting bar was packed with afternoon customers.

Rose City Teas was a dream come true.

Landon's dad waved from the door to the tasting room, wiped his hands on the towel he always kept over his shoulder, and came to greet us.

He squeezed Landon's shoulder—he and Landon had never hugged each other in front of me, which I thought was kind of weird—and then squeezed mine too.

"Hey, son. Looking sharp, Darius. How're you doing?"

"Thanks, Mr. E. I'm okay. How about you?"

"B-plus, A-minus," he said with a wink.

Elliott Edwards had the same gray eyes as his son. And the same auburn hair, though his thick eyebrows and well-kept beard were more brownish. And I couldn't say for sure, but I suspected that underneath his beard he had the same excellent cheekbones as Landon too.

Landon Edwards had television cheekbones. They were

angular and beautiful and always looked like he was blushing. Just a tiny bit.

"I thought you were going to Darius's tonight?"

"I am," Landon said.

We were still holding hands.

I really liked holding Landon's hand.

"We were close. Thought we might as well stop by."

"Well, perfect timing. Come try this. Polli, can you handle things?"

Polli was one of the managers at Rose City. She was an older white lady—probably about my grandmothers' age—who always wore all black except for her scarves, which were wildly colorful, and her glasses, which were huge neon-yellow squares.

She seemed like the kind of person who should have been a judge on some kind of reality show. Or owned an antique bookshop, where she catalogued and dispensed esoteric knowledge while sipping espressos from tiny cups.

Polli waved at us and kept talking to a customer about the benefits of local honey.

Mr. Edwards led us into the tasting room, a small room partitioned from the main dining room by a frosted glass wall with the Rose City logo etched into it. The table was set with a row of gaiwans, full of damp, bright green leaves; and in front of those, tasting cups full of steaming emerald liquor.

"Here." He handed us both ceramic spoons. I let Landon go first, dipping his spoon into each cup one by one and slurping up the tea. It was a robust, grassy green.

"Oh, wow," I said when I tasted the third one, which had this burst of something—maybe fruity?—on the finish.

Mr. E's eyebrows danced. "Right? Any guesses?"

"Hm." I tasted number four, but number three was definitely the best. "Gyokuro?"

Gyokuro was a green tea from Japan, famous for being shaded for three weeks before plucking, which made it taste sweeter and smoother.

"Close. It's Kabusecha."

"What's that?"

"It's like Gyokuro but with only a week of shading."

"Oh."

I took another slurp of number three.

"It's awesome."

Mr. Edwards smiled. "I thought you'd like it."

"Are you gonna get some?"

He sighed and shook his head. "Too pricey to be worth it."

"Oh."

One of the things I'd learned from interning at Rose City was, sometimes the best teas weren't the most practical for a business.

I guess I understood that.

"You want the rest?" He grabbed a paper pouch covered in Japanese writing.

"You sure?"

"Positive."

"Thanks!"

"All right," Landon said. "We'd better go. Pick me up at nine?"

"Sure. Have fun. Make smart choices. Be safe."

"Don't be weird."

Mr. Edwards just laughed as Landon led me out.

Dad's car was gone when I punched in the code to the garage door.

I untied my black Sambas and stuck them in the shoe rack while the door rumbled shut behind us.

Landon kicked off his shoes and slotted them next to mine, then followed me into the living room.

"Sorry it's kind of a mess," I said, even though I'd vacuumed over the weekend.

"Don't be."

I checked the fridge for a note or something.

"Everything okay?"

"My dad was supposed to be home."

I sent him a text to ask where he was.

Landon had come over before, but Mom or Dad had always been home.

The back of my neck prickled.

I checked all the counters, and the table too, but there was no sign of where Dad had gone, just a pile of dishes in the sink. As soon as Landon saw them, he rolled up his sleeves and started washing them.

"I can do those," I said.

"I like doing them."

"I'll dry, then."

I stood next to Landon, taking plates and bowls and glasses and drying them with one of the blue-and-white tea towels Mom seemed to have an endless supply of.

Our dishwasher had broken over the summer, and with Mom and Dad's savings depleted from our trip to Iran, we hadn't been able to replace it.

Who knew Shirin Kellner's tea towel collection would prove so useful?

After I dried the last plate, Landon took the towel from me and wiped up the sink and counters and backsplash. He looked up at me. "You okay?"

"Yeah."

What did you do when you were home alone with the guy you were seeing, and there were no more chores to do?

I grabbed my messenger bag off the chair. "I guess I better put this away."

Landon followed me up the stairs. My pulse pounded against my eardrums.

"You sure?"

"Yeah. Why?"

"Your face is all red."

"Oh." I swallowed. "It's just. Dad didn't leave a note or anything. And we've never been alone like this before."

Landon sat on my bed. I hung my bag on the hook in my closet and turned to face him.

"And I feel like maybe we should be kissing or something."

Landon laughed at that. "We don't have to if you don't want to. We can just talk."

"I like kissing you, though."

Landon smiled and bit his lip.

"I like kissing you too."

He brought his hand up to my face, and then ran his fingers

along the edges of my fade. I hadn't had bare skin there in a long time, and it made me tingle all over.

I really liked that.

I also really liked how Landon was very slow and deliberate with his lips. He had the fullest lips I'd ever seen on a white guy.

I didn't like it as much when Landon put his other hand on my stomach, because I had to suck in my gut, and that made it a little harder to breathe and still keep up with the kissing.

I did like how it felt when my tongue met his. How careful he was with it.

But then I didn't like it when Landon moved his hand lower, and his fingertips brushed the skin beneath my waistband.

I couldn't tell if he was doing it on purpose or not, but I didn't know how to stop him. Especially since, like I said, I really did like the kissing part a great deal, and to say something I would have had to stop.

And then, of course, I didn't like it at all when Dad popped his head into my room.

"Darius, can you come help me with Lal—oh."

Landon yelped as I accidentally bit down on his tongue. We sprang apart.

I covered my lap with my hands.

"Oh." Dad's face was at Red Alert. He looked down the hall. His eyes flicked back to my face and then away again. "Sorry."

My own face was at Red Alert too.

"Your sister got sick at gymnastics. I had to pick her up early."

"Oh." Normally Laleh had gymnastics classes on Tuesday evenings, and got a ride home with one of her friends' parents.

"Can you come downstairs? When you're, ah, decent?"

My face burned even hotter.

Being caught making out by my father had deflated my indecency in zero point six eight seconds.

"Yeah," I croaked.

Dad closed the door behind him.

"Sorry," I said. "Are you okay?"

"Yeah. But I didn't know you were a biter."

I tried to smile. But then, I don't know why, I wanted to cry a little bit.

I'd switched medications for my depression over the summer, and while I mostly liked the new prescription, and felt ten to twenty percent better on average, sometimes I got very overwhelmed and wanted to cry.

"Hey. It's okay." Landon swiped a tear off my cheek.

"I know." I mean, obviously my parents already knew about Landon and me. They'd seen us kiss before.

But not *kiss* kiss.

"I know." I took another breath. "I'm gonna help my dad. You wanna stay here?"

"Nah, I'll come help too."

"Thanks."

One of the best things about Landon Edwards was how good he was in the kitchen.

Not just doing dishes: He was an awesome cook too.

While Dad took Laleh upstairs to get changed, I washed and peeled vegetables for Landon, who chopped them to make chicken noodle soup.

"What's this?" He pulled down an unlabeled mason jar of brown spice and unscrewed the lid.

"Careful," I said, but it was too late. Landon took a sniff, which led to a cascade sinus failure.

"Bless you."

"Thanks. Whew."

"It's my mom's advieh."

"Advieh?"

"Like a family spice mix. For Persian cooking."

"It's different."

He shook out a handful and tossed it in with the onions and carrots, then got to work chopping celery.

While Landon cooked, I set the table and watched him work. He had become so comfortable in our kitchen, it was like he lived there. He had this soft smile, and he hummed as he pulled apart leftover chicken breast to add it to the pot.

As Landon worked, Dad came down the stairs, his ears red.

"Hey, boys," he said. He leaned down to kiss my forehead. "Wow. Your hair looks great."

"Thanks."

"Hey, Stephen," Landon said.

"Sorry for surprising you."

"It's all good." Landon rummaged through the spice cabinet and pulled out the bag of bay leaves sitting in the back.

I didn't know how he could be so cool about everything.

I couldn't meet Dad's eyes.

"Is Laleh okay?"

"I hope it's not strep again. Be sure to wash your hands plenty."

"Okay."

"And thanks for making soup, Landon. It smells good."

"Sure thing."

Laleh eventually made her way downstairs in her green pajamas and poured herself into her seat at the kitchen table.

I kissed her head. "Hey, Laleh."

She made the kind of dramatic groan I usually associated with adults who hadn't had their coffee in the morning.

Sometimes it was hard to tell if my sister was nine or thirty-nine.

"Sorry you're not feeling well."

"Thanks," she said. Her voice was hoarse and throaty.

"Landon's making soup for you."

"Yum," she said, but with none of her usual manic enthusiasm for Landon's cooking.

By eight o'clock, the soup was done, and Mom was finally home from work. She and Dad had been working a lot more hours since our trip to Iran.

Mom looked so tired, it was hard to decide who needed soup more, her or Laleh. But as soon as she tasted it, she smiled.

"This is good, Landon," she said. "You made it in an hour?"

"Yeah. Well, you had good chicken for it."

Like I said, Landon was a great cook. I think that's the main reason he won Mom over.

It's not like Shirin Kellner was mad or upset when I told her I was gay.

And it's not like she was weird about me and Landon hanging out.

But sometimes there was this tension between us, some

perturbation in the gravity of our orbits, that I couldn't figure out.

At least Landon could cook.

Every Persian mother wants her son to marry someone who can cook.

To be clear, I was not considering marriage, to Landon or anyone else. But cooking skills are an absolute requirement in prospective partners as far as Iranian parents are concerned.

"Landon found your advieh," I said.

"It's Mamou's recipe. My mother," she said to Landon. "She used to mix it up in a big mortar and pestle."

"I miss Mamou," Laleh said between slurps of noodle. "I wish we could go see her again."

The table got kind of quiet.

I think we all wished that.

The thing is, we only went to Iran last spring because Babou—my grandfather—had a brain tumor. He was dying. And Mom wanted us to meet him before it was too late.

"I wish we could go again too," Mom said at last.

She turned back to me and ran her finger along the edge of my fade, where it met the long curls up top.

"I can't believe you finally got a haircut."

I was finishing up my homework when Dad knocked on my open door frame.

"You got a minute?"

"Sure."

He closed the door behind him and sat on my bed.

"So." He rubbed his palms on his knees. "I know we've talked some about dating. And sex. And consent. But I figured we had better revisit."

My face burned.

"Dad."

"I know it's awkward. But it's important, Darius."

I spun my desk chair around and hunched over with my elbows on my knees.

"But, I mean." I swallowed. "Nothing's changed since the last time we talked."

That was over the summer, right after Landon and I had our first onion-tinged kiss.

We'd had talks before that too. Like when I was eight, and about to have a baby sister, and asked where babies came from. And again, after Sex Ed in middle school.

The worst was when I was thirteen and woke up with sticky sheets.

It was the most painfully awkward conversation in me and Dad's catalogue of painfully awkward conversations, and before our trip to Iran that was pretty much all our conversations.

To be honest, even after Iran—after there were no more walls between us—talking about sex was still awkward.

Dad cleared his throat. "Landon didn't have his hand under your pants when I walked in?"

"No," I said.

And then I said, "I mean, he hadn't gotten very far."

And then I said, "And I don't really know if I want to do that kind of stuff yet."

Dad nodded. "Okay. You know it's healthy and normal if you do. And healthy and normal if you don't. Right?"

I nodded and stared at my feet.

Dad let out a slow breath. "Did you tell him?"

I shook my head. "We were kissing."

"Okay." He stared out my window for a second. The curtains were open, and dusk was settling over the neighborhood like a blanket. "First, it's okay to hit pause on kissing so you can communicate. Relationships, or even just casual, you know, whatevers, need communication. And second, if you don't know what to say, you can use your hands to guide his. So if you don't want them . . . uh . . . in your pants, you can gently guide him to somewhere better, like your back or your knee or whatever."

"Okay."

Dad gave me a shaky grin.

As hard as it was to have conversations like this, he never made it seem like he didn't want to do it.

"Have you ever talked to Landon about his past relationships?"

"A little," I said.

"Did you talk about how intimate they were?"

That made me feel a little sick to my stomach.

"Some," I said.

Landon told me he'd done more with girls than with guys. That he had his first kiss in sixth grade.

Sometimes I wished I'd started dating sooner. Maybe then I would've had some practice at all this.

Maybe then I would've known what to do and what to say.

Dad ran his hand through his hair.

"Does it make you nervous, that Landon's more experienced?"

"No. Maybe. I don't know."

"I know this isn't fun to talk about with your dad," he said. "But I want you to be healthy and safe and happy. Okay?"

"I know," I said.

"Good. Okay. Good." He took a deep breath. "Next time, just tell him you'd like things to go a little slower. Let him know you enjoy, uh, kissing and stuff, and you want to wait for the rest."

"All right."

Dad patted his legs and stood up. He kissed me on top of my head and then rubbed the back of it. "I forgot you had skin back there," he said.

"Ears too. I look like the Grand Nagus."

Dad snorted. The Grand Nagus was the leader of the Ferengi, this alien race with huge ears and an obsession with profit.

"You're perfect just the way you are," Dad said.

"Thanks, Dad."

"Now finish up your homework so we can watch some *Deep Space Nine*."

Most mornings I went for a run before my shower.

I don't know that I actually liked running.

It wasn't so bad when we ran at practice, and the guys were there, and we could shout and laugh and egg each other on. But there was something about being all alone with my thoughts, in the rosy morning light, that made me kind of sad.

Still, I wanted to improve my speed.

And, if I'm being completely honest, I hoped it would help me lose weight, so maybe I could look more like the rest of the guys on the team, who were pretty much all lean and long-limbed and flat-stomached.

Maybe then I wouldn't have to suck in my stomach when Landon touched me.

The house was quiet when I got home. Mom's car was already gone, Laleh was still in bed, and Dad's door was closed.

It was weird, taking a shower with so much less hair. Way quicker. When I was dry, I rubbed in some of the curl cream Mikaela had recommended.

My hair looked nice. Really nice.

I got dressed and sat at my computer to call Sohrab.

It rang and rang—well, it made that weird *doot-doot-doot* music—and then:

"Hello, Darioush!"

I heard Sohrab's heavily compressed voice before I saw his face, which emerged from the Pixelated Black Void.

"Hey."

Sohrab Rezaei was my best friend in the whole world.

I hated that he lived half a world away.

Iran was eleven and a half hours ahead of Portland (I still didn't get the point and purpose of a half-hour time difference), so it was evening in Yazd.

"Are you eating dinner? Can you talk?"

"I can talk. Dinner is not ready yet. We're having ash-e reshteh."

Ash-e reshteh is Persian noodle soup.

"Oh good. We had soup last night. Laleh was sick."

"Is she okay?"

"I think so. She's going to the doctor today."

"Good." Sohrab studied me for a second. "Eh! You cut your hairs!"

I grinned.

"Do you like it?"

"It looks good, Darioush. Very stylish."

My cheeks burned.

"How does Landon like it?"

Sohrab was the first person I told about Landon.

Actually, Sohrab was the first person I told I was gay.

It was super scary, even though I knew he would be cool with it.

(I hoped he would be cool with it.)

But he said, "Thank you for telling me, Darioush. Have you told your mom? Your dad?"

"Not yet."

"Are you scared?"

"No. Maybe. I don't know."

We talked for a while, about how I wanted to tell people, and who I wanted to tell, but then I think Sohrab realized it was making me nervous, because he switched topics to Babou's latest appointment.

"The doctors think it's time for him to be on . . . what do you call it? Hospice?"

"Oh."

I don't know why that made me want to cry. I knew Babou wasn't going to get better.

But I guess there was a little part of me hoping for a miracle.

"I'm sorry, Darioush."

"It's okay."

It wasn't okay, and Sohrab knew it. But we didn't have to say it out loud.

We talked about other stuff after that: about the weather in Yazd; about the fortunes of Team Melli; about the latest argument he'd had with Ali-Reza and Hossein, the boys he played soccer/Iranian football with in Yazd; about school, and his uncle's store, and his mom's cooking.

Right before we hung up, Sohrab looked at me. And he said, "I'm glad you told me, Darioush. I will always be your friend."

I told Sohrab about Landon taking me for my haircut, and about visiting Rose City after, and how Dad had walked in on us making out.

When I told him I accidentally bit Landon's tongue, he laughed so hard he had to wipe tears away from his eyes, and that made me laugh too.

And I told him about having another Awkward Talk with Stephen Kellner.

Sohrab and I told each other everything.

"But enough about me. How are you doing?"

"I'm fine. I saw Babou yesterday."

"How is he?"

"Not very good." He sighed. "Mamou thinks it won't be long now."

"Oh. Is she okay?"

"Your grandma is strong. Like you, Darioush. But . . ." He looked off to the side for a moment. "It's hard for her. She won't tell anyone when she needs help. Maman and I have to force her to slow down."

"I'm sorry."

"Don't be. I love your grandma. And your grandpa."

"Me too." I wiped at my eyes. "I wish I could be there."

"I wish you could too."

"Thank you. For taking care of them."

Sohrab's brown eyes crinkled up into a squint as he smiled at me.

Sohrab Rezaei always smiled with his whole face.

"Always, Darioush. Ghorbanat beram. Always."

Ghorbanat beram is one of those perfect Farsi phrases you can't quite translate into English.

The closest thing is: I would give my life for yours.

Sometimes it was just hyperbole.

But for Sohrab, it was literal.

And it was literal for me too.

That is what it means to have a best friend.

THE GOOD TABLE

I was a little nervous about going to school Wednesday morning.

First, because we had our opening game that evening. And second, because Trent Bolger had been fiddling suspiciously with his phone when he saw me with Landon, and Trent loved spreading misinformation.

But when I got to school, no one said anything at all.

Either Trent hadn't made his move yet, or he had and no one cared.

By the time I got to Conditioning class, which I shared with Trent and a couple guys from the soccer team, it seemed like it was the latter: He'd been disappointed by the results of his rumormongering. Trent kept glaring at me, especially when I greeted Jaden and Gabe, two seniors on the team.

"All good, Darius?" Gabe asked. Our starting forward was brown-skinned and the shortest guy on the team, but he was also the fastest runner I had ever seen.

"A little nervous."

"Don't be. You'll be fine," Jaden said. He was a Fractional Korean—he laughed when I called him that the first time, but then he adopted it himself—and tall, but not as tall as me or Chip. He played midfield.

"Thanks."

Gabe glanced over at Trent, then lowered his voice.

"You know Trent's going around telling people he saw you with a guy last night?"

"I kind of figured he would."

Gabe grinned. "You got a boyfriend?"

"Maybe. I dunno. We're just hanging out."

"Anyone we know?"

"I don't think so. He goes to private school in Vancouver."

"Cool. You don't mind people knowing?"

"Not really."

"All right. We got your back, though. Just say the word."

I didn't know what to say to that.

It still felt weird for people at school to actually have my back.

"Thanks."

"Partner up for front squats," Coach Winfield said. "Light load. Ten reps. Three-second hold."

I stifled a groan. Squats were the worst, but front squats with a three-second hold at the bottom were tantamount to a crime against humanity.

At least they were good for my butt.

You could tell Coach Winfield was a football coach, because whenever there was a football game, there would always be stretching or jogging or some kind of "active recovery" for Conditioning. But that sort of collusion never extended to soccer games.

I partnered up with Jaden, since we could use the same rack height, and Gabe was next to us, partnered with Trent.

It was hard to tell who was more unhappy with that arrangement.

To be fair, Trent Bolger never seemed happy these days. I'd

always been Trent's Priority One Target, but now that I was friends with Chip, and part of the soccer team, I had people on my side.

Trent hadn't been able to find a new Target, though. He just spent his time trying to make me miserable, and never quite succeeding.

There had been this great gravitational shift in the stellar alignment of Chapel Hill High School, but Trent was operating off old star charts.

I almost felt sorry for him.

Almost.

"Don't look at my ass, Dairy Queen," Trent muttered when Coach Winfield was out of earshot.

"Then try moving it," Gabe said. "Some of us would like to get a set in."

I stopped myself from laughing, but I didn't stop myself from grinning. Trent just didn't know how to navigate this new paradigm.

And I wanted to cry a little bit too.

It felt good, having Gabe stand up for me.

It felt good to have a team.

Game days for the Chapel Hill High School varsity men's soccer team were a lot less intense than for the football team, but I didn't mind that. The football players had to wear their jerseys all day, and the cheerleaders their uniforms, and there were Spirit Assemblies and altered schedules to accommodate them.

There were no Spirit Assemblies for the soccer team. So the

day of our first game, I finished fourth block like usual, then headed to the bike racks to meet Chip.

Flat gray clouds had rolled in while we were in class. I pulled my hood up to protect myself from the cold drizzle tapping a soft, steady rhythm against the back of my neck.

As I unchained my bike, Chip came down the stairs, his keys jangling from the carabiner clip on his messenger bag. He had at least ten keys on there, even though only two of them were actually useful. The rest were random keys he'd found and added to his keychain—like a blackened skeleton key that looked like something from the eighteenth century—"for the aesthetic."

"Sorry. Had to ask Mr. Gerke about an assignment, but somehow we got on the topic of Germany and the European Union's economy and I'm still not sure how."

"Mr. Gerke can be like that. Come on. We better hurry if we want to get the Good Table."

I tightened my messenger bag against my back, while Chip unchained his bike and got helmeted up.

I led the way to Mindspace, this little coffee shop about a mile away from Chapel Hill High School, in the opposite direction from home. It only sat about ten people, so if you didn't get there at the right time you might not be able to get seats.

I was categorically opposed to drinking coffee, but I actually liked the smell of the roaster they kept going pretty much all the time at Mindspace. And I liked the way the roaster kept the whole shop warm, especially on rainy days. The sound was a nice constant white noise that made it easier to study.

The best part, though, was that Mindspace carried Rose City

Teas. It was the only place close to school to get a reliable cup of tea, unless I carried my own with me.

(I mean, I did carry my own with me, but it was nice not to need it.)

I got in line while Chip made a beeline for the Good Table: a polished mahogany dining room table butted up against one wall, with a bench on one side and mismatched chairs with red cushions on the other. Chip grabbed one cushioned seat and set his bag in the other to save it for me.

I ordered a cup of Ali Shan (an excellent Chinese oolong) for me and a Mocha for Chip, and grabbed a couple of napkins to wipe down the Good Table before we got to work.

"What've you got?" Chip asked as I pulled out my tablet.

"Algebra II."

"Algebra II was the worst."

"Still is."

Chip nodded and sipped his Mocha. He pulled out his own tablet, popped in his earbuds, and got to work.

Here's the thing: I'm still not entirely sure how I ended up doing homework with Cyprian Cusumano at Mindspace several days a week. In fact, I'm not entirely sure how we ended up friends.

Growing up, Chip had teased me almost as much as Trent did. And then somehow, after I got back from Iran, things changed. Chip started being nice to me. He said hi in the halls, and we hung out at practice, and we biked home together—Chip's house was in the same direction as mine—and talked about soccer or homework or whatever.

One day after practice, when we both had American Lit essays to work on, Chip asked if I wanted to work on them together, and I had suggested Mindspace, and somehow, a tradition was born.

I kind of liked hanging out and doing homework with Chip.

I don't know why, but I did.

That's normal.

Right?

Chip and I got back to the locker room at six o'clock.

My stomach felt like it had a small neutron star in it.

He squeezed my shoulder. "You okay?"

I nodded and rubbed my hand against the back of my head.

I still wasn't used to the bristly feeling back there. It felt good.

Relaxing, even.

"You look kind of green."

"Just nerves, I guess."

Chip grinned at me. "You'll do great."

"Thanks."

I got changed into my kit—crimson and black for our home games—and sat on the bench to lace up my cleats.

Next to me, Gabe peeled off his sweater. I kept my eyes on my cleats, because Gabe was pretty good-looking, his stomach flat and brown with a little bit of hair right above his waistline, and it was kind of distracting.

Besides, I was dating Landon. So it was wrong to look at another guy. Wasn't it?

"Is your boy coming to the game?"

My cheeks heated. "Landon? No, he's got band rehearsal. Mom and Dad are, though. And my sister."

"Older or younger?"

"Younger. She's nine."

"Cool." Gabe sat next to me to pull his own cleats on. I stood up and stretched, then turned away for a second to make sure I was arranged okay in my compression shorts.

Chafing was no joke.

"Ready?"

"Ready."

HOT BEVERAGE POD
EXTRACTION DEVICE

My old gym teacher, Coach Fortes, was the one who convinced me to try out for the soccer team, but over the summer his wife had gotten a job in Eastern Washington, so he followed her there.

Coach Bentley had been hired to replace him (and to teach History and Citizenship). She was a Black woman with warm, dark skin, a shaved head, and the kind of face that could go from glowing praise to nuclear rage in less than a second, especially if she thought you weren't giving a hundred percent out on the field.

At her last school she led her teams to multiple Oregon State Championships, and now she was determined to make Chapel Hill High School Soccer a name to be feared. She had the determination of a Klingon warrior and the analytical prowess of a Vulcan scholar.

As I warmed up, kicking a ball back and forth with Chip, she kept shouting at us.

"Faster feet! Faster feet!"

I nodded and sped up our drill.

I was pretty sure I liked Coach Bentley.

Really.

But she could be a little intense too.

Across the field, the team from Crestwood High School,

Chapel Hill's district rival, warmed up in their white away kits trimmed with green and yellow.

I never really got the rivalry thing, which I suspected was because of our schools' football teams, but their mascot was the Spartan, so I was genetically predisposed to dislike them.

Persians (even Fractional ones) and Spartans (even fake ones) are natural enemies. Whole epics have been written about it. Some racist movies too.

Coach Bentley blew her whistle. "All right, Chargers, circle up!"

Circling up is this thing Coach Bentley has us do before practices and games. We convene behind our goal and stand in a circle, arms crossed, holding hands with the people on either side of us. And we each go around in a circle, saying something nice a teammate did for us.

Coach Bentley brought it with her from her old school. She said it's to promote team unity and fight the cult of toxic masculinity in sports.

I ended up between Chip and Gabe, across from Coach Bentley, who went first: "When we started off this season, you didn't know me and I didn't know you. But you welcomed me, and now we're about to win our first game. I'm proud of you all."

We went clockwise from there: Guys described favors someone did, notes shared, advice on footwork, even being a wingman for getting a date.

When it got to Chip, he said, "Ricky loaned me his charger when my tablet was about to die. Thanks, Ricky." Ricky, our left wingback, nodded from across the circle.

And then it was my turn.

"Today in Conditioning, this guy from the football team was being kind of rude to me."

I couldn't name Trent, because there was this rule for Circle: You couldn't say anything bad about other people. At least not by name.

Even then, Coach Bentley opened her mouth like she was about to correct me, so I said, "But Gabe and Jaden had my back. And that was really cool. It meant a lot to me. So, thanks, guys."

Next to me, Chip shifted back and forth on his feet, and his hand twitched in mine.

He had to know I was talking about Trent.

Right?

On my other side, Gabe bumped shoulders with me and then said, "Speaking of which, Darius stayed and helped me clean up my weights in Conditioning, even though he was running late. That was really cool of him. Thanks, man."

I nodded and looked at my feet.

I wasn't used to getting compliments from the guys at school.

My chest felt like a plasma reactor.

I wanted to cry—just a little bit—but managed not to. I didn't want to have a stuffy nose for the start of the game.

When we finished, Coach Bentley counted to three, and we all shouted together.

"Go Chargers!"

We were ahead by one, thanks to some excellent goalkeeping by Christian and a sweet goal in the first half by Gabe, but by the last few minutes of the second half, the Crestwood Spartans were living up to their names by not giving up.

I played sweeper for our team—a position Coach Bentley said I was uniquely suited for, whatever that meant—and the Spartans had been hammering our defense, trying to get a goal in.

I was drenched in sweat. My black shorts were stained green, the result of a tricky (but successful) slide tackle against one of Crestwood's forwards. Sohrab had taught it to me, back in Yazd.

A few minutes later, that same forward slipped around Jaden and faked out Chip, but it was like I got a sensor lock on him. When he dove to my left, to take a shot at our goal, I dove with him.

I got a kick to my shin, but my guard caught it, and I managed to send the ball offsides.

Still, I groaned. The guard caught the worst of it, but I was going to have a nice-sized bruise.

"Hey." Chip jogged over to me. "You okay?"

I flopped over onto my back. "I think so."

Chip offered me a hand up.

"You sure?"

I stepped back and forth a few times. The pain was starting to fade.

"I'm sure."

Chip bumped my fist. "Nice save."

"Thanks."

We won the game, 1–0.

I had never seen Coach Bentley smile so much in all the months we'd been practicing.

After we shook hands with the Crestwood Spartans, I ran over to the stands where Mom and Dad were waiting for me, with Laleh in tow behind them.

Despite me being disgustingly sweaty, Mom pulled me into a hug, but she definitely didn't kiss me.

Dad laughed, though, and planted a kiss right into my messy hair.

"Good game, son," he said. "Green's a good color on you."

"Thanks." I looked down at my grass-stained shorts and arms and then back up. "Maybe I have a future as an Orion slave dancer."

"Might need to work on your dance moves a little."

"Hey!"

"Really, Darius. You looked great out there. Like you were having fun." He mussed my hair and rested his hand on my shoulder. "I'm so proud of you."

I got that burning plasma reactor feeling in my chest again, but I managed to smile too.

"Thanks, Dad." I knelt down so I was level with Laleh. "What did you think? How'd I do?"

"Good," she said, but then she coughed into the crook of her elbow.

"She wouldn't stay home," Mom said. "But at least her fever broke."

"That's good."

I turned back to Laleh.

"I'm glad you came."

She nodded at me and gave me a weak smile, but then she coughed again.

"We'd better get you home. I'm gonna shower."

"We'll get your bike loaded up," Dad said. "Meet us in the parking lot?"

"Sure."

"You hungry?" Mom said. "You need anything?"

"I'm good. Thanks, Mom."

I ran to catch up with the other guys as we did a warm-down and some stretches and then headed for the locker room.

Chapel Hill High School had nice showers, where we all got our own stall, but the shower heads were apparently made for Student Athletes shorter than I was. I had to bend down to get my head under the spray, and the hot water didn't last nearly long enough, which meant by the time I was clean I was also cold and slightly miserable.

I dried off and wrapped myself in my towel, sucked in my stomach, and went to get dressed.

Most of the guys were gone, but I passed Chip pulling his shirt on as I padded to my locker.

"Hey," he said.

"Hey," I said, and turned into my row. Gabe was already gone, which was good, because I hated getting dressed next to him.

Between playing soccer every day and my new medication, I had lost a little weight, but it wasn't like I was suddenly skinny. I still had way more stomach than I wanted, and now the stretch marks had gotten way more noticeable, despite the scar cream I put on at night.

I kind of hated the way I looked.

That's normal.

Right?

I pulled on my shirt first, even before my underwear, because the risk of someone seeing my cold penis still seemed less alarming than having them see my stomach.

From the other side of the lockers, Chip said, "You headed home after this? You wanna grab a bite or something?"

"My family's waiting for me."

"Oh. Cool. Maybe some other time?"

"Maybe."

Chip got quiet again as I packed my dirty kit into its mesh bag.

And then he said, "What you said in Circle?"

"Yeah?"

"Was that about Trent?"

"Oh. Yeah." I slung my messenger bag over one shoulder and my soccer bag over the other and stepped around the partition.

"Well. Sorry about that."

"You don't need to be," I said.

And I meant it.

Really.

I didn't expect Chip to apologize for the things Trent did.

I just wished I knew why the two of them were friends in the first place.

I didn't know quite what to make of Cyprian Cusumano.

I tossed my bags into the trunk of Dad's car and then opened the passenger-side door.

"Sorry for the wait."

Dad shook his head. "No worries."

But as soon as I closed the door, I felt trapped.

No one said anything, but I could feel it: an invisible particle field of frustration or anger, I wasn't sure which. It pressed against my ears and thrummed in my chest.

I rolled down my window a bit. "Is this okay?"

"Laleh's got an earache," Mom said from the back, where she sat with Laleh to give me more leg room up front.

"Oh." I rolled the window back up and turned the air on low instead. "This better?"

"Thanks, sweetie."

As Dad pulled out of the parking lot, I saw Chip emerge from the locker room, headed toward his bike. I waved, but I don't think he saw me, because he didn't wave back or anything.

With no music playing, and no one talking, the vibration in my chest started getting worse.

I didn't know what was going on with my family, but I didn't like it.

So I said, "Thanks for coming. It means a lot."

"Of course we came," Mom said.

"Wouldn't miss it for the world." Dad glanced a smile my way and then looked back to the road. Behind me, Mom ran her fingers through Laleh's hair while she slept against the window. Quiet crept back over the car. I pulled out my phone to text Landon about the game and tried to ignore the prickly feeling in my stomach.

What was going on?

※ ※ ※

When we got home, Mom got Laleh ready for an early bedtime, while I warmed up some of the leftovers from Landon's soup. Once the adrenaline of the game had drained out of me, I was starving.

While I stirred my little pot of soup, Dad stood at the sink, doing the dishes.

"I can do those," I said. "I'm making more anyway."

"No, it's okay. I should have done them during the day. Just didn't get around to it."

Dad huffed and reached into the sudsy water to pull out a mug.

Stephen Kellner always liked to fill one side of the sink with sudsy water and soak the dishes in it. I wasn't a fan of that method, because I hated reaching into dirty, soapy water and not knowing what I was going to find.

But Grandma and Oma did dishes the same way, so it must have been genetic.

Grandma and Oma also used one of those wand things, the kind that you filled with soap that had a sponge on the end, but Mom was adamant that those didn't get the corners clean, so she bought us regular washcloths instead.

Shirin Kellner had strong opinions about dish-washing, opinions I had apparently inherited from her, since I did the dishes a lot more like her than I did like Dad.

The Level Nine Awkward Silence had followed us from the car to the house, like a shrouded Jem'Hadar warrior lurking in the shadows, observing our weaknesses and waiting for the perfect moment to strike.

All the joy I'd felt from winning our first game had leeched out too, until I was left feeling as prickly and unsettled as the rest of my family.

I cleared my throat. "How was work?"

"Didn't get much done today," Dad said. "Had to take care of your sister."

"Oh."

"Richard thinks we might have a project lined up in California soon. A community center outside LA."

"Oh. Cool."

Richard Newton was my dad's partner at Kellner & Newton, the architecture firm where he worked.

I guess he kind of owned it.

To be honest, I wasn't entirely sure how his business was structured. I just knew that he didn't get to work from home as much anymore. That he was always tired, like Mom.

"I'll be doing a site visit next week. Need anything from Tehrangeles?"

Dad had been traveling a lot more for work too.

"I'm good. Mom will probably have a list, though."

Dad smirked. "She already gave it to me."

"Oh. Good."

I transferred my soup to a bowl. "Want to watch a *DS9*?"

"Sure. Give me a minute to finish up?"

"I'll make some tea."

I filled my electric kettle and set it to 165 degrees. "Want to try something new?"

"What is it?"

"Kabusecha. Mr. Edwards gave it to me."

"Tell me about it."

I did my best to explain what Mr. Edwards had said, about shade-growing and theanine and flavor compounds, but I had already forgotten some of it since I hadn't taken any notes.

It was almost embarrassing, how little it turned out I knew before starting at Rose City. My first day I thought I would be able to jump right in, but I ended up needing a ton of training. There was so much more to learn when you're at a place that actually makes the tea. I had to learn about seasons and the fickle politics of tea growers and the magic of *terroir*.

For some reason, people always said *terroir* like you could actually hear the italics.

I didn't even know that was possible.

"The kiss of the earth itself," Mr. Edwards said. "Words can only approximate it."

I didn't really know what he meant by that.

Not really.

But I wanted to.

Once Dad finished the dishes, and I had steeped the Kabusecha in a small pot for two, we curled up on the couch to watch *Star Trek: Deep Space Nine*.

It took some doing, but I'd managed to convince Dad to watch the entire series in one go, instead of interspersing it with *The Next Generation* and *Voyager* in broadcast order, like we usually did.

"It's one big story," I had said. "And what if Laleh wants to watch with us?"

Dad was still on the fence until soccer practice started up, and we weren't always guaranteed a window to watch an episode each night. Then he finally relented. Sticking to one series made it easier to follow.

As I poured Dad's tea, he cued up "Distant Voices."

"My twin," I said, pointing at Quark—*DS9*'s Ferengi bartender—when he showed up in the teaser.

Dad snorted.

"Your ears are perfect," Mom said from behind us. She reached over and tugged on one of them.

"Want to watch?" I scooted closer to Dad to make room for her.

"Not tonight. Your sister's still sick."

"Can I help?"

"Let me take care of her," Dad said, but Mom put her hand on his shoulder.

"It's okay. You two watch your show. I've got work to do anyway."

Mom wandered into the kitchen and I heard the distinctive sounds of her Hot Beverage Pod Extraction Device, which I refused to either name or use strictly on principle. As the opening credits finished, she passed back through, kissed me on the head and Dad on the temple, and headed upstairs with a steaming mug of coffee cupped in her hands.

Dad's eyes followed her up the stairs. He bit his lip and rubbed his stubbled chin for a second. Then he put his arm over my shoulder and turned back to the TV.

And we both tried to relax.

THE MOST HARROWING
SOUND IN THE UNIVERSE

I had trouble falling asleep that night.

One, my nerves were still humming like a warp core in the aftermath of the game.

Two, I'd tried to Skype Sohrab, but he didn't answer, so I spent half an hour writing him an email instead.

Three, my parents were arguing.

Well, maybe arguing is the wrong description, because I don't think they were actually mad at each other. They were frustrated, and worried, and they were doing that weird Parental Voice where they're agitated but trying to keep their voices down, like they could shield me and Laleh from knowing bad things if only they whispered.

I had gone to the bathroom to brush my teeth and pee before bed, and I heard them talking (my bathroom shared a vent with theirs), which is how I ended up sitting on the toilet listening to them.

"I just don't see how we can make it work," Dad said. "I've already got the California project lined up, and another after that in Arkansas if it gets confirmed. You're working overtime. And we still can't—"

Mom sighed. "I know. I know. I just hate not being there."

"I know, love."

Dad murmured something too quiet for me to make out.

"Not good. Mamou says it won't be long. Most days he doesn't even wake up long enough to eat."

They were talking about Babou again.

Things got muffled after that, but I could hear the sound of Mom crying.

It was the most harrowing sound in the universe.

I pulled off a handful of toilet paper to wipe my own tears, but I accidentally bumped the tank on the toilet.

I flushed the empty toilet, just to keep my cover, but that meant I heard even less.

When the roaring water quieted down, I caught a little bit more between my own sniffles.

" . . . kids about it sooner or later," Mom said.

"Tomorrow," Dad said. "Let me check with my parents first."

Things got quiet after that. Either they'd started to whisper, or they'd moved away from their bathroom.

I washed my hands and took a couple deep breaths and went to bed.

But I still couldn't sleep.

When I got home from practice the next afternoon, Laleh was sitting upright at the table, drinking tea and reading an over-large paperback book. The color had come back to her cheeks, and she perked up a little when she saw me.

"Hey," she said.

"Hey, Laleh." I leaned down to kiss her head. "Feeling better?"

"Yeah."

What're you reading?"

"Dune."

"Oh."

I blinked.

"Is it any good?"

Laleh shrugged. "Kind of boring."

"Oh."

I went to the teapot and poured myself a cup.

Ever since our trip to Iran, Laleh had taken it upon herself to make tea when I wasn't home to do it.

She always made Persian tea—black tea bursting with cardamom. It felt like being back in Iran, with Mamou and Babou (when he was sick but could still do things). In their house, the kettle was always on.

I swallowed away my sadness.

"This is good, Laleh," I said. "Thanks."

She didn't look up. "Not too much hel?"

"It's just right."

Laleh nodded and kept reading.

I thought about sitting with her, but she seemed like she didn't want company.

She wasn't sick anymore, but there was something going on with her. Something she wasn't saying out loud.

I studied my sister, but she just sipped her tea and turned the pages of her book.

So I went upstairs to do my Algebra II homework. Ms. Albertson had assigned us a bunch of exercises, but I couldn't quite wrap my brain around the point and purpose of conics.

Who goes around slicing a cone to see what it looks like on the inside?

I ran a hand through my hair, tracing the line of my fade. I liked the way my skin tingled.

Dad knocked on my door frame. "What're you working on?"

"Parabolas," I groaned.

"That bad?"

I shrugged.

"Want me to look?"

"Sure."

Dad stood over my desk, resting his hand on the back of my neck. He gave it a squeeze as he read over my equations.

The light from my desk lamp cast his face into sharp relief. The lines around his eyes looked deeper, and I remembered the weird tension in the car ride home from my game, and how he and Mom had been whispering last night.

"Is everything okay?" I blurted out.

"What?"

"Just . . ." I swallowed. "Things seem weird. With you. And Mom."

Dad sighed.

He moved his hand down to my back.

"Things are okay," he said. "Money's just a little tight right now, after the trip to Iran, and sending money to help out Mamou."

I nodded.

Dad drummed his fingers on my back. I didn't think he knew he was doing it. "With your mom working so much overtime, and me being out of town, we thought it would be good if your grandparents came to stay with us for a while."

"Oh," I said.

The thing about Dad's moms was, even though I knew they loved me and Laleh, I never got the feeling they actually liked us.

They lived in Bend, which was three hours away, but we only saw them a few times a year: birthdays and, for some weird reason, Easter. (Like Dad, Grandma and Oma were secular humanists, but Easter brunch was still a favorite meal for them.)

I couldn't remember a time where I didn't know my grandmothers were queer. Even before I figured that out about myself, they were just part of the fabric of my life.

Well, maybe they were the trim on the fabric of my life: forever on the edges, an embellishment you might notice if you're looking for it.

I thought, when I told them I was gay, it might bring us closer.

That we could share this thing that set us apart from everyone else.

That they would talk about when Oma came out.

That they would tell me about the history I was too young to witness going on around me: Prop 8, and Don't Ask, Don't Tell, and the fight for marriage equality.

But all Grandma said was "I thought you might be," and all Oma said was "We love you just the same," and then we drank our tea in silence like always.

I didn't know what I'd done to make my grandmas so disinterested in me.

And it wasn't like they were any more interested in Laleh, which was strange, because everyone liked Laleh.

Even Babou adored Laleh at first sight, and he didn't like anyone until he'd warmed up to them.

In fact, the only thing my grandmothers and I had in common were tea and soccer.

They were almost excited when I told them I had made Chapel Hill High School's varsity men's soccer team.

Almost.

"We'll have to come see a game," Grandma had said.

"If you make it to the championships, for sure," Oma had added.

I didn't know how to feel about that: their excitement being conditional on us winning.

I was on the team because it was fun, because I liked my teammates, and I liked Coach Bentley.

I didn't know if I had it in me to be a winner.

"It'll be nice to see them, huh?" Dad said.

His fingers kept drumming against me, like I was a console on the bridge of a starship, and he was trying to plot a course through some kind of unstable stellar phenomenon.

To be honest, I never got the feeling Grandma and Oma actually liked Dad either.

I don't know why I thought that.

It was an awful thing to think.

So I said, "Yeah."

They were coming to help us out. To help Mom be less tired.

To give Dad a chance to breathe.

"Yeah," I said again.

And I tried to mean it.

JUST HYPERBOLE

It was still dark out when I got back from my morning run, just in time to say bye to Mom as she pulled out of the driveway.

"Hey," she said out the window. "Will you check on your dad after you shower? He's sleeping in a little."

Dad never slept in.

"Okay."

Mom gave me a sad smile. "See you tonight."

I swallowed away the lump in my throat.

I hated seeing my parents so tired.

"Yeah."

I showered and packed my soccer bag, and tucked my curl cream in too. I'd be seeing Landon after practice and wanted to look nice. I knocked on Dad's door, but he hollered he was up and getting ready.

And then, since I hadn't heard from Sohrab in three days, I sat down and tried him again.

This time he answered right away.

"Eh! Hello Darioush."

"Hey! Chetori toh?"

I didn't speak much Farsi, but what few words I could say— heavy with my American accent—I felt okay practicing with Sohrab, who never criticized my pronunciation.

Sohrab let out a dramatic sigh. "Darioush. Have I ever told you about my Ameh Mona?"

"I don't think so."

"She lives in Manshad. You know Manshad?"

I shook my head.

"It's across the mountains from Yazd. It's very beautiful. But it's a long drive." Sohrab glanced behind him and hollered something to his mom.

"Maman says hi."

"Oh. Tell her hi too?"

Sohrab shouted back at his mom.

"Anyway. Ameh Mona broke her leg."

"What happened?"

"She tripped over her cat."

"She what?"

Sohrab shook his head, and then he snorted.

"She tripped over her cat." He snorted again. The snort turned into a chuckle.

And then his eyes crinkled up and he started laughing. He laughed so hard it made me start laughing too, even though tripping over a cat and breaking your leg sounded awful. I laughed so hard I had tears in my eyes.

But eventually the laughter petered out, and Sohrab said, "We hadn't seen her in a long time."

His image jittered for a second as he looked to the side. I thought he was going to say something, but he just sat there, his jaw twitching. He'd been keeping it more stubbly, like he was trying to grow a beard but couldn't quite manage it.

His face looked longer too. Either he'd gotten taller or he'd lost some weight.

Maybe both.

Eventually he turned back and said, "How was football?"

"It was good. We won our first game!"

I told Sohrab everything: about circling up, about how I used the tackle he showed me, about how the team was starting to feel like actual friends.

"I'm glad you're making friends, Darioush."

"Me too." I swallowed. "I was kind of scared."

"Why?"

"I don't know," I said. "You were my first real friend. I thought, maybe I didn't know how to make more. Maybe you were special." I cleared my throat. "You are special. But I thought . . . I don't know."

Sohrab's eyes crinkled up again. "Best friends are special, Darioush. But you're a nice guy. Of course you are making more friends. I'm happy for you."

Sohrab always knew what to say.

"Thanks."

Sohrab looked away again, his jaw twitching.

Sohrab's jaw twitched when he ground his teeth.

Sohrab ground his teeth when he was thinking about his dad, who died just before we left Yazd. He had been in prison when he died: Sohrab's family was Bahá'í, and the Iranian government had a tendency to harass and imprison Bahá'ís.

It cast a shadow over him, one that came and went.

I knew him well enough to sit with him until it passed.

That's the kind of friends Sohrab and I were.

Finally he said, "Darioush. How did you know you were depressed?"

"Oh."

I didn't know what to say at first.

I never thought I'd hear Sohrab ask me that question.

I don't know why. Lots of people deal with depression.

"Well," I said. "There's a difference between being depressed and having depression. And for having it, a doctor can diagnose you, but I think it's usually because you've been depressed enough times or over a long period of time."

I swallowed.

"You know how it looks in the mornings in Yazd, when it's still a little foggy, and you can see things but they're kind of grayed out and blurry around the edges?"

Sohrab nodded.

"That's what it felt like for me. When it was bad. It was like I could make out the shape of life but I could never quite see it. It's different for different people, though. My dad told me when he was depressed, he was just tired all the time. And he never wanted to do anything." I swallowed again. "Do you think you might be depressed? Or have depression?"

"I don't know," he said. "Maybe. Sometimes I feel like that. The fog."

"Can you see a doctor about it?"

"I don't think so."

"What about your mom? Can you talk to her at least?"

"Maybe." He sighed.

Sohrab was one of the happiest people I knew, but even he had his sadnesses.

To be honest, it felt like I'd been seeing them more and more lately. That, and his angers.

Sohrab had a lot of anger inside him, anger he didn't always know how to talk about, unless I could pry it out of him.

I hated how far away my best friend was.

"You know you can talk to me, right? Ghorbanat beram."

"I know, Darioush. Always."

BLACK SHIRT AESTHETIC

Landon was waiting for me at the bike rack outside Rose City Teas when I pulled up.

He had this big smile. "Hey."

"Hey."

He pulled me into a hug. I rested my chin in his hair, which smelled like almonds and orange blossoms and boy. He looked up and kissed me, first on my cheek and then on my lips.

"I missed you. Sorry I couldn't make it to your game."

"It's okay. I missed you too."

Landon wrapped his hands around my neck and kissed me again. I put my hands on his waist and kissed him back.

It felt like a scene out of a movie, kissing each other under the awning while rain soaked the streets. Until someone cleared their throat.

Mr. Edwards was standing in the doorway.

The back of my neck prickled.

"Um." I cleared my throat and stepped away from Landon, pulling the hem of my hoodie down as I did. "I better get changed."

"Come to the tasting room when you're ready."

At my old job, at Tea Haven, we had to wear black button-up shirts and bright blue aprons. Rose City kept the Black Shirt Aesthetic, but it was a V-neck T-shirt with the Rose City Teas logo (a teacup with a rose blooming out of the top) silk-screened on the back, and little teapots on the sleeves. We also had to wear dark-wash jeans.

I liked the way that dark-wash jeans looked on me. Especially my butt, which, like I said, had seen some benefit from all the squats I'd been doing.

Landon liked how I looked in them too. (Again, especially my butt.)

I laced up my Sambas, checked my hair in the mirror, straightened out my magnetic name tag, and went to check in.

"Come on, Darius. We've got something special today," Mr. Edwards said as he poured water into a set of gaiwans. Landon was already seated at the tasting table with his notebook open. I sat down next to him and got my own notebook out.

Landon pressed his knee against mine. I grabbed his left hand and rubbed circles into it with my thumb.

I must've had a goofy grin, because Mr. Edwards caught my eye and winked at me.

Mr. Edwards seemed super happy that I was dating his son, so happy it made me feel kind of weird.

I mean, Mom and Dad liked Landon, but they never winked at him.

And they weren't Landon's boss either.

It was weird.

Mr. Edwards cleared his throat. "This is Long Jing." He grabbed the first gaiwan—a white porcelain bowl with a lid and saucer beneath it—tilted the lid a hair with his thumb, and poured the tea into the tasting cup, capturing the leaves in the gaiwan. "Also known as . . . ?"

My mind blanked.

I loved tastings, but they made me nervous too. I felt like I was in class, and Mr. Edwards was a teacher I really didn't want to disappoint.

"Dragonwell," Landon said.

"Right. This was harvested before the Qingming Festival."

I made a note to look up what that was, because Mr. Edwards kept going. He talked about leaf shape, and pan roasting, and pricing, and biodynamic growing.

I wrote as fast as I could.

Finally, we got to the best part: We got to actually taste the tea.

It was buttery and sweet and just a tiny bit nutty.

"Oh, wow," I said. I went for another spoonful.

Landon slurped next to me. "Hmm. Eggplant?"

Mr. Edwards nodded.

"Bok choi?"

He nodded again.

I slurped another taste. I didn't get either of those. And as a Persian, I was keenly attuned to the taste of eggplant, which we called bademjoon in Farsi, and to which I was categorically opposed.

Mr. Edwards looked at me.

"Um. Chestnut?"

"Hm." He slurped, swirled the tea on his palate, and swallowed. "Interesting."

He poured out the next gaiwan.

I swallowed and kept making notes.

After we cleaned up the tasting room, Mr. Edwards said, "Mind manning the register? Landon can do some stocking."

"Sure."

Interns weren't technically supposed to man the register, but sometimes we had to fill in if it got super busy. Usually we helped with stocking, and serving, and cleanup, and stuff like that.

The register was one of those tablet setups on an angled swivel mount, which felt very Starfleet to me, and almost made up for how boring it was.

Almost.

I rang up a Business Casual Couple buying a sampler of Chinese green teas and a gaiwan to steep them in; and a hipster with a beard and beanie making the transition from coffee to tea for "health reasons." Mr. Edwards grabbed a tin of Second Flush Darjeeling from the shelf and had me mark it off inventory.

Every so often, Landon came out from the back with his little pushcart of tins to restock the shelves. He smiled when he came by, and brushed my arm, or gave me a kiss on the cheek.

One time, he even smacked me on the butt.

"Hey!" I said, but he just smirked and kept walking, like he hadn't done anything.

"Excuse me," a customer said. They wore a pink sweater with black galaxy-print leggings, which I thought was a pretty cool look. "Do you have any more Bai Hao?"

Bai Hao was one of our best-selling oolongs. It was grown in Taiwan, and every year these little bugs came and chewed on the leaves, until the leaves activated a natural chemical defense that drove them away. That chemical changed the flavor of the tea, made it fruity and floral and awesome.

I glanced at the shelf, but Landon still hadn't gotten to it yet.

"We have some in the back. I can go grab it."

I waved down Alexis, who was running the tasting bar, and asked her to keep an eye on the register for me.

"Sure thing," she said.

I found a couple boxes of Bai Hao tins in the stock room, along with Landon, who was leaning against the wall, looking at his phone.

"Hey," he said. "Need something?"

"Some Bai Hao." I reached up to grab them—they were on the top shelf, where Landon couldn't reach without the step stool—and stacked a few extras on the pushcart to get stocked later.

"Cool." Landon slipped his phone into his pocket and stood up. He wrapped his fingers into my belt loops and pulled himself closer to me. I lifted the boxes of tea overhead so he wouldn't bump into them. "You work too hard."

"I was just helping someone."

"You're always helping someone." He smiled. "That was the first thing I noticed about you."

I met Landon my first day at Rose City—Mr. Edwards introduced us while he gave me a tour—but we got to know each other when we worked the Rose City Teas booth at Portland Pride, serving a bright pink iced hibiscus tisane.

Landon had been to Pride before—he came out as bi when he was in middle school—but it was my first time. I had only come out to my parents like two weeks before.

"Don't be nervous," Landon told me. "We don't bite."

"I'm not. I'm gay," I said. "It's just my first time is all."

"Oh, really?" He smiled at me.

Landon Edwards had the kind of smile that could shake a comet from its orbit and send it plummeting toward the sun.

"Um. Yeah."

"Cool. I'm bi."

"Oh. Cool."

We spent the whole day talking—interrupted by my running to get more bags of ice or jugs of water.

"You don't have to keep doing that," he said. "Alexis and I can help too."

"I don't mind," I said.

Landon smiled at me again.

"Well, thanks. At least drink some tea and cool off."

That was before my hair was cut, when I had a big halo of curly black hair, which did get pretty warm in the summer.

"Okay. Thanks."

Landon leaned up to kiss me, and then his hands went from my belt loops to the small of my back. I kissed him with my lips closed, but then he started to add some tongue, and to squeeze my butt, and I leaned away.

"Hey," I said. "I've gotta go back out there. I can't . . ."

"Can't what?"

I swallowed and glanced at the open stockroom door. "I can't have an erection on the job."

Landon smirked again—he had the most charming smirk in the world—and let me go. "Sorry. But we haven't done that in a while."

"I know." I thought back to what Dad and I had talked about. Communicating. I took a deep breath and said, "But I need us to take things a little slow. Okay? You're my first boyfriend."

Landon got this smile on his face. "What?"

"What what?"

"You called me your boyfriend."

Red Alert.

"Um. Is that okay?"

Landon gave me this look.

Another comet fell toward the inner solar system.

"Yeah. Yeah, it's okay. Boyfriends." He bit his lip. "Sometimes I forget this is all new to you."

"I'm sorry."

"Don't be. We'll go at your pace. Okay?"

"Okay."

Landon gave me one last peck on the lips.

"Later?"

"Later."

"Darius. Can I talk to you for a moment?"

"Sure."

Mr. Edwards's office was a little nook tucked behind the

tasting room, glass-walled and glass-doored but with exposed brick for the other two walls. The brick was covered in maps of tea-growing regions across the world, and photos (including some cute ones of Landon when he was younger), and little sticky notes with to-do lists on them. Mr. Edwards always drew little squares as bullets for his to-do lists, so he could check them off with a flourish.

"You've been here for three months now, so I wanted to check in. Are you still happy?"

"Yeah! Yes. Definitely. I'm learning a lot."

"Good. The team likes you."

"I like working with them."

"And obviously Landon likes you too."

I blushed.

"I mean . . ."

Mr. Edwards winked at me. "Well, you've become a valuable part of our operation. So I was thinking. How would you like to turn your internship into something more official?"

"Like what?"

Mr. Edwards laughed. "Like a job."

"I thought I had to be eighteen, though."

"You do for some things, like operating the machinery. But you're already basically working. Way more than an intern is supposed to. You deserve to get paid."

I played with the hem of my shirt and studied the white stripes on my Sambas.

"Really?"

"Really."

I couldn't help it.

I smiled.

"Okay."

I was filling the dishwasher after closing when Landon came and hugged me from behind.

"Hey," he said. "Did my dad talk to you?"

"Yeah."

"You said yes, right? I told him you would."

"You did?"

"He talked to me about it last night."

I closed the dishwasher and turned around.

"I still can't believe it."

"Why?"

I shrugged. "I don't know."

Landon wrapped his hands around my neck. "You'll be awesome."

"Thank you."

He kissed me, and I kissed him. He giggled when I nuzzled into his neck, and sighed when I stroked under his chin with the back of my hand.

"My boyfriend," he whispered, and I smiled against his mouth.

Landon stepped toward me, which pushed me up against the dishwasher. It beeped shut, but we ignored it and kept kissing. I angled my hips so I wasn't pressing against Landon, because I didn't want him to feel how excited I was. Not after I just told him I wanted us to take things slowly.

The lights in the store turned off, and Mr. Edwards hollered at us that it was time to go.

I kissed Landon one more time, and he gave my butt a quick squeeze before we straightened out our clothes and followed Mr. Edwards out the back door.

It was an uncomfortable ride home, with my messenger bag slung in front of my lap as I rode the bus.

Dad had some dinner heated up for me, and the tea ready to go. We had a two-parter to watch—"Improbable Cause" and "The Die is Cast"—and it was already late.

But I couldn't sit still. I kept replaying the night in my head.

"Darius?"

"Yeah?"

"Are you mad at me about something?"

"What? No. Why?"

"You're so quiet. And your leg is jiggling."

I stilled my knee and paused the episode. "Sorry. Just, a lot happened at work. Mr. Edwards kind of offered me a job."

"That's terrific!" Dad pulled me in to kiss my forehead. "I'm so proud of you. Why didn't you tell me sooner?"

"I don't know. It still feels weird. And, well. This other thing happened too."

"What's that?"

I almost jiggled my leg again, but stopped myself. "Landon and I are officially boyfriends now."

Dad leaned back to look me in the eyes.

"How does that make you feel?"

"Happy," I said. "Really happy."

"That's wonderful. You deserve to be happy."

"Thanks, Dad."

I hit play, and we finished the episodes, and I kept my hands folded across my lap, because I kept thinking about Landon.

I really needed to go number three.

I usually did it before bed, and sometimes in the mornings, too, after my run. Well, most mornings, if I'm being honest.

Ever since Dr. Howell had changed my prescription, it was like my sex drive had gone from impulse to warp.

I wondered if other guys felt this way.

I wondered if Landon did.

I wondered what it was that made me imagine Landon touching me when I masturbated, but cringe when he reached below my waist in real life.

That's normal.

Right?

THE TAXONOMY OF
BREAKFAST FOODS

S aturday morning, instead of sleeping in, I woke up to the smell of something amazing: cinnamon rolls.

In the taxonomy of breakfast foods, cinnamon rolls are the only food more exalted than bacon.

I grabbed my hoodie off the floor, pulled on yesterday's joggers, and followed my watering mouth to the kitchen. Cinnamon rolls could only mean one thing: Grandma and Oma were here.

Sure enough, Oma was at the sink, scrubbing out a pan Dad had left soaking overnight, and Grandma was filling the kettle.

I cleared my throat. "Morning."

Grandma turned around. "Morning, Darius." Melanie Kellner was tall—nearly six feet—with gray hair cut in a pixie style and sky-blue eyes. She had a pair of clear-framed glasses pushed up onto her forehead, and she pulled them down to study me. "You've gotten taller."

"Maybe."

Oma peered over her shoulder at me. "And you finally got a haircut."

I rubbed at the back of my head. "Yeah."

She turned back to the dishes while I gave her a kiss on the cheek. Oma was taller than Grandma, but only just. She had longer hair, down to her shoulders, and it was a sort of light brown, though there were streaks of gray in it. She had blue eyes too, but they were darker, more like Dad's. And she had Dad's Teutonic jaw too.

I kissed Grandma hello and gave her one of those awkward side hugs.

My grandmothers only ever did side hugs.

"You've got quite a collection," Grandma said, inventorying my tea cabinet. It was crammed full of tins and pouches and mason jars. Not to mention the jar of Persian tea we kept on the counter because it was too big to fit in the cabinet.

"What's new?"

"Here." I pulled down a mason jar filled with a single-estate Assam. "This is nice and brisk."

She unscrewed the lid and sniffed. "Mmm. The cinnamon rolls are almost done."

"Where's Stephen?" Oma asked. She rinsed off the pot and then pulled the plug to let the sink drain. "And your mom and Laleh?"

"Dad likes to let Mom sleep in on the weekends."

"Hm."

But as soon as I said that, Mom stepped into the kitchen, already dressed for work.

I hated when she had to work on weekends.

"Those smell so good," she said, kissing Grandma and Oma hello. "Save one for me?"

"Of course," Oma said.

Mom kissed me on the forehead on her way out the door. "Have fun with your grandmothers."

"I will. Thanks."

While I made a pot of Assam, Laleh came downstairs, no doubt lured by the same tantalizing scent that had roused me from bed.

"You want to help ice them, Laleh?" Grandma asked. She handed Laleh the little plastic canister of icing.

"Yeah."

Laleh used a fork to drizzle zigzags of icing over the rolls in their circular pan while I set the table for five.

"Your dad's not still in bed, is he?" Grandma asked.

"Just taking a shower," Dad said from the doorway. He was in his blue sweatpants and a gray Kellner & Newton T-shirt, his short hair still damp and messy. He usually kept his blond hair combed and styled with a perfect side-part, but that was before he and Mom were tired all the time.

"Did you leave the fan on?" Oma asked. "We're going to clean the bathrooms after breakfast."

"You don't have to do that, Linda."

Dad always called Oma by her first name.

"Someone's got to."

Dad cleared his throat and rested his hand on my head. "Who's hungry?"

After breakfast, I ran upstairs to make sure the bathroom was okay before Grandma or Oma got to it.

I mean, I'd been keeping my bathroom tidy since I was fourteen, when I noticed just how much leg hair I was shedding and felt weird that Mom and Dad had to sweep it up all the time.

And, since I shared the bathroom with Laleh, I was pretty careful not to leave anything awkward in view.

Not that I owned anything that awkward, anyway. Just an open box of condoms with only one missing, because Dad made me practice putting one on a cucumber during one of our talks.

Persians are more likely to have cucumbers around the house than bananas.

There was no way I would use any of them before they expired. I told Dad that. But he said to hold on to them "just in case." Which is why I had a box of condoms hidden in my nightstand with only one missing.

Okay. Two missing.

I practiced on myself, one time.

"Just in case."

"Darius?"

I banged my elbow against the counter.

"Ow." I looked up. "Hey, Laleh."

"What're you doing?" she asked.

"Just making sure I . . . um, we had cleaning supplies and stuff. For Oma and Grandma."

"I think cleaning is their favorite."

"I guess." I set the all-purpose cleaner on the counter.

"Are you almost done? I have to pee."

"Yeah. Sorry."

"Thanks."

After dinner—one of those frozen lasagnas you bake in the oven, a staple of Grandma and Oma's culinary repertoire—I made a big pot of Dragonwell.

"What's this?" Oma asked as she sipped.

"Dragonwell. Long Jing. We tasted it yesterday."

"It's lovely."

"Yeah."

Grandma poked her head out of the fridge, which she had decided to scour from top to bottom. "Your dad said you got a job."

"Yeah."

"That's great."

Oma nodded at me, and we sipped our tea in silence.

It wasn't an Awkward Silence, but it was an uncomfortable one.

Once Melanie or Linda Kellner said what they had to say, that was it.

They were as averse to small talk as Vulcans.

Dad popped his head in from the living room. "Darius. You ready for *Star Trek*?"

"Yeah. You want a cup?"

He nodded. "Mom? Linda? Want to watch with us?"

"No thanks," Oma said.

And Grandma had already buried her head back in the fridge.

So I poured Dad's tea, and topped off my cup, and settled on the couch to watch "Explorers," this really excellent episode about Captain Sisko and his son, Jake, taking a voyage together in a replica of an old solar-sailing ship.

In the morning, Dad would be taking a voyage without me.

I felt melancholy and unsettled as I sat there with Dad's arm around me, and I scooted closer to him so I could rest my head against his shoulder, although I had to kind of scoot forward on the couch in order to reach.

Ever since I grew taller than Dad, all my habits had to shift.

It made me melancholy.

And unsettled.

Sunday morning, the lights were on when I got home from my run. The garage door was up, and Mom's car was in the driveway with the trunk open. I stopped at the curb to stretch my calves, but Mom looked out the door and waved me in.

"Can you help with your dad's suitcase?"

"Oh. Sure." I kicked off my running shoes, wiped my face, and jogged upstairs. Dad was sealing his toiletries in their clear plastic bag when I knocked on the door frame.

"Hey. Can I help?"

"Sure. Give me a second."

He tossed his brown leather shaving kit into the suitcase—he hadn't shaved yet, and his golden whiskers caught in the glow of the bathroom lights—and zipped it up.

I reached down for the suitcase, but he stopped me.

"You gonna be okay?"

"Yeah," I said. "It's only a month. And you'll be home weekends. Right?"

"As much as I can."

"Okay."

Dad had gone on business trips before, but that was back when he and I didn't get along, and him being out of town was like a little vacation for both of us.

Now the thought of him being gone for so long made my heart ache.

He pulled me closer, his hand resting on the back of my head where the fade had started to grow from bristly to fuzzy.

It seemed like he held on to me longer than usual.

And I got this feeling, this flutter in my diaphragm. I couldn't explain it.

When he let me go, I asked, "What about you? Are you gonna be okay?"

"Of course. But I'm going to miss you."

"We'll have a lot of *Star Trek* to catch up on when you get back."

"You know it." Dad slung his messenger bag over his shoulder. "Come on. Let's get these loaded."

While Mom took Dad to the airport, Grandma and Oma decided to vacuum the living room.

I helped as best I could, moving the couch and the chairs, until they shooed me out because I was in the way.

So I made a pot of Persian tea instead.

Laleh had a cup, with a leftover cinnamon roll, while I made myself some scrambled eggs.

"Doing okay, Laleh?"

"Yeah."

"Are you sad about Dad leaving?"

She shrugged. "I guess."

Laleh wouldn't look up at me. And I thought again that maybe there was something more bothering her.

Something she still wouldn't say out loud.

Mom got back a little after nine. By that point Grandma and Oma had moved onto a deep-clean of the kitchen, so I grabbed a cup of tea for Mom before they erected their quarantine field.

"Thank you," Mom said. "I'm going to call Mamou. You want to say hello?"

My chest tightened.

"Yeah."

I really did want to talk to Mamou.

But every time we did, I was terrified the news would be bad.

We situated ourselves in the office with the door closed to silence the sound of dishes clattering downstairs. Mom's nostrils flared every time a particularly loud bang rattled the floor.

After a couple rings, Mamou's face appeared on the computer screen.

"Eh! Salaam Shirin-jan, chetori toh?"

Mamou and Mom talked for a minute in Farsi, and I listened and smiled. Mamou's voice was warm and happy, even if her eyes were tired.

"Hi Darioush-jan, how are you doing maman?"

"I'm okay. How are you?"

"You know, I am okay. Keeping busy, all the time. How's your school? Do you have a girlfriend?"

Mamou asked me that just about every time we talked.

I hadn't told her about Landon yet.

I hadn't told her I was gay.

Fariba Bahrami was Iranian, and I knew enough about Iran to know that being gay was a subject of some contention. No one ever really talked about it.

The only reason I told Sohrab was because I told Sohrab everything.

It's not that I thought Mamou would stop loving me.

Not really.

But I couldn't shake the fear that maybe, just maybe, she would have a problem with it.

I didn't think I could take it if Mamou looked at me differently. I didn't think my heart could survive that.

Mom shifted. I could feel her eyes on me like a targeting lock.

So I said, "No. Just focusing on school right now."

And then, to change the subject, I said, "How is Babou?"

Mamou sighed.

Sometimes when we talked to Mamou, she started crying.

It was a terrible thing, to see your grandmother cry. To be separated by miles and borders and sanctions from reaching out and giving her a hug.

But lately she just sighed instead.

"He has not changed much. He doesn't wake up very often."

"Oh."

"He asks about you."

"He does?"

"You and Laleh."

I felt my own containment breach coming. I sniffed.

"We're doing okay, Mamou. Will you tell him? And tell him we love him?"

Mamou smiled at me, but her warm eyes shone, and the corners stayed turned down.

I wiped at the corners of my own eyes with the crook of my finger.

"I will tell him, maman."

LOLLY

"Laleh," Mom called. "We're going to be late!"

I couldn't hear Laleh's reply from my bedroom, where I was getting dressed for school, but I could tell it didn't make Mom very happy, because she called out "Come on!"

Mom had waited to go into the office so she could take Laleh to school—usually it was Dad who did it—but that meant she'd be fighting rush hour to get to work.

I grabbed my stuff and headed downstairs. Laleh was sitting on the little stool by the garage door tying her right shoe through her sniffles.

"Can't I just stay home?"

My sister's face was red and tear-streaked.

I must have missed a Laleh-pocalypse while I was in the shower.

"No," Mom said, stacking plates in the sink. "You better be ready when I come back down."

Mom's voice was pinched, and her face was a storm cloud.

"Morning, Darius," she said as she ran back upstairs.

"Hey, Laleh," I said softly. I knelt down next to her, took her left shoe, and slipped it onto her foot. "What's up?"

Laleh sniffled but didn't answer. She watched my hands as I tied her shoe.

"Too tight?"

She shook her head.

I retied her right shoe, then took her hands in mine and bounced them a little.

"Laleh?"

"I just don't wanna go to school today."

"Why?"

"I don't like it."

I was surprised to hear my sister say that, because she had always enjoyed school before.

Laleh had the gift of being good at taking tests—a genetic trait our parents had failed to pass on to me—and always got gold stars on her assignments. Her teachers and classmates liked her too.

I pulled my sleeve down over my palm and brushed away Laleh's tears.

Maybe this was why she'd been so quiet lately.

"How come?"

"I don't know."

"Did your teacher do something?"

She shrugged.

"Did one of your classmates?"

She shrugged again, but then nodded.

"Want to tell me?"

Laleh looked up at me and then back down at her shoes. "Micah and Emily won't talk to me anymore."

"Why? What happened?"

"I don't know." Laleh's voice cracked. "They keep calling me Lolly."

That was preposterous. Micah and Emily had been Laleh's

friends since first grade. They knew how to pronounce her name correctly.

"That's rude." I frowned. "Why are they doing that?"

"It started ever since we went to Iran."

"Oh."

After our trip to Iran, I had to deal with my fair share of ostracism and rumor mongering. (Trent Bolger even tried to start a rumor that I had joined ISIS.) But I hated that it was happening to my sister.

No matter how old you are, it's never good to remind your classmates that you're different.

Otherwise you run the risk of becoming a Target.

I got Laleh cleaned up as best I could, gave her a kiss on her head, and helped her into Mom's car.

Mom came out, her hair in a messy bun—she'd been wearing it in a bun a lot lately, instead of down and styled like she used to—and gave me a quick hug.

"Thank you for calming your sister down," she said. "I think she's tired. She's always up too late, reading her books."

"It's not that," I said. "Her classmates are being racist."

Mom shook her head. "They're third graders."

"Still."

Mom kissed me on the cheek. "I know you're just looking out for her. Don't worry, we'll talk tonight. Love you."

I watched Mom and Laleh drive away. Once the car disappeared around the corner, I pulled my bike off the rack and headed to school.

It was drizzling, the sort of fall drizzle that smells like the inside of a freezer, and I pulled my hood over my helmet. About a mile from Chapel Hill High School, I saw Chip pedaling ahead of me, and sped up to catch him. Beneath his helmet, his hair was pasted to his forehead, but he still tossed a grin my way.

I never knew anyone that grinned as much as Cyprian Cusumano.

"Hey, Darius."

"Hey."

"Good weekend?"

"Okay. You?"

Chip shrugged.

"Not bad."

"Cool."

Chip grinned at me again and then faced forward as we hit The Big Hill.

I downshifted and fell behind him so we could stay closer to the sidewalk, because there were few things in life more terrifying than being on a bike on the road to Chapel Hill High School when a senior was running late for first block.

Chip's shirt rode up his back as he pedaled. He had these little dimples in his lower back.

I swallowed and kept my eyes on the road.

"See you at practice?" he asked as we locked our bikes up.

"Yeah. See you."

Coach Winfield must've liked torturing Chapel Hill High School's Student Athletes. That's the only explanation I could come up with for why he had us doing an hour of wind sprints.

Only Trent Bolger got off light, because apparently he had a "bad case of shin splints."

The Sportsball-Industrial Complex at work.

By the time Coach Winfield blew his whistle, I thought I was going to throw up. Even Gabe was bent over his knees, gulping for air and looking a little green, and like I said, he was the fastest guy I knew.

"All right, gentlemen," Coach Winfield shouted. "Get cleaned up and get out of here."

I limped to the locker room, trailing behind Jaden and Gabe. Both of them had their hands behind their heads in Surrender Cobra, which was unfair, because they both had really nice shoulder muscles.

I wished mine looked that nice.

"Perv alert," Trent said behind me.

"Shut up, Trent."

"Make me, Dairy Queen." He jogged ahead of me, flashing me his middle finger.

Jaden turned around. "Did he—"

"Yeah," Gabe said, glaring at Trent's retreating back. "How can you let him get away with stuff like that?"

I shrugged. "It could be worse. Last year he kept calling me a terrorist."

Jaden frowned. "Really?"

"Yeah."

The thing about Gabe and Jaden was, they were nice guys, but they never had to deal with being Targets. They never knew what that was like until they met me and saw how Trent treated me.

I think they understood something about me just then.

Jaden slowed until I came alongside him and rested his arm across my shoulder.

"You're a cool guy, Darius," he said. "You don't deserve that."

And Gabe took my other side and said, "We've got your back."

I wanted to cry.

Just a little bit.

But I couldn't do that in front of them.

So instead I said, "Thanks. But it's best not to dwell on such minutiae."

CATASTROPHIC
HULL BREACH

"How'd you do?" Chip asked. He was already dressed for practice, leaning up against a locker with his arms folded as I laced up my cleats.

"Hm?"

"On your algebra."

"Got a C. Hanging in there."

"You want to go over it later?"

"You don't have to do that."

"I don't mind."

I studied Chip.

He wasn't grinning at me—not really—but there was something going on in his brown eyes. The ghost of a grin, maybe. Or a temporal echo of a grin he hadn't actually grinned yet.

"Okay," I said. "Sure. Thanks."

I adjusted my shin guards and followed Chip out to the field.

"Coach Winfield had us doing wind sprints today," I said. "If I die during practice, tell my tea I love it."

"If you die during practice, can I have your locker?"

Chip's was at the other end of the locker room, with all the football players—one last legacy of his time on the Chapel Hill High School junior varsity football team. At least once a week he complained the smell was getting to him.

"All right, Chargers!" Coach Bentley called as we hit the field. "Give me a couple laps and then circle up at the whistle!"

Chip patted my back and then broke into a jog. I kept pace with him despite the burning in my legs. We passed Jaden, who looked like he was hurting as bad as me. Gabe ran like he always did, sure-footed and swift and tireless, like he hadn't done an hour of wind sprints after lunch.

Halfway through our fifth lap, Coach blew her whistle twice, and we circled up by one of the goalposts.

The rainy morning had given way to an overcast afternoon, and the cool breeze cut right through my jersey and had me shivering where I stood. We linked hands, and I was grateful to be squeezed between Chip's and James's warm bodies.

Coach started us off. "You all won our first game, and I'm proud of you for that. But I'm more proud of all the hard work you've put in. Let's keep it going."

Jonny Without an H told us all how Jaden had spotted him lunch money; and Gabe told us how Ricky had proofread his assignment in their Creative Writing class.

Next to me, Chip said, "I was in a really bad mood this morning, but I ran into Darius and we biked to school together. It made me feel a lot better. Thanks, Darius."

He gave my hand a little squeeze.

My ears burned.

I hadn't done it on purpose.

I didn't deserve Chip's praise.

Then it was my turn, so I said, "Chip said he'd help me with Algebra II. I could really use the help. So, thanks, Chip."

I tried to squeeze his hand back, but since our arms were crossed, I did the wrong one and accidentally squeezed James's hand instead.

I don't think he noticed, though, or he just thought I was telling him it was his turn, because he told us how Coach Bentley had taken time to work on his back heel kick with him.

By the time we made it all the way around the circle, my jaw was clenching up from the chill. Thankfully Coach Bentley said, "Count off and let's go."

We divided up into Ones and Twos—me and the other Twos wearing bright blue vests to help tell us all apart—and took the field. Christian, our captain and goalie, led us through some warm-up drills until Coach blew her whistle again.

"Okay," Christian said. "Bring it in." He was a Black guy, a senior, with light brown skin and the most amazing cheekbones I had ever encountered. He always had a friendly smile, but it was the kind of smile that was more a shield than an invitation.

Not that I blamed him: People always think of Portland as this super liberal place, and it is, but it's also super white.

As bad as it was being The Once and Future Target, I knew—I knew—that Christian had experienced worse.

Sometimes I wanted to talk to him about it. To let him know I had his back, the way Gabe and Jaden had mine.

But I didn't know how to say that out loud.

"Gabe likes to play it aggressive," Christian said, glancing across the field at the Ones. "Let's be smart. We've got the better defenders. Keep it cool and look for your opening."

We all nodded.

"Darius?"

"Yeah?"

"Cover me."

"Okay."

At least Christian knew I had his back on the field.

Maybe that was enough for now.

"One two three," he said.

"Chargers!"

For Coach Bentley, scrimmages were a skill-building tool. They were supposed to be fun and educational.

But for Gabe and Christian, who'd been playing together since middle school, they were a contest of wills, a battle of celestial forces that could only end when one or the other was utterly annihilated.

As soon as the whistle blew, our teams clashed, galaxies colliding with Gabe's and Christian's egos as the supermassive black holes at their centers. I stayed back, Christian's last line of defense, as Gabe broke past our midfielders, passing the ball back and forth with Chip, feinting to Zack and then surging forward.

Gabe tried to get between me and Bruno—one of our center backs—but Bruno stole the ball and passed it to Jaden.

The scrimmage went back and forth. Christian called out plays and encouragement and the occasional groan whenever we narrowly missed scoring on the Ones. He let in one goal from Gabe, but stopped way more than that.

We had better luck, though, with two goals on their goalie Diego. He was a sophomore who'd just moved up from JV, and everyone thought he was going to replace Christian as goalie next year.

Not as captain, though: Diego was the least inspiring speaker

I'd ever met. Even when he said something nice, like during Circle, he always managed to sound like he was complaining.

I actually thought maybe Chip would make captain next year. Everyone liked him, and he was a great motivator.

Especially when he was trying to get past you to score: When Gabe passed him the ball, and I was the only one between him and Christian, I was extremely motivated to stop him.

He tried to get around me, but I stayed with him. Bruno had Gabe covered, so Chip couldn't pass the ball back.

Chip grinned at me, faked left and then took off right, but I knew what he was going to do. I slipped in and hooked the ball away from him.

That was a mistake, though, because I hooked it right as he was going for a kick.

His eyes widened for a microsecond, like he knew what he was about to do to me.

And then his knee got me. Right between the legs.

I dropped to the grass, like every muscle in my body had reverted to a semi-gelatinous state.

I squeezed my eyes shut and tried to breathe.

I was certain my testicles had just experienced a catastrophic hull breach.

"Oh my god I'm so sorry are you okay?" Chip knelt next to me, his hands fluttering from my back to my shoulder to my neck, like he thought he should be doing something but didn't know what.

There was nothing he could do.

There was nothing anyone could do.

"Easy, Darius," Coach said. I couldn't remember her ever using my first name before. "Can you talk?"

I swallowed away the burning taste of bile.

"Yeah," I groaned.

"Can you move?"

I nodded.

"Can we take you off the field, or do you need to stay here a while? Do we need to call a doctor?"

"I'm okay," I said. "I can get up."

"I'll help him," Chip said. "It was an accident, Coach. Really."

"I know," she said. "Why don't you get cleaned up, Darius? Do you need me to call your parents?"

"No. I mean, yeah. I'll get cleaned up. You don't need to call my parents."

"All right. Cusumano, get him to the locker room and see if you can find Coach Steiner."

Chip helped me up.

"I can walk," I said.

"Okay." Chip pulled my arm over his shoulder, anyway. His back was drenched with sweat, and he didn't smell particularly nice, but I probably didn't either. "Come on."

Chip led me to my locker in silence.

The pain was starting to wear off, but a wave of nausea was replacing it, radiating out from somewhere deep behind my belly button. I leaned my head against the cool metal of my locker and closed my eyes.

"Hey, don't fall asleep," Chip said. "That's how you die."

"I think that's concussions."

I kept my eyes closed, but I could just picture Chip's eternal grin.

"Well, I concussed your balls pretty bad."

"Yeah."

"For real, though. I'll be right back. Will you be okay for a second?"

"Yeah." I pulled away from my locker and took out my towel and soap. "I'm gonna shower off."

"Okay, but if you see blood going down the drain, make sure to scream really loud."

"Gross."

I showered off as gently as I could. There was, mercifully, no blood. My testicles felt tender, and suddenly very precious, but whole.

I toweled off and padded back to my locker. I was stepping into my boxer briefs when I heard Chip's voice coming around the corner.

"I got you an ice pack, in case you . . . oh."

Chip and I stared at each other for a second.

I mean, we'd been in locker rooms together before, but I don't think he'd ever seen me naked.

In that moment I felt very naked indeed.

Chip's eyes darted downward.

"Huh," he said, under his breath.

That nauseated feeling came back as I pulled my underwear the rest of the way up and turned away so he was looking at my back instead.

The air felt thick and weird.

Why was it so weird being around Chip? We were teammates, and friends.

I mean, other guys had seen me naked before. That's what happened when you were on a soccer team.

Even my best friend, Sohrab, had seen me naked, when we played soccer together back in Iran.

But nothing had ever made me feel quite as sticky as when Chip looked at me and said *"Huh."*

I tugged my joggers on, then my shirt, and ran a hand through my hair.

Behind me, Chip finally spoke.

"At least they're not turning blue."

Just like that, the tension vanished.

I snorted. It hurt to laugh.

"Not yet."

Chip set the ice pack down on the bench. "You need water or anything? I can grab you some."

"Um."

He looked at me again, real quick.

I was certain he glanced down at my pants.

Just for a second.

"I'm okay. Thanks, though."

What was happening?

TEUTONIC PUNCTUALITY

While Chip went to find Coach Steiner, I sat outside Coach Bentley's office and iced my testicles.

Coach Steiner was Chapel Hill High School's athletic trainer. Ostensibly he was in charge of monitoring the health and safety of Chapel Hill High School's Student Athletes.

Go Chargers.

My pain had more or less gone away, as long as I didn't move. Or cough. Or think.

As the team shuffled in at the end of practice, they lined up to fist-bump me one by one and express their condolences.

They actually said that: "Sorry for your loss." One after another, Christian and Robby and Jaden and Jonny Without an H and all the guys said it, and by the time Gabe brought up the end of the line I was smiling and it didn't hurt so much when I laughed.

"You okay, Kellner?" Coach said.

Now that I wasn't prone on the grass, she was back to calling me by my last name, like coaches always do.

"Yeah."

"What did Coach Steiner say?"

"I don't know. Chip hasn't come back yet."

Coach Bentley's nostrils flared.

Coach Steiner was supposed to be available to all the teams equally, but he always seemed to be with the football team, monitoring for potential concussions.

"I swear . . ." Coach Bentley began, but the door opened and Chip trudged back inside.

"Sorry. Coach Winfield was there, and he got on me about 'abandoning the sport' again. You know how he is."

Coach Bentley cocked her eyebrows. "Hmm. What about Coach Steiner?"

Chip glanced at me, his cheeks turning pink.

"He said if there was no, uh, blood, to ice the, uh, affected area."

Coach shook her head. "Darius, what do you want? Should we call a doctor?"

I shifted in my seat.

"I think I'm okay. Really."

I did not want to discuss my testicles with Coach Bentley any more than was absolutely necessary.

"You have a ride home?"

I had not considered my return home.

The thought of riding my bicycle caused a little twinge of pain.

"No . . ."

"Why don't you walk back to my place?" Chip said. "Your parents can pick you up from there?"

"You sure?"

Chip nodded.

"Thanks."

Chip and I walked our bikes down The Big Hill. He insisted on carrying my messenger bag for me, so he had his and mine slung over each shoulder, the straps making an X across his chest like some sort of anime hero.

The afternoon light caught the fine hairs on the back of his neck, where his fade had started to grow out, and painted his skin gold.

Cyprian Cusumano was a beautiful guy. It was impossible to ignore that about him, even though I was with Landon.

That's normal.

Right?

We didn't talk much on our walk, just trudged down the hill. Sometimes Chip would glance at me and give me one of his grins.

I didn't know what to make of Cyprian Cusumano.

And my chest felt tight, walking alone with him in a loaded silence, knowing he had seen me naked earlier, when my own boyfriend hadn't seen me naked.

Why did it make me feel so weird?

And wrong?

And excited?

"It's this way," Chip said, turning us onto a side street that led up another, smaller hill. It was shorter than The Big Hill, but way steeper. "We're at the top, sorry."

"It's okay. I bet it sucks riding up this after practice."

"It's not so bad after practice. Way worse back when I was on the football team, and Coach Winfield made us do sled pushes."

"Coach Winfield is the worst."

"Dude, I know. Trent says he can always tell when Coach Winfield is in a bad mood, because that's when he makes everyone do squats. Says it brings a sense of order to his universe."

I didn't say anything to that.

I really didn't get how Chip could be friends with a Soulless Minion of Orthodoxy like Trent Bolger, or how he could just bring up Trent in conversation with me when he knew—he knew—how Trent treated me.

Chip cleared his throat. "Hey. Can I ask you something kind of personal?"

"Um. I guess?"

"I kind of saw you in the locker room."

The back of my neck prickled.

I didn't know where this conversation was headed, but I had the strong urge to throw myself back down the hill we were climbing.

I glanced sideways at Chip—his face was bright red—and then looked back at my feet.

"Are you . . . uncut?"

"I mean. Yeah?" I swallowed. "But I think intact is a better word."

"Oh," he said.

And then he said, "I wish my parents had left me intact."

My whole body was on fire.

I swallowed again.

Chip stepped around a pothole and brushed shoulders with me.

"Sorry if I made it weird."

It was super weird.

I would rather have gotten another knee to the balls than discuss my foreskin with Cyprian Cusumano.

"It's fine," I squeaked. "It's not weird. I mean."

I didn't know what I meant.

I cleared my throat.

Chip just shrugged and led me up his driveway. He dug through his messenger bag for a moment and must have had a remote for the garage door, because the left one started opening.

"You can leave your bike in here," he said. "What time . . ."

Before he could finish, the door from the garage to the house burst open, and a small blur darted for Chip.

He laughed and scooped up a little toddler—they couldn't have been more than two years old—with light brown skin and dark, curly hair.

Chip was white. At least, I thought he was white, with his pale skin and soft brown hair. So I kind of wondered who the kid was.

Not that I could ask that kind of question out loud.

"Hi," I said as the kid looked over Chip's shoulder at me. I gave a little wave. "I'm Darius."

The kid's eyes got big.

Chip laughed again and angled himself so both he and his passenger could see me.

"Say hi, Evie," Chip said. His grin was so big it wasn't even a grin anymore: He was totally beaming.

"Hi," Evie whispered.

Chip planted a loud smooch on Evie's cheek, which got a giggle. "This is my niece."

"Oh. Cool."

Chip led me into the house as Evie talked his ear off. I couldn't make out a word she said: She was talking too fast, and in that funny way toddlers have, where they know what they want to say but can't quite form the words all the way. Chip was smiling so big his eyes were squinting up.

I really liked seeing him smile like that.

He never smiled like that at school.

"You doing okay? Need another ice pack?"

"I think I'm good."

Chip shifted Evie a little bit to free up one hand, and pulled a cheese stick out of the fridge. He peeled it open and handed it to Evie.

"Where's your mommy?" he asked.

"Upstairs." Evie squirmed a bit. Chip kissed her one more time and set her down. She ran out of the kitchen, doing that funny run little kids do, where they lift their knees up really high and stomp their tiny feet as they go.

Chip grabbed a red Gatorade out of the fridge and handed me a purple one.

"I didn't know you had a sister."

"Really? She graduated last year. Ana."

"Oh," I said. "From Chapel Hill?"

Chip nodded, like I should have remembered. "I've got an older brother too. But he graduated before we started."

My ears burned.

I had a whole bunch of questions, but I didn't know how to ask them.

In fact, I was pretty sure it would be rude to ask them.

So I said, "How old is she?"

"Ana?"

"Evie."

"Oh. She'll be two in December."

"That's a good age," I said, because that's what everyone always says, no matter what age is being discussed.

"Yeah."

We looked at each other for a long moment as the kitchen walls closed in on us. The air in the room grew heavy and pregnant.

Which was a weird thought to have, since I was just thinking about Chip's sister being pregnant while she was in high school. And wondering lots of things that weren't my business.

My heart thudded against my sternum.

Chip kept looking at me.

I looked down at my hands.

"I should probably let my grandmas know where to pick me up."

A dark blue Camry pulled into Chip's driveway: Oma's car. She honked twice.

Linda Kellner was a paragon of Teutonic punctuality.

"Oh. That's my ride," I said.

I dumped my ziplock baggie full of half-melted ice into the sink—I'd started aching again as we went over my Algebra II answers—while Chip gathered up our Gatorade bottles.

"Thanks for letting me hang out," I said. "I don't think I would have survived a bike ride tonight."

"It's all good."

"And thanks for your help. Really."

Chip grinned. "I had fun."

I groaned. "Math is not fun."

"Well, I enjoyed the company at least."

Chip kept grinning at me, but it wasn't his usual grin. There was something gentler about it. Almost like a question.

"Well. Thanks."

"Anytime. You wanna leave your bike here? You can get it after practice tomorrow?"

My face heated at that. I wasn't sure why.

But I said "Sure," because Oma didn't have a bike rack.

As I laced up my shoes, Evie ran down the stairs. Chip scooped her up mid-dash and swung her up to cover her face with kisses. She squealed and laughed and said "Noooo!"

Chip stopped. "No?"

"Not now."

"Okay." Chip set her down, and she scampered off into the kitchen.

I liked that he respected her boundaries, even though she was a toddler.

I thought that was really cool.

"Say bye to Darius!"

"Bye, Evie!" I called after her, but she ignored us both. Chip just shook his head.

In the driveway, Oma honked again.

"Well." I slung my bag over my shoulder. "See you tomorrow."

IRON GODDESS
OF MERCY

Linda Kellner didn't like to listen to music in the car. She always listened to the news.

She also didn't like to talk very much.

"Hi, Oma," I said as I buckled up. "Thanks for coming to get me."

Oma nodded and then turned up her NPR.

That meant the conversation was over.

Like I said, I'd never been very close with Oma. Or with Grandma.

Linda and Melanie Kellner weren't very demonstrative with their affection.

I thought maybe that was just how grandparents were, until I went to Iran. Mamou had practically smothered me with hugs and kisses, and even Babou's reserve had cracked as we spent time together.

When we got home, Oma parked on Dad's side of the driveway. I got out and punched in the code to open the door.

Grandma was at the kitchen table doing a puzzle while Laleh read. It looked like she had finished *Dune*, but I couldn't tell what the new book was.

"Hi, Grandma," I said, and gave her a kiss on the cheek. "Hi, Laleh."

Laleh nodded but kept reading.

"Go get ready for dinner," Oma said. "It'll be done soon."

"Okay."

I didn't actually have that much to do to get ready—just drop off my stuff in my room—but I took the opportunity for privacy to check the status of my testicles.

They were still red, but less angry-looking, and they didn't hurt so much when I pressed on them.

I sighed with relief.

It was bad enough, explaining to Oma what happened and why I needed a ride.

I did not want to reopen the subject and ask her to take me to the doctor for broken testicles.

"Dinner!"

I put on a pair of clean compression shorts, to keep things supported, and headed downstairs.

My grandmothers had made ground beef tacos.

Mom always said the only spices Grandma and Oma knew about were salt and pepper, but that wasn't technically true, if you counted the pouch of taco seasoning Grandma used.

I handed out plates, made two tacos for myself, and took my seat. I shifted a little, and tried not to wince, but Oma noticed.

"How're you feeling?"

"Okay," I said. "Just sore."

"What happened?" Laleh asked.

My ears burned. "I got hit in practice today. I'm okay, though."

"Stephen said you won your first game," Grandma said. "He sent pictures. It looked like a good one."

"Yeah."

While Laleh crunched on her taco—which was mostly cheese

and shell, with a little bit of lettuce and tomato and a sprinkling of beef—Oma asked, "When's your next one?"

"Friday."

"Well, keep on winning. If you do well this season, you might be in line for a scholarship."

Oma said, "Especially if you get your GPA up."

I crunched my taco so I wouldn't have to respond.

The thing is, I wasn't sure I wanted to go to college. In fact, I was pretty sure it would be a bad fit for me.

I knew my grandmothers were only trying to help, but somehow that only made me feel worse.

I swallowed.

"Maybe."

While Grandma put away the leftovers and Oma did the dishes, I made us a pot of tea.

"What's that you're making?" Oma asked over her shoulder.

"Ti Kwan Yin."

Ti Kwan Yin means "Iron Goddess of Mercy." It's a Chinese oolong with pretty much the coolest name ever.

Normally I made it in a gaiwan, but with three of us it wasn't practical.

Grandma and Oma settled on the couch, each at one end, and I took the chair. After a while, Oma reached for the TV remote and turned on a cooking competition.

For people who didn't use seasoning, Grandma and Oma really liked cooking shows.

We sipped and sipped as the silence between us built, a cascading wave of missed opportunities.

I wanted my grandmothers to ask me to sit with them.

I wanted them to pause the show so we could talk.

I wanted them to be more like Mamou and Babou.

But I didn't know how to say that out loud.

So instead I said, "I'm gonna see if Laleh wants any tea."

My sister's door was half-open, but I still knocked on the frame: one-three-three, which was our special knock. "You want some tea?"

"Yeah."

Laleh curled her legs under her and let me sit on her bed. She had one of those huge pillows with armrests built into it, soft pink with a purple fringe on top. It was dented in the middle from all the hours she'd spent sitting against it reading.

I handed her a tasting cup—a ceramic one emblazoned with the Rose City logo—and tilted my head to look at the spine of her book.

"*The Shining*?" I asked. "Is it good?"

"It's okay."

"Scary?"

"Nah."

Laleh blew on her tea and took a sip. I took a bigger slurp from my own cup.

"Hmm," Laleh said. She smacked her lips. "It's sweet."

"It's got notes of honey," I said. "And milk too. But I didn't put any sugar in it."

"Really?"

I nodded.

Laleh took another sip. "It's okay. Not as good as Persian tea."

"Noted." We sat together, enjoying our tea.

Then I said, "Is school any better?"

Laleh shrugged.

"Are Micah and Emily treating you better?"

Laleh shook her head.

"I'm sorry."

"It's okay."

But it wasn't okay.

"Have you talked to your teacher?"

"No." She sighed. "Emily's her favorite. She never gets in trouble."

"Oh."

I wanted to build a force field around my sister, to shield her from Micah and Emily and her teacher and all the other Soulless Minions of Orthodoxy lurking in her future.

I hated how helpless I was.

"Is there something I can do?"

Laleh shook her head again, and then turned back to her book, like she didn't want to talk about it anymore.

I leaned over and kissed the crown of her head.

"Love you, Laleh," I whispered into her hair.

It was nearly nine o'clock when the garage door finally rumbled. Everyone else was in bed, but I was sitting in the kitchen, icing myself again.

I dumped the ice in the sink and pulled out the leftover taco meat for Mom.

"Hey, sweetie." I wrapped my mom in a hug, but her whole body was like a polarized hull plate, rigid and brittle. After a moment she finally relaxed against me. But then the microwave beeped.

"You don't need to do that for me."

"I want to."

"All right. How was your day?"

"It was okay," I said. Mom didn't seem like she was in the mood to hear about my testicular trauma.

I wasn't in the mood to talk about it anyway.

"How was yours?"

"Long."

I pulled down a plate for her and grabbed the rest of the taco fixings out of the fridge while she checked something on her phone. She looked up and frowned at me. "I can make my own dinner, you know."

"I don't mind. Want some tea?"

Mom sighed and sat down. "I better not. Thanks."

I grabbed my cup—a second steeping of Ti Kwan Yin, which had more mellow floral notes than the first steeping—and sat next to her.

"How did your test go?"

"I got a C."

"Do you need some help? We can go over your problems together."

"It's okay. I went to Chip's after practice and we worked on it together."

"Oh. That's nice." Mom took a bite of taco and studied me as she chewed. "You've been spending a lot of time with him lately."

I don't know why it felt like such an accusation when she said that.

I don't know why I felt like I had to defend myself.

"He's been really helpful," I said. "Oh. I left my bike at his house. Think you can drop me off in the morning?"

Mom frowned. "I can't tomorrow. Early meeting. Oma or Grandma will have to."

"Oh."

"I wish I could, though."

"It's okay. Really."

I let Mom eat in silence after that.

There was something she wasn't saying out loud, something I was supposed to know but didn't.

When she finished, she wiped her hands and mouth, careful to avoid her lipstick.

"I better go put Laleh to bed."

"Oma already did. She even got her to take a bath."

"Really?"

"Yeah."

"Well then." Mom glanced toward the stairs.

I sipped my tea.

"Want to watch something? *Star Trek*?"

"Um."

Mom had never asked me to watch *Star Trek* before.

That was always me and Dad's thing.

I didn't know what to say.

I was trying to figure out if we should continue where Dad and I left off, or start a different series, but then Mom said, "Never mind. Sorry."

She got up before I could say anything.

Before I could tell her I wanted to watch *Star Trek* with her.

Mom ran her fingers through my hair and kissed my forehead. "I'm going to go to bed."

BROKEN FURNITURE

In the morning, Oma dropped me off at Chip's to grab my bike.

"Hey." Chip answered the door in a pair of soft gray sweatpants that looked really nice on him.

Like, not-wearing-any-underwear nice.

He wasn't wearing a shirt either, and like I said, Cyprian Cusumano had a very nice stomach and chest. The kind I wished I had.

The kind guys like me were supposed to have.

"Sorry, I know I'm late. Evie's been a handful."

My ears felt like twin plasma fires.

"I've just gotta throw some clothes on. You want anything?"

I shook my head. I couldn't speak.

How could Chip act so casual around me when he was half-naked like that?

And why couldn't I look away?

I wondered what Landon looked like without his shirt on.

If he had hair on his chest, or if he was smooth.

I sucked on the tassels of my hoodie.

"Sorry," Chip said when he ran down the stairs in black joggers and a white V-neck T-shirt that was just a bit too small for him.

It was only slightly less distracting.

He'd done his hair too, styling his fade into a soft brown quiff that was just a little messy.

Cyprian Cusumano really was a beautiful guy.

I hated myself for thinking so.

"Sorry. I'm ready."

"It's cool."

Everyone at practice treated me like I was made of glass. Perhaps seeing me take a knee to the balls had brought the guys face-to-face with their own frail mortality.

That kind of thing could be deeply unsettling.

When Coach called a time-out, I grabbed my water bottle and wandered over to the bleachers to stretch my calves. Coach followed me.

"How's it going, Darius?"

She was using my first name again, like I needed to be handled.

"Okay."

"Will you be able to play this Friday?"

"Yeah. For sure."

"Good." She nodded at me and then wandered away, her clipboard tucked under her arm, to shout at Jaden and Gabe for horsing around.

I held on to the bleachers for a hammy stretch.

Even though I was kind of annoyed everyone was taking it easy on me, I really did love that Coach and the team cared about me like that.

It was pretty cool, having a team.

I'd never had something like that before.

After practice was over, Christian called all us together.

"Good work today, guys," he said.

He had this warm, calming voice when he talked normally— like he was doing now—which was nothing like his Captain Voice.

Christian's Captain Voice would not have been out of place on the bridge of a starship.

"Game against Meadowbrook this Friday. Let's crush it!"

We all cheered.

"And party after. My place. I got the new FIFA."

"Woo!" Jaden shouted, and high-fived Christian.

I looked at Chip, who shrugged and grinned.

I had never been to a party before.

Was it the kind of party people had on TV? With drugs and alcohol and sex and broken furniture?

"What if I suck at FIFA?" Chip whispered to me.

"I've never played."

"Well, it can't be worse than the wrestling parties."

During the winter, Chip was on the Chapel Hill High School varsity wrestling team.

"Why?"

"Most of the guys didn't shower after meets."

"Gross."

"Right?" Chip laughed and ran his hands through his sweaty hair. "Soccer guys are way cleaner."

Chip squeezed my shoulder and grinned at me, then followed the rest of the guys toward the locker room.

I stayed where I was, shaking my head.

Sometimes I didn't know what to make of Cyprian Cusumano.

Wednesday afternoon I had my first shift as a real employee at Rose City Teas. I worked the tea bar, chatting with customers and figuring out what kind of tea they wanted: black or green or oolong, flavored or unflavored, an old favorite or a new adventure.

While I worked the bar, Mr. Edwards was cupping a new batch of Phoenix Mountain, a Chinese oolong that was supposed to be fruity and delicious. Landon kept poking his head out of the tasting room, waving at me to join them, but every time I was about to, another customer showed up needing help, and Polli was too busy making lattes to cover for me.

Finally, Landon gave up and closed the door.

I don't know why it made me so sad. It was just one tasting.

But I really did want to try the Phoenix Mountain Oolong.

Instead I prepared a gaiwan service for a man about Oma's age, who peppered me with questions about oolong processing, and Chinese versus Taiwanese producers. I was trying to explain about Bai Hao and the little bugs that tried to eat the leaves when Polli cleared her throat and pointed out there was a line forming.

I excused myself and started taking more orders.

As I steeped a single-serve pot of Earl Grey and did a wake-up steep for another gaiwan service, Landon emerged from the tasting room, holding a white porcelain Rose City–branded teacup.

"Here," he said. "This was the winner."

"Thanks."

Landon handled the gaiwan for me while I sipped with one hand and poured out the Earl Grey with the other. The tea was bursting with lychee flavor, which was kind of a surprise to me.

I'd never tasted lychee in a tea before.

I wondered what the other batches had tasted like.

I wondered what Landon got to learn about Phoenix Mountain tea and where it came from.

I wondered what I had missed.

Finally the line at the tea bar petered out, so Mr. Edwards sent me and Landon to do some inventory. As I counted tins of Genmaicha, Mr. Edwards poked his head in. "Can one of you grab some Dragonwell?"

"Sure, Dad."

Landon went over to the shelves and reached for the top, where the boxes of Dragonwell sat. His shirt rode up, exposing a tiny patch of smooth skin on his back, and the metallic silver waistband of his underwear.

I thought about Chip's gray sweatpants, and how he didn't wear underwear with them.

And I thought about Chip, seeing me naked, when I'd never even taken my shirt off around Landon.

My ears burned.

"Darius?"

"Hm?"

"Can you . . . ?" he asked, turning toward me, showing a few inches of pale stomach.

He had this line of fine hair that disappeared behind his belt buckle.

Landon Edwards was a beautiful guy. Way more attractive than me.

Sometimes I wondered what he saw in me anyway.

"Yeah," I squeaked. I cleared my throat. "Hey. What're you doing Friday?"

"Coming to your game?"

"I meant after."

"I don't know." Landon wrapped his arms around my waist. I sucked in my stomach. "What am I doing after?"

I swallowed.

"You wanna come to a party? It'll just be the team, I think. Playing FIFA and stuff."

He let out this funny snort. "Really?"

"I guess."

Landon squeezed my waist. I hated that it wasn't hard and smooth like his.

"I'd love to."

"Really?"

"Yeah."

My cheeks warmed.

I couldn't stop myself from smiling.

"Okay."

L ike I said, I'd never been to a high school party before.

I had envisioned some sort of Level Seven Debauchery, with dried-out red Solo cups and used joints and people passed out on every flat surface.

Instead, there were twenty of us crammed into a half-finished basement, sitting on folding chairs or sprawled on the floor, using pillows from the living room couches to cushion us from the cold smooth concrete.

A few of the other guys had invited their girlfriends, and everyone was smiling and laughing and happy we'd won another game.

Christian's parents were upstairs, swapping out batches of pizza rolls and popcorn chicken in the oven, and talking with some of the other team parents.

And there was no alcohol. We drank Gatorade, and took turns playing FIFA on Christian's PlayStation, which was hooked into a tiny projector that James—who was a theater kid in the off-season—had managed to borrow for the weekend. It was pointed at the blank drywall, and we could barely hear the tinny built-in speakers over everyone's talking.

Landon and I sat on the floor against the wall, cuddling and watching it all play out. We leaned our heads against each other and occasionally kissed, but not too often, because every time we did one of the guys would start whooping and clapping at us.

It reminded me of being at an Iranian wedding, where

the married couple would have to kiss whenever people started clinking their glasses with their forks and shouting "Shoo-loo-loo-loo-loo!"

"You good?" Landon's hair tickled my lips as I spoke into his ear.

"I'm good," he said.

"I'm gonna grab another drink."

I untangled my limbs from his and went upstairs to pull another purple Gatorade—the best flavor—out of the fridge. A few guys were upstairs, hovering in the kitchen or sprawled out in the living room playing on their phones.

The door to the patio was wide open, to circulate some air and relieve the overwhelming smell of pizza rolls and tightly packed boys.

Chip was outside, talking to Trent Bolger, who had somehow rated an invite to the party. They were arguing, as best I could tell.

"—ditched me again, dude," Trent said.

"I don't complain when you have football practice."

"Why are you playing soccer anyway? It sucks."

"I like soccer. I told you football wasn't for me."

Trent grunted.

"Yeah, well, what about Monday? You were supposed to text me when you got out."

"I told you I was sorry. I kneed Darius in the balls. What was I supposed to do, leave him on the side of the road?"

Trent snorted at that. "I wish I'd seen it."

"It was awful. You don't even know."

"I didn't know you were so desperate to get to third base."

My ears burned.

Chip mumbled something I couldn't catch, but it made Trent laugh again.

"Whatever." Trent rounded the corner and saw me holding my purple Gatorade up to my lips without drinking. "What's up, D-cheese."

That was a new one.

Objectively speaking, Trent had said worse. Dairy Queen was at least a Level Three Homophobic Insult.

But D-Cheese offended me more.

I had excellent personal hygiene, and that hadn't been a problem for me since I was like twelve.

Not that I could tell that to Trent Bolger.

I never wanted to discuss my penis with Trent Bolger.

"Be cool, man," Chip said. "Hey, Darius."

I took a sip of my Gatorade. "Hey."

The burning in my ears had spread down to my neck.

I looked from Trent to Chip and back to Trent. He had this smirk on his face, like he knew what I was thinking.

I didn't like it.

Behind me, the oven beeped, and I heard Christian's mom call from upstairs. "That's the pizza rolls!"

"I'll get them!" I hollered. I put on an oven mitt and pulled the sheet of molten nuggets out while Trent grabbed Chip's shoulder.

"Come on."

Chip gave me a little closed-lip smile and followed his friend downstairs.

I turned off the oven and tossed my Gatorade in the recycling bin. The sound of Trent's hyena laugh echoed up from the basement.

I went upstairs to use the bathroom.

I didn't actually have to pee.

I mean, I did pee, but I didn't actually have to.

I just needed to get away.

I washed my hands and sat on the edge of the bathtub with my phone. I read an article Coach Bentley had sent out to the team about post-game recovery, sent Mom a text to let her know the party was fine and Christian's parents were home, took a quiz to find out *Which* Star Trek: Deep Space Nine *Supporting Character Are You?*

I thought about hiding in the bathroom for the rest of the party, but someone knocked on the door.

"Just a sec," I said, and flushed the toilet again, so they wouldn't know I'd been hiding. I washed my hands again too.

"Thanks," Gabe said, and closed the door behind him.

I found Landon in the kitchen, drinking a bottle of orange Gatorade.

"Hey. Sorry."

"No worries." He pulled me in for an orangey kiss. "You good?"

"Yeah. Just needed a second away from the crowd."

Landon's arms slid down to my hips. He kissed me one more time, then pulled me toward the living room. I settled on the corner of the big beige couch, and Landon sat on my lap, his knees on either side of my hips and his butt resting on my thighs.

"Hey." He kissed my nose. "You were awesome today."

"Yeah?"

He kissed me again, on the corner of the mouth.

"Yeah. I loved watching you play."

"Really?"

"Really. Have you seen yourself in those shorts?"

I couldn't breathe.

"You like them?" I squeaked.

Landon's eyes twinkled. "I do." And then he kissed me again, and his tongue slipped into my mouth, and I decided breathing wasn't all that important anyway.

I'm not going to lie: With all the kissing, I got an erection pretty quickly.

And I couldn't tell for sure, but I thought Landon had one too. It was either that or his belt buckle rubbing against me as he rocked back and forth on his hips.

"Is this okay?" he whispered.

"Um."

What Landon was doing felt good.

Really good.

If he didn't stop, I was facing a containment breach of an entirely different sort.

Landon's hands were wrapped around my love handles, and I couldn't breathe because I was keeping my stomach sucked in.

And the whole team was downstairs.

Chip and Trent were downstairs.

"Wait." I rested my hands on his hips to stop his rocking.

"Too much?"

I nodded.

"Sorry." He smiled and kissed me again. His kisses trailed

from my mouth to my neck, and then down to my collarbone, which felt weird. I giggled.

"What?"

"Sorry. That tickles."

He sat back, biting his lip, and glanced down at my lap.

I wished I had worn jeans instead of my joggers.

"Do you want to go somewhere less . . . exposed?"

"Um."

My heart thundered.

The idea was exhilarating.

And terrifying.

Sweat beaded on my forehead.

Before I could answer, though, the sound of footsteps drumming against the basement stairs echoed up to us.

Chip poked his head into the living room, with Trent right behind him.

"Oh. Hey dude," Chip said. He wasn't grinning. Instead, his brows were scrunched up. "Landon, right?"

Landon cleared his throat. "Yeah." I loved how red his cheeks were.

"Don't let us stop you," Trent said from behind Chip. "Dairy Queen could use some breaking in."

My own cheeks reddened.

"Shame no one's broken you in," Landon muttered.

I snorted, and Chip grinned, but Trent said, "What?"

"Come on." Chip dragged Trent away, mouthing *sorry* at us as he disappeared into the kitchen.

"Assholes," Landon said.

"Trent is the worst," I agreed. "But Chip's not so bad."

I don't know why I felt like I had to defend Chip.

I was kind of mad at him too.

But I didn't want Landon to be.

"Isn't he the one who hit you in the balls, though?"

I winced.

"He's nice, though. Usually."

Landon stared at me for a long moment, biting his lip.

And then he let out this tiny sigh. "Hey. I better head home."

"Already?"

"Yeah. I've got rehearsal tomorrow morning."

"Oh."

Landon kissed me and got off my lap.

Our encounter with Trent and Chip had removed any barriers that might have previously hindered that maneuver.

I waited in the kitchen with Landon until his ride showed up.

"You sure everything's okay?" I asked.

"Yeah. Why?"

"Just checking."

Landon kissed me on the cheek, zipped up his puffy coat, and left.

And I got this feeling. Like I had done something wrong.

Behind me, Chip cleared his throat.

"Hey. Sorry about all that."

"Yeah. Well."

I didn't know what else to say.

I really did like Cyprian Cusumano, but he would never see Trent Bolger for who he truly was.

"I convinced the guys to switch to Mario Kart. Wanna play?"

"I guess."

BIG RED ROBE

When I got home, I had a cup of tea and then lay in bed staring at the ceiling, going over things in my head, trying to figure out what I had done wrong. Why Landon had left so suddenly.

It was a restless night, and a worse morning, mowing the still-damp lawn before heading downtown for my shift.

I'd never been nervous going into Rose City Teas before.

"Hey, Darius." Kerry was working the front register. She was a twenty-something white woman with piercings up and down both ears. She wore this garish, itchy-looking cardigan over her black Rose City T-shirt, the kind where you can see the fibers stretching upward like trees reaching for the sun.

"Hey." I looked around. "Where do you need me?"

"Stock room. But later." She cocked her head toward the tasting room. "Mr. Edwards has a tasting for you."

"Cool."

After missing the last tasting, I had been kind of worried, so it was a relief when I knocked on the tasting room door and Mr. Edwards swept me inside.

"You're in for a treat today. We just got a new batch of Wuyis in."

Wuyi rock tea is a kind of oolong from the Wuyi Mountains in China, known for its heavy minerality, smokiness, and stone fruit notes. The Wuyi Mountains are also, supposedly, the home of the original tea bushes in China, which they use to make a tea called Da Hong Pao, or Big Red Robe.

The finest leaves sell for something like $30,000 an ounce.

Mr. Edwards had only tasted the expensive stuff once, through sheer luck, on a visit to China a few years back.

He said it was the taste of a lifetime.

"Mind grabbing some gaiwans?"

"Okay."

I pulled down the gaiwans from the top shelf of the cupboard.

"It's nice to have a tall guy here to help. Don't need the step stool as much."

I rinsed each gaiwan in warm water and then dried them as carefully as I could with a soft towel. As I set the table, Landon poked his head in.

"Hey, Dad," he said. "What're we doing?"

"Da Hong Pao. Come on in."

Landon nodded at me and took a seat at the long table, while I pulled out tasting cups and spoons for us. Mr. Edwards grabbed the kettle and started pouring while I picked up my notebook and sat next to Landon.

"Hey," I said.

"Hey."

My skin hummed.

I wasn't sure if things were still weird between us or not.

But then Landon reached over and put his hand on mine. I rubbed the top of his hand with my thumb.

Mr. Edwards handed around each cup of leaves for us to smell before he poured the first steeping. We sipped, and took notes, while Mr. Edwards poured the second steeping.

"Kind of bashful," Landon said. His dad slurped a spoonful and nodded. I took my own taste.

I didn't even know what bashful tasted like.

"Um. Smoky?"

"Yes, it's a roasted oolong, but what do you get beyond that?"

"Um."

I swallowed and looked down at my scribbled notes.

I felt like I was back in Algebra II, trying to figure out the equation of a parabola.

"Good mouthfeel?"

Mr. Edwards nodded, but I could sense the disappointment hanging off his shoulders as he began a second steeping.

We did three more steepings, each longer than the last. The leaves unfurled their green splendor until there was barely room to pour water over them.

When we finished the last taste, Mr. Edwards set his spoon down.

"Okay. Which one would you buy?"

"Number four tasted best," I said.

"Landon?"

He flipped through his own notes.

"Number two."

"Why?"

"Better operation."

"Right. They've got higher volume, better pricing, they're investing in new equipment."

I looked down at my mess of a tasting notebook.

I wondered if I was ever going to get this right.

What was the point and purpose of loving tea if you weren't sharing the best taste with people?

Tea was love, not money.

I blinked away my frustration before I experienced a containment breach in the tasting room.

"Good tasting, both of you." Mr. Edwards stood and pushed his chair in. "Can you handle cleanup and then hit the stock room?"

"Sure," Landon said.

Mr. Edwards squeezed Landon's shoulder on the way out the door.

I took the gaiwans to the dishwasher.

"Hey." Landon brought the spoons over. "Sorry about last night."

"Did I do something wrong?"

"No. It's just, I felt out of place, and then that guy was such an asshole when he interrupted us."

"Trent?"

"Yeah. I didn't like seeing him treat you that way."

"I'm used to it."

Landon stepped closer to me, so our hips were touching. He rested his hands on my waist.

"You shouldn't be."

"Thanks."

"I was having a good time, though."

"Me too."

"I could tell."

My ears burned, and Landon's cheeks flushed. He bit his lip.

"I kind of wish we'd been alone."

I got this prickly feeling.

Like maybe I wished that too.

I wasn't sure.

I didn't know how to explain it to Landon that I just wasn't ready for us to do things.

I didn't know how to explain it to myself.

Landon squeezed my butt a little bit. "Maybe next time . . ."

Kerry popped her head in. Landon let go of me.

"Hey Darius," she said. "We're getting slammed at the tasting bar. You mind helping out?"

"Oh. Sure." I kissed Landon. "Sorry."

Landon kissed me again. "Can we talk about this, though? Tonight?"

I swallowed.

"Yeah. Sure. Tonight."

After our shift, Landon came home with me, along with a bag full of groceries to make Breakfast for Dinner, which was his favorite. The house was quiet, Laleh and Grandma and Oma all doing their own things, and I couldn't shake the feeling that a cloud was hanging over our family.

But then Landon started cooking. He made scrambled eggs and hash browns and bacon and Brussels sprouts and brioche French toast.

Eventually Laleh came down, no doubt drawn by the smell of bacon.

"Can I help?" she asked.

Landon smiled at her. "Sure." He had her dip the brioche and season the hash browns and even taste-test the Brussels sprouts.

Laleh loved cooking with Landon.

I couldn't remember the last time my sister had smiled so much.

When Mom got home, she saw them cooking together and smiled, too.

I couldn't remember the last time my mom had smiled so much either.

Even Oma and Grandma seemed happier when they sat down to a table laden with bacon and eggs and French toast.

Landon Edwards was magic.

After dinner, Mom insisted on doing the dishes herself. "You and Landon worked so hard," she said. "Relax."

"You sure?"

"Yes. He's a keeper, huh?"

My ears burned.

"Thanks."

I pulled Landon away from the living room, where he was telling Oma about the Wuyi we'd tasted (Oma was a big oolong fan), and led him up to my room.

"Hey," he said when I closed the door and turned back to him.

"Hey. Thank you."

"Sure."

I wrapped my arms around him and rested my chin in his hair.

"This was really nice."

"Yeah?"

"Yeah. Everyone was so happy."

Landon's eyes twinkled. "I like making your family happy."

"Thank you." I leaned down and kissed him.

His mouth still tasted a bit like bacon, but I kind of liked it.

I led him to my bed and scooted into the corner, letting him rest against my chest. I wrapped my arms around him, kissed his cheek, his jaw, his neck, and then I rested my head against his and closed my eyes.

I loved cuddling with Landon.

But it always turned into kissing sooner or later.

This time was no different: After a few minutes, Landon shifted and brought his lips toward mine. He was so slow and deliberate and tender, with the way he ran his hands through my hair, and grazed my lips with his, and rested his forehead against mine.

I kind of melted.

When he pulled away, his lips were puffy, and his cheeks were flushed, and his eyes were soft like a cat's. He smiled and reached out for me, taking my hand and pulling it toward his stomach. He slipped our hands under his shirt. The hairs above his waistband tickled my palm.

My breath hitched.

"Is this okay?" he asked.

"I don't know," I whispered.

"Can I do it to you?"

I shook my head.

He sighed and let me go. I pulled my hand back and sat on it.

"Is it something I'm doing? Or not doing?" he asked.

"No. I just . . . It's hard."

Landon giggled.

"Not like that. I don't know . . ."

"I really like you, Darius."

"I really like you too."

Landon pushed my hair back off my forehead.

I melted a little more.

"I don't ever want to pressure you. But I have to be honest and, well, sex is important to me. As part of a relationship."

"I'm sorry. I'm just not ready."

"What do you need to be ready?"

"I don't know."

I wanted to cry.

"I don't know."

Landon tugged my arm until he pulled my hand out from under me. He kissed my palm, and then he reached up and brushed a tear off my cheek. "Okay." He wrapped his arms around me, and rested his head on my chest, and let out a little sigh.

When Landon headed home, and everyone else had gone to bed, I steeped a cup of Bai Mu Dan—this soothing, delicate white tea—to settle in for the night.

My bedroom still smelled faintly of Landon's cologne, and I felt a little sticky and unsettled as I breathed in his scent.

I kind of wanted to go number three.

But Saturday night in Portland meant Sunday morning in Iran, and that meant Sohrab would be awake.

It took a couple rings before he answered.

"Hello, Darioush! Chetori?"

"I'm okay. How're you? What did you do today?"

"Maman made kuku sabzi and took it for Mamou. We spent some time there."

"How was it?"

"It was okay. Quiet. Babou was sleeping the whole time. Mamou says he is not eating much anymore."

My chest squeezed.

And I had this really horrible thought: that the waiting was worse than Babou actually dying.

That it would be easier for everyone if he just passed away quietly.

I hated that I thought that.

I was so ashamed of myself.

"What's wrong, Darioush?"

I shook my head and bit my lip to keep from crying.

What kind of person thinks that?

"Darioush?"

"Sorry." I cleared my throat. "I had an ugly thought, that's all."

Sohrab studied me for a second. "I have those too, sometimes."

"Yeah." I sniffed. "How's school?"

Sohrab sighed. "Maman doesn't want me to go anymore."

"Really? Why?"

"The police have been bothering Amou Ashkan a lot lately. She's worried they will start to bother me too."

Sohrab's Amou Ashkan ran a store in Yazd.

"But why now?"

"I don't know, Darioush. Sometimes they just do. To remind people they can. Or because people are unhappy, and they say it's the fault of the Bahá'ís."

"I'm sorry," I said.

And then I said, "I wish you could be here instead."

Sohrab got this sad smile.

"Sometimes I wish that too."

"Really?"

"Yeah. You know, it's hard for Bahá'ís to go to university here. To make a future. And we have to do military service." He chewed on his lip.

We had talked about Iranian compulsory service before. I hated that it haunted his future.

I hated that he had to worry about his future.

It made my own worries seem small and inadequate.

"My mom has a sister who left Iran. Khaleh Safa. She and her family went to Pakistan and became refugees. Now they live in Toronto."

"Oh. Wow."

"My dad always said, he didn't understand why anyone would want to leave Iran. And I used to agree with him. But now I think about Khaleh Safa a lot."

"You want to move, then?"

"I don't know. I wish I could go to United States for university."

"I wish you could too."

Sohrab chewed on his lip.

"Enough sad things. How is Landon?"

The back of my neck prickled. "He's okay."

Sohrab looked at me, like he knew there was more.

Sohrab always knew.

"We talked some. About stuff."

He kept looking at me.

"Sex stuff."

Sohrab's eyes got big for a second and he let out this little cough.

"Oh." Sohrab's camera wasn't good enough for me to tell if his face was getting red, but his voice was distinctly pinched when he said, "Are you . . ."

He couldn't finish the sentence, though.

"No. We just talked. Landon . . . he wants to."

"What do you want?"

"I don't know."

Sohrab looked away for a minute. He shifted in his chair.

I could tell he was uncomfortable.

Sohrab didn't have many walls inside, but one of them was about sex. He always got nervous if the conversation veered anywhere near the topic.

I felt kind of bad, bringing it up.

So I said, "I just want him to be happy."

And Sohrab said, "I want you to be happy too, Darioush."

"Thanks."

A silence hung between us, laden with the things we couldn't say out loud.

I swallowed.

"Mamou and Babou don't know."

"I know."

"I don't know how to tell them."

"I know."

MIRROR UNIVERSE

Our next soccer match was an away game, against Poplar Grove High School down in Salem.

After school, we grabbed our away kits and boarded the bus waiting in the student parking lot. I ended up in the middle of the bus, with Chip right across the aisle from me. At the front, Coach Bentley cleared her throat.

"It's your first away game, gentlemen," she said. "I'm not going to bore you with the Code of Conduct or anything. You all know what's expected of you. So why don't we go make it three and oh?"

We all cheered. The airbrakes hissed, the door hinged shut, and the bus lurched into motion, but Coach Bentley stayed standing, swaying as the bus mounted the speed bumps at the parking lot's exit.

"Some of you have been asking about recruiters." She glanced around, her eyes lingering on Gabe. He was, empirically speaking, our best player, and had a real chance of getting scouted. "I suspect there will be some today. I know it's pointless telling you not to feel pressured. But I hope you'll remember that this isn't a singular opportunity, for any of you. There will be other games, other recruiters, and other paths to the future you want. So just get out there, play hard, and have fun. Go Chargers!"

"Go Chargers!" we shouted.

The bus bounced as we got onto the highway, and the guys

settled into the ride, playing on their phones or talking or, sometimes, shouting from one end of the bus to the other.

In front of me, Gabe and Jaden speculated about which schools might have scouts at our game.

"Probably UW and UO, at least," Jaden said. "Maybe Idaho?"

Gabe laughed. "Do they have schools in Idaho?"

"No idea. Hey, Darius."

"Yeah?"

"Who do you think is gonna be at the game?"

"Oh," I said. "I dunno."

I was a junior. And besides, I was a defender. No one ever paid attention to defenders.

Plus, like I said, I was pretty sure college wasn't for me. I knew Mom and Dad wanted me to go, but I just couldn't see myself being happy there.

Across from me, Chip frowned at his phone, thumbs jabbing the screen. He huffed, crossed his arms, and stared out the window.

I watched him for a second, and then looked out my own window. It was one of those perfectly clear fall days where you can just barely make out Mount Hood to the east. I watched it as best I could, my view interrupted by billboards every so often, but the back of my neck prickled.

Chip huffed again, and then sighed.

I leaned across the aisle. "You okay?"

"Yeah," he said, but he kept his arms crossed and his shoulders up around his ears.

And then he said, "You've got a sister, right?"

"Yeah. Laleh."

"She ever do anything that just makes you want to, like, murder her?"

"Not really. She's nine."

"Yeah, well, that's okay then." Chip puffed his cheeks and blew out a heavy breath. "My brother was supposed to look after Evie tonight, since Ana and Jason both have class, but now he says he's sick and wants me to do it instead. Like I could just turn this bus around. Like our game calendar isn't on the fridge."

"That sucks," I said.

And then I said, "Who's Jason?"

"Jason Bolger? Evie's dad?"

My brain executed a swift and painful change in inertia.

"Is he related to Trent?"

"Yeah, Trent's brother. Graduated when we were first years?"

I had about a million questions.

I couldn't ask any of them.

So instead I just said "Oh."

Chip blew out another sigh.

"I guess I should be used to this."

"Sorry."

I didn't know what else to say.

I thought maybe Chip didn't want me to say anything else. Just listen.

Sometimes people just need you to listen to them.

Chip shrugged and turned back to the window. I watched him for a second. The sunlight silhouetted him in gold and caught the fine hairs at the nape of his neck.

My chest gave a little squeeze.

I shrugged myself, and blinked, and turned away.

Our game against Poplar Grove High School was a complete and total victory for us.

I almost felt bad for the other team.

Almost.

Gabe got a hat trick in the first half, while James and Jaden each scored a goal in the second.

We shook hands with our vanquished opponents, and then Coach pulled some of the guys (including Gabe) aside to talk to a pair of track-suited adults in the first row of the stands. I couldn't make out the logos on their breasts, but it was pretty clear they were recruiters.

As we walked to the guest lockers, Chip put his arm over my shoulder.

He'd never done that to me before.

It reminded me of the way Sohrab always did that to me.

"Good game, huh?"

"I guess."

"What do you mean?"

I shrugged. "I only touched the ball twice. But Gabe was awesome."

"Yeah."

Chip's arm left my shoulder, but then he put his hand on my back.

"Um."

"Hm?" Chip said.

"I didn't say anything." I swallowed.

The silence between us hummed against my skin where Chip's hand warmed it.

Poplar Grove High School's locker room smelled so sterile it made my eyes water, like someone had poured ammonia over every single surface, and then maybe added some rubbing alcohol on top of that, and then filled the sprinkler systems with bleach and ran that for a couple hours too.

The back of my throat burned, and I hacked and coughed as I changed. Chip stood right next to me, radiating body heat and a faint scent of sweat and deodorant as he pulled his shirt over his head.

I slipped my joggers on and got out of there as fast as I could, because I didn't want anyone to see my erection.

What was wrong with me?

It was dark when the bus pulled back into the student parking lot at Chapel Hill High School.

"Good job today, guys. Get some sleep."

A row of cars lined the curb, parents picking up their sons. Some of the seniors headed deeper into the lot to pick up their cars and give their friends rides. I grabbed my bag and one of Coach's and helped her inside.

"Good work today, Darius," she said.

"Thanks, Coach, but I didn't do much."

She smiled.

"You never give yourself enough credit."

"Well."

"Your parents waiting for you?"

"I rode my bike."

"All right. See you tomorrow."

"Yeah. See you."

I grabbed my messenger bag and helmet out of my locker and went out to the bike racks.

Chip Cusumano was there too. He'd unlocked his bike, but it was lying on its side in the grass next to the curb, where he was sitting with his chin in his hands.

"Hey," I said.

"Hey."

I sat down next to him, but with a good foot between us, because I was still feeling weird about getting an erection when I was changing next to him, and the way my skin hummed when he was close to me.

I didn't like it.

I didn't like that my body responded to him the same way it did to Landon. Like it didn't matter who it was I actually liked.

Like it didn't matter who I wanted.

"You okay?" I asked.

"Yeah. I guess."

He looked out into the parking lot. Orange cones of light dotted the empty asphalt, catching the misty rain that had begun to fall.

I ran my hands through my hair at the same time Chip did, trying to get the damp bits out of our eyes.

Chip made a popping sound with his lips. "It just sucks."

"What does?"

"My sister is mad I couldn't take care of Evie. Like it wasn't my brother's night in the first place. And my mom is taking her side."

"That doesn't seem fair."

"Right? It's like, it's not my job to fix all their messes. But for some reason everyone expects me to be 'the mature one.' The one who's got it all figured out." He sighed and flopped back, stretching his arms over his head into the wet grass behind him. "I never get to be the one who needs help."

I leaned back too, using my hoodie to protect the back of my head, and rested my hands on my stomach. The misty rain tickled my eyelashes.

"That sucks."

"Yeah." Chip leaned over to look at me. "Whoa."

"What?"

"You just have really long eyelashes, dude."

My cheeks burned.

"Oh. It's a Persian thing."

"Huh."

Chip stared upward again.

"Sorin's always been a mess. And Ana was never really responsible until she had Evie. And Mom's got her hands full with both of them, and now Evie too."

Chip ran a hand through his hair again, leaving it even messier than before.

Somehow, it made his whole face look more open.

Vulnerable, even.

"It's like, they already sucked up all the air in the house. Now there's Evie too. And I love her, god I love her, but what's left for me? Nothing."

"I'm sorry. That really sucks."

"Yeah. Well. I'm pretty sure I'm Evie's favorite at least. She can't even say Sorin's name."

"Sorin's your brother?"

"Yeah."

"That's kind of a cool name, though."

Chip snorted.

"Sorin?"

"Yeah."

"Better than Cyprian at least."

"What do you mean? I like Cyprian."

"No one can spell it."

"What does it mean?"

"Man from Cyprus."

"It suits you. I mean, you seem like a Cyprian."

"Thanks," Chip said.

And then he said, "Hard to beat being named after a king, though."

"Technically Darius the Great was an emperor."

"Yeah, well. Darius suits you too."

My ears burned. I thought maybe the rain would start steaming off them. "Thanks."

"And it's cool you have this, like, connection. With your family back in Iran."

"I guess. It's hard sometimes too. I'm still only a Fractional Persian. And sometimes the Persian part is all that matters. And sometimes, the American part is too much of a barrier."

Chip looked at me for a second.

I blinked away the rain.

"You know what?" he asked.

But before he could finish, his phone buzzed. He pulled it out and held it above his head, typing into it as a grin crept across his face.

He sat back up. "Sorry. That was Trent."

"Oh."

I still couldn't wrap my brain around the idea of Trent Bolger, Soulless Uncle of Orthodoxy.

It seemed to violate some fundamental law of the universe.

I sat up and wiped my palms on my knees.

"I'm gonna go hang out with him. You want to come?"

I stared at Cyprian Cusumano as my brain experienced a cascade failure.

Maybe when you're a guy like Chip Cusumano, and Trent Bolger has always been your friend, you can't conceive of why anyone would want to avoid him like a hull breach.

"I think I'm gonna head home. I need to shower anyway." I stood and pulled my helmet on.

"Aww, come on."

Another cascade failure.

Why would Chip want me to come along, anyway?

Chip reached his hand out, and I helped him up. "Maybe next time?" he asked, his eyebrows all perked up in hope.

"Maybe."

Like if we ever found ourselves in mirror universe where people had goatees and inverted senses of morality.

"Cool." Chip hopped onto his bike. "See you, Darius."

"See you, Cyprian."

He grinned at me and pedaled away.

I shook my head, wiped off my face, and headed home.

Grandma and Oma were at the dining room table when I got home, sipping mint tea and reading.

Oma was always reading mysteries—the more twisted, the better—while Grandma was into biographies.

I'd never managed to convince either of them to read any science fiction or fantasy. They said they preferred "real books."

I don't know why that made me so mad.

Neither of them looked up when I walked in. I pulled the door shut behind me, and they didn't respond.

That aura of quiet unhappiness had returned to our house, an oppressive miasma that hung in the air like a coolant leak.

I cleared my throat and said, "Hi."

"How'd it go today?" Oma said.

"We won."

"Good. That makes three in a row, right?"

"Yeah. Gabe—that's our forward—he even got a hat trick."

Grandma whistled but kept reading.

"How about you?" Oma asked. "How'd you do?"

I shrugged. "The ball barely made it to me."

"You should be more aggressive."

That was something my old coach, from when I played as a kid, would say. Be aggressive.

Coach Bentley never said anything like that.

I really liked that about her.

"Where's Laleh?" I asked.

Grandma sighed. "In her room. She's been there most of the night."

"How come?"

Oma folded down the page she was reading and closed her book. "She got into a fight at school today."

First of all, I never folded pages—I always used bookmarks—and there was a moment where I wondered if Oma and I were even related to each other.

Second, Laleh had never been in a fight in her life. Not ever. What Oma said was impossible.

So I said, "What?"

And then I said, "Laleh's never been in a fight before."

Oma nodded. "She won't tell us what happened."

Grandma said, "Her teacher couldn't get the full story either."

So then I said, "Maybe she'll talk to me."

My sister never kept her door closed, not even at night. She always left it cracked open.

But when I went to see her, the door was all the way shut.

I guess I always knew there would be a point where she closed a door between us. When she would grow too tall for me to carry piggyback, or for Mom and Dad to tuck in at night.

I knocked, but there was no answer.

"Laleh? It's me. Can I come in?"

"I guess," she murmured.

I opened her door and poked my head into her room. The only light came from the night-light on her bedside table—this weird carousel-looking thing that played creepy tinkling music when you cranked a knob on it.

Laleh never used that feature, except on Halloween, when she would play the music and I would pretend to be terrified of it, and she would shriek with laughter at the way I cringed and flailed and hid under her blankets.

Laleh was already in bed, the lump of her facing away from me, toward the lamp.

I sat on the edge of her bed, and then kind of laughed at myself, because Mom and Dad always did that.

Standard Parental Maneuver Alpha.

"Don't laugh at me," Laleh mumbled.

"I'm not. Mom and Dad always sit like this when they come talk to me."

Laleh didn't say anything.

"You wanna tell me what happened?"

Nothing.

"Did I ever tell you about the time I got in trouble for hitting someone?"

At that, Laleh turned over, leaving her book open behind her. "You hit someone?"

"This guy named Vance Henderson." I scrunched up my nose. "He always made fun of me, which was bad enough. But one time he started making fun of Mom. Her accent."

Laleh scrunched up her face too.

"I know. So I gave him a kotak."

Laleh giggled. "Kotak mekhai? Ba posta das?"

While we were in Iran, one of our cousins taught Laleh that phrase. It means "Do you want a slap? With the back of my hand?"

For months after we got home, she kept saying it to people

whenever they annoyed her. And after a while she started saying it whenever she wanted to be funny. And then eventually her use kind of petered out.

But I liked that the memory of it could still make my sister smile.

"Technically I hit him with my palm. But still."

Laleh giggled.

"Will you tell me what happened? I promise not to judge. Or get mad."

Laleh looked at her hands for a moment, and then her shoulders loosened up a bit.

"I didn't hit anyone," she said. "Not even a kotak."

I was glad to hear that, but I didn't say it, because I promised not to judge.

"I just told Micah to shut up. We're not allowed to tell people to shut up. Miss Hawn says it's a bad word. But that doesn't make any sense. It's two words."

I nodded.

"How come?"

"How come it's a bad word?"

"How come you told him to shut up?"

"He was calling me Lolly again. He kept saying it." Laleh's voice got smaller. "And he said our family was terrorists."

I breathed in sharply.

I was almost used to being called a terrorist.

Almost.

But I hated for someone to call my sister one.

I hated that people could look at her, look at our family, and say that.

"I'm sorry, Laleh. That hurts. People say that to me sometimes. And other stuff too. Did you tell Miss Hawn what happened?"

Laleh shook her head. "She wouldn't let me. She gave me a demerit!"

Demerits were these little pieces of paper that basically said the teacher was disappointed in you.

They didn't actually mean anything, not unless you got three of them in a week, and then you got sent to the principal's office.

But I remembered being Laleh's age, and thinking they were the worst thing that could ever happen.

"That's not fair," I said.

Laleh's lip quivered.

I ran my hand through her hair. When she was a baby, it was fine and light, but now it felt a lot like mine: curly and thick and strong.

"So Miss Hawn didn't say anything at all to Micah?"

Laleh shook her head and wiped her eyes.

"And no one will listen to me. Grandma and Oma are just disappointed. And Mom is at work."

"And I was at soccer," I finished for her. "I'm sorry. But I'm here now. I'm listening to you."

She sniffed.

"Hey. It's okay." I held my arms open. "Do you want a hug?"

Laleh pulled herself out from her covers and wrapped her arms around me. I pulled her in close and held her against my chest and rocked her back and forth.

"It's gonna be okay," I said. "I'll talk to Mom. We'll figure it out." I kissed the crown of Laleh's head.

I would have done anything in the world to shield my sister

from Soulless Minions of Orthodoxy like Micah Whatever-his-last-name-was.

I never wanted her to feel the way I felt.

Like a Target.

"I love you, Laleh."

I put Laleh to bed and kissed her forehead and left her door cracked, the way she liked it.

I tried calling Sohrab. No answer, but he was probably in school anyway.

Oma and Grandma had already gone to bed, but I stayed in the kitchen with a cup of New Vithanakande, a tea from Ceylon that has this great round, mellow mouthfeel and notes of chocolate on the palate.

I sipped my tea and worked on my Algebra II. We'd moved on to logarithms, which I didn't get at all. I kind of wished Chip was around to help me.

But that made me feel weird.

Ashamed of myself.

I was finishing up when the garage door rumbled.

"Hi, sweetie. How was your day?"

"Okay," I said. "Better than Laleh's. You heard what happened?"

Mom sighed and went to the fridge. She opened the bag of leftover bacon, pulled a piece out, and ate it cold.

My lips quirked.

"What?"

"You used to yell at me when I did that."

"I did not."

I grinned.

"Did I?"

"Yeah. And then Dad would ask me why I wasn't eating a piece of fruit or a celery stick instead."

Mom sighed. Her shoulders slumped.

I had never seen my mother look so exhausted before.

"We've been pretty crappy parents, haven't we?"

I blinked.

Mom had never said something like that to me before.

"Of course not."

Mom grabbed another piece of bacon and tossed the bag back in the fridge.

"Really," I said.

"Thank you, sweetie." She plopped onto the chair next to me. "I'm just tired. And now your sister's teacher wants me to come in for a conference."

"Did she tell you what happened?"

"She said Laleh's been having trouble in class lately. And today she got into a fight."

"One of Laleh's classmates called her a terrorist," I said. "And some of them have been calling her Lolly."

Mom shook her head and looked toward the stairs.

I swallowed.

"She said it's been happening ever since we went to Iran."

Mom snapped back to me.

"What are you saying? We shouldn't have gone?"

I didn't know why she was so angry.

I didn't know what I'd done wrong.

"I'm not saying that."

Mom huffed.

"Really." I twisted the hem of my shirt around my finger. "If we hadn't gone to see Babou? I think we would have regretted it forever."

I watched the anger drain from Mom's face.

"It's just. Well, Laleh never stood out before that. She got treated like all the white kids. But now . . ."

"Iranians are white, though."

I bit my lip.

Just because that's the blank we fill out on forms at the doctor's office doesn't make it true. No one at school ever treated me like I was white once they found out my mom was from Iran.

Laleh's classmates weren't treating her like she was white.

So I said, "Laleh is getting singled out. And the teacher is punishing her instead of the kids teasing her."

"You're right." Mom pursed her lips. "But I don't know what to do. I have a meeting with a client tomorrow afternoon. Grandma is going with Laleh instead."

I thought about Melanie Kellner, trying to explain racism to Laleh's teacher.

I thought about how none of my own teachers ever got what it was like. How they never protected me from being a Target.

"Want me to go with them?"

"You don't have to do that, sweetie. Don't you have practice?"

"Coach Bentley will understand," I said. "I want to. Really. I'm the only one who knows what it's like."

Mom started running her fingers through my hair.

"Was school like that for you too?"

"Sometimes." It still was, kind of. "Sometimes people just don't like Iranians. Or anyone from the Middle East, really."

"I'm sorry."

"Don't be."

Mom stared out the kitchen window.

"You know, when I first moved here, people said things to me too. Especially after 9/11."

She kept playing with my hair.

"I guess I just got used to it. And I worked hard to be as white as I could. That's one reason I didn't teach you Farsi like I should have."

Mom had told me that before: that she didn't want me to feel different from the other kids.

"I even went by Sharon for a while, because my professors couldn't say Shirin right."

"Sharon Bahrami?"

Mom snorted. "It lasted about two weeks, before your dad talked me out of it." She smiled and twisted a lock of my hair around her finger, then let it go and admired the curl. She rested her palm against my cheek.

"Maybe I should have learned more, so I could prepare you and your sister better. But no one wants to think that their kids are going to get called terrorists at school. And that they can't protect them from it."

"You don't have to protect me, Mom."

Mom pulled my head down to kiss my forehead.

"Yes I do," she said. "Always."

"Well." I swallowed. "I have to protect Laleh."

Mom gave me this sad smile.

I had never noticed the little creases in the corners of her eyes before.

"You're a good brother."

"Thanks, Mom."

SPONGEBOB SQUAREPANTS

Rising Hill Elementary School was something of a misnomer. The school sat in a valley between two smaller hills, neither of which were actually named Rising Hill—or named anything at all, as far as I could tell.

The school was new: They finished it right before Laleh started first grade. The exterior was all endless gleaming windows and repurposed lumber, with solar panels on the roof and geothermal heating and cooling inside.

The parking lot was still full as Grandma pulled Oma's Camry into a visitor's spot.

Laleh squirmed in the back seat.

"We're late." Grandma clicked her tongue. "Better hurry."

Our meeting with Laleh's teacher was at 5:00.

It was 4:55.

Melanie Kellner was compulsively early to everything.

I opened Laleh's door for her and offered my hand as we walked inside, but she shook her head, hunched her shoulders, and trudged ahead between me and Grandma with her hands in her coat pockets.

Everything inside Rising Hill Elementary looked so small: Signs were posted lower on the walls, hallways were narrower, drinking fountains were down at knee height.

Had my own elementary school been that small?

A friendly young white man in a bow tie and thick-framed glasses greeted us.

"Here for a meeting?" he asked. He had a mellow voice, and there was something in it that kind of made me wonder if he was queer too.

Sometimes I did this thing where I imagined other people I met were queer. Just because I liked to think there were lots of us around.

I wondered if other people did that.

I wondered if Grandma and Oma did that.

"Here to see Miss Hawn," Grandma said, like we were at a doctor's office.

"Sure thing." The guy took Grandma's driver's license and my student ID and put them through this little scanner/printer to make visitor stickers for us. "Here you go."

The guy looked down at Laleh. "You think you can take them to your classroom, Lalah?"

I bristled. He said my sister's name like it rhymed with Challah bread.

Laleh just nodded. But I said, "It's pronounced Laleh."

The guy blinked. "Oh. I'm so sorry. Laleh."

"Yeah."

"Thanks. I won't mess it up again."

"Cool." I gave the guy one of those closed-mouth smiles and followed Laleh to her classroom.

Miss Hawn's classroom was a nightmare.

Here's the thing: I never understood the point and purpose of *SpongeBob SquarePants*.

I never watched it when I was little. According to Dad, I used to cry when it came on, and he had to change the channel.

To be honest, I still found it deeply unnerving.

So when we stepped into Miss Hawn's classroom, and I saw a SpongeBob SquarePants figurine on her desk, and a poster of him with the phrase READING IS MAGIC suspended on a rainbow between his hands, I kind of shuddered.

Miss Hawn sat at her desk, looking up at us with a practiced smile. She had blue eyes and blond hair that was parted in the middle and curled up on the sides.

She looked like a banana split.

I thought that was kind of a mean thing to think, that Laleh's teacher looked like a dessert that contained dairy products and (most likely) nuts, but it was hard to think anything nice about her after holding Laleh while she cried herself to sleep.

"Have a seat," Miss Hawn said. "You must be . . ."

"Melanie Kellner," Grandma said. "Laleh's grandmother."

"Nice to meet you," she said, extending her hand over her desk. Grandma shook it and then took a seat in an uncomfortable-looking metal folding chair. "And you must be Darius."

"Yeah."

Her eyes crinkled up. "If I had known you were coming I would have gotten you a better seat."

"It's okay."

I sat next to Laleh on one of the third-grader-sized seats. My knees were nearly in my chest, and Laleh giggled at me. I wanted to make a face at her, but we were here to be serious, so I just put my hands on my knees and tried to look as professional as I could in my work jeans and a light green button-up I'd gotten for soccer functions where we had to dress Business Casual.

As someone with years of experience attempting to decipher

various interpretations of Persian Casual—the complex set of intersecting Social Cues that dictated attire at various Iranian functions—I found the simplicity of Business Casual a welcome relief.

"So." Miss Hawn typed into her computer, clicked her mouse a few times, and turned back to us. She put her hands on her desk, one on top of the other. "I'm sorry to ask you to come in. Normally we handle discipline matters in class, but there are some other concerns I have."

"Other concerns?" Grandma said.

"Her unusual behavior yesterday aside, Laleh is at the top of her class. She's the first one to turn in assignments. She's reading well above grade level. And I'm worried she's not being challenged in class." Miss Hawn cleared her throat and tucked a stray lock of banana split behind her ear. "I think that might be playing into some of her behavior lately."

Next to me, Laleh crossed her arms and looked at her feet. She was wearing her favorite white sneakers, and she kept tapping her heels together, like Dorothy trying to wish herself back home.

I raised my hand.

Some habits die hard.

Miss Hawn's nose scrunched up as she half smiled. "Yes?"

"Well." I swallowed. "What about the other kids?"

She blinked.

"What about them?"

"Well, what happened to the kids who keep calling Laleh 'Lolly' on purpose?"

She blinked again. "I don't . . . hmm. I haven't noticed that. I promise I'll pay closer attention."

"What about Micah calling her a terrorist?"

Miss Hawn's eyes went wide.

"Micah said that?"

Laleh was still staring at her feet. I felt her shake a little next to me, so I put my hand on her knee and squeezed it. After a second, she nodded.

"That's certainly unacceptable," Miss Hawn said. "But I don't think he understands the context of what he's saying."

My voice shook. "I think he does." Grandma put her hand on my shoulder, but I kept going. "He sees stuff like that on TV all the time. That's how white people see people like Laleh and me."

Miss Hawn clenched her hands.

"Not all of us," she said.

"That's not—"

But Grandma cut me off. "I think what Darius is trying to say is that it seems you're singling her out by only punishing her."

I blinked at Grandma.

That wasn't what I was trying to say at all.

I was trying to explain what it was like for Laleh.

For me.

Grandma never seemed to want to know about that, though.

Miss Hawn cleared her throat again. "I'll talk to Micah tomorrow. But I'd like for us to focus on Laleh's future."

"What about it?" Grandma asked.

"I'd like for Laleh to take the test for the district's gifted program. Her OAKS scores are exemplary, and her other teachers think it would be good for her too."

Grandma looked at me and then at Laleh, who kicked her heels together again.

And then she nodded to herself and turned back to Miss Hawn.

"What would that entail?"

The drive home was quiet.

Grandma didn't speak, because much like Oma, she never talked while she drove.

Unlike Oma, she didn't listen to NPR: She left the radio off because she didn't want distractions.

And Laleh didn't speak. I got the feeling she was still kind of mad at Miss Hawn, too mad to process any of the good stuff Miss Hawn said about her. And mad at Grandma, for acting like everything was fine. And maybe mad at me too, for letting her down.

Miss Hawn wouldn't listen to me. And Grandma totally derailed what I wanted to talk about. Nothing was going to change.

I was so ashamed.

I didn't speak either.

When we got home, Laleh ran straight up to her room. I walked inside with Grandma.

"I'm going to call your mother," she said.

I made a pot of tea—some Moroccan Mint that Laleh liked— and loaded a tray with cups and spoons and a jar of local wild-flower honey.

My sister's door was all the way closed again. I wondered if that was the new normal for her.

"Laleh? My hands are full. Can I come in?"

For a second I thought she was going to say no. Or just ignore me. But then the door unlatched and rested against the jamb.

I shouldered the door open, then closed it behind me with my foot.

"Want some tea?"

"Sure."

Laleh flopped back down on her bed face-first, right back onto the damp spot she'd been crying into.

"Honey?"

Laleh nodded. I poured her a cup and spooned a dollop of honey into it.

"You want to stir?"

Laleh sat up and took her cup, clanging the spoon against the rim as she stirred.

She always clanged her spoon against the cup. At least that hadn't changed.

"Hey." I sat on her floor and leaned against her bed. "I'm really sorry, Laleh."

"Why?"

"I let you down. With Miss Hawn."

Laleh shook her head. "Why wouldn't she listen to you?"

"I don't know. I wish I did."

I sipped my tea.

Laleh sipped hers.

"Sometimes people think they're doing a good thing, and so they ignore that they're doing a bad thing too. Miss Hawn and Grandma were excited about the gifted program, so they just ignored all the microaggressions and stuff."

Laleh frowned.

"I deal with stuff like that too. You know people call me names sometimes?"

I couldn't get too specific with my sister. I didn't want to explain why D-Cheese was an insult.

I never wanted to discuss anything penis-related with Laleh Kellner.

"I can't always make them stop. But I can find better friends. And better teachers. And better places."

"Like Sohrab?"

"Yeah. And like soccer too. My coach and my teammates. Maybe this gifted program isn't all bad. Maybe it's a chance for you to find a new place. Make some new friends."

"But I don't want to be in a different class."

I got it. Really, I did.

Laleh didn't want to be different.

Being different made you a Target.

But if my sister was going to be a Target, at least it could be for something good. Something special.

"Will you at least think about it some? For me?"

Laleh looked up at me through her eyelashes. She had long dark eyelashes like me. Like Mom.

"All right."

"You need some more tea?"

"Yes please."

FAMILY BUSINESS

That night, Landon came over and made dinner for us again: Mom's recipe for khoresh-e-karafs, or celery stew.

"Smells good," I said, and kissed him on the temple.

He was wearing Dad's *Star Trek* apron and stirring in another handful of fresh parsley.

"Thanks. Am I doing the rice right?"

Next to the khoresh, a pot of rice steamed underneath one of Mom's tea towels.

"I think so. I've never made it myself." I went to lift the lid, but Landon put his hand on my arm.

"It says to leave the lid on until it's ready."

"How do you know it's ready if you can't take the lid off?"

Landon shrugged. "The recipe is a little vague on that point."

Like I said, Landon Edwards was magic.

The rice turned out perfectly—a resplendent golden disc—and he upended the pot onto a platter right as Mom got home.

"Wow," Mom said. "This is amazing."

Landon's cheeks turned pink. "Thank you."

I set the table as Mom changed into sweatpants, and we all settled to eat. Landon dished out perfect wedges of tah dig and great big scoops of stew.

"Thank you again for taking Laleh," Mom said.

"It's fine, Shirin," Grandma said. "I put the papers about the gifted program on your desk."

My ears burned.

Grandma was acting like that was all that mattered.

But Mom just nodded.

"Oh, are you doing that, Laleh?" Landon asked.

"I don't know." Laleh looked up at me and then down at her food. "Maybe. I guess."

I pushed some stew onto my spoon.

"I used to do that. All the way through eighth grade." Landon squeezed my knee under the table. "Were you in it too?"

I shook my head.

"Oh." Landon looked down at his plate. "Well. It's really cool, Laleh. I think you'll like it."

Laleh said, "Okay."

I stared into my stew. It was verdant green, with seared chunks of beef like dark brown islands in a lush swamp.

Lots of Persian stews look like swamps, even—no, especially—the most delicious ones.

I swallowed away the lump in my throat.

I wanted to cry.

I don't know why.

But I couldn't cry at the dinner table.

Landon had band practice early the next morning, so we could only steal a few minutes in my room before his dad picked him up. I waved at Mr. Edwards as they drove off and then went to help Mom wash the dishes.

While we worked, Grandma and Oma planted themselves in the living room to watch reruns of *Law & Order*. The original one.

I could see where Dad got his television habits from, because they watched a single episode every night. And there were a lot of episodes of *Law & Order*.

"What did you think of the meeting?"

"I think Miss Hawn doesn't get that Laleh's classmates are being racist. Or maybe she doesn't care."

Mom sighed. "I don't think she knows. Or at least she doesn't know how to deal with it. But I do think she cares about Laleh."

I chewed on my lip and dunked my sponge into the rice pot, which I had cleaned and filled with sudsy water.

Mom turned the sink back on and started rinsing again.

"Landon did a good job with the khoresh."

"Yeah."

"He's something special, huh?"

"Yeah."

"How'd your test go, by the way?"

"Okay. Chip helped me study."

"How come you never ask Landon to help you study? Sounds like he's smart too."

I swallowed away the lump in my throat again.

"I don't know. His classes are all different."

"Hm."

The back of my neck prickled.

"Remind me when your next game is?"

"Friday."

"Maybe your dad can catch it while he's home."

"Maybe."

※ ※ ※

Our game against the Beaverton East Eagles was tough. Neither team scored, so we ended up in a shoot-out.

The Eagles' first shooter scored with a tricky shot that ricocheted off the corner and into the net, but Gabe got them back with a slick shot of his own. No one else scored after that: James and Nick and Jaden all missed, and so did Beaverton's shooters.

But then it was Chip's turn.

I held my breath as he sized up the goal and took the shot.

And scored.

The stands went wild—at least the small cluster of parents and friends did. People didn't care about the Chapel Hill High School varsity men's soccer team the way they cared about the football team.

Dad was conspicuously absent. His flight got delayed.

The guys all clustered around Chip, laughing and shoving each other and high-fiving and exchanging sweaty hugs.

I hung back a little bit. I don't know why.

But then Jaden saw me. He laughed and pulled me into the scrum too, and he slapped my back and hung his arm around my neck, and Gabe fist-bumped me, and Chip grinned at me, and I smiled back in spite of myself, and we shouted and jumped until Coach came and told us to calm down so we could shake hands with the other team.

She was grinning too, though.

And for a second, at least, it was okay that Dad was gone.

Just for a second.

Chip found me at the bike rack.

"Hey," he said.

"Hey. You were awesome."

"Lucky shot."

I shook my head.

"You doing anything tonight?"

"Headed home. My dad's supposed to be in town."

"In town?"

"Yeah. He's been in California for a job."

"Oh." Chip's grin dropped just a bit.

"Why?"

"Trent's coming over. We're gonna watch Evie and play games or something. I was gonna see if you wanted to come."

I blinked.

Sometimes Chip just didn't make sense.

"You know he hates me, right?"

Chip shook his head. "He doesn't hate you. And Evie loves you."

"I don't think . . ."

But Chip's phone dinged at him. He grimaced and looked at the message.

"Sorry, I gotta go. Guess no one actually got any dinner."

"Oh. Sorry. See you."

Chip sighed.

"Yeah. See you."

Like I said.

I didn't know what to make of Cyprian Cusumano.

Dad was at the table eating leftover khoresh-e-karafs when I got home. He leaped up from the table and wrapped me in a Level Seven Hug.

I held him tight.

"Hey, Dad."

He held my face for a second and then kissed my forehead.

"How'd you do?"

"Won it in a shoot-out."

Dad beamed. But then his shoulders kind of slumped.

"I hate that I missed it."

"It's okay."

Dad squeezed my shoulder. "I'm almost done. I'll do the dishes if you make the tea."

"Okay."

I made us a pot of Genmaicha and we settled onto the couch for "Family Business," which is about Quark's mother earning profit even though it's against the law for Ferengi females to do so.

"What do you think would happen if I started calling Mom 'Moogie'?" I asked.

Moogie is what Quark called his mom.

Dad snorted. "I wouldn't try it."

When it was over, we sat on the couch together, drinking our tea. Dad had his arm wrapped around me.

"How're you doing? Really?"

"Okay." I chewed on my lip for a second. "Miss you."

Dad nodded and sighed. He looked like he hadn't shaved for a couple days, and now that I was sitting right next to him, I could see dark crescents under his eyes.

My father looked rumpled.

I didn't know people could look rumpled.

"Dad? Are you okay?"

"Me? I'm fine. Tired."

But there was this thing in his voice, this unquantifiable timbre that sent a chill down my spine.

I scratched the back of my neck.

Dad sighed again.

Stephen Kellner never sighed.

"It's rough being on the road."

He squeezed my shoulder.

"Being away from you all . . . it's harder than I thought it was going to be. I would've turned this job down, but we need the money."

Dad drummed his fingers against his teacup.

And then he sighed again.

"Sorry. I just . . . I'm having a bit of an episode right now. It's going to be okay."

"A depressive episode?"

He nodded.

"Can I help?"

Dad squeezed my shoulder again.

"No. I've got it under control, and I've been talking with Dr. Howell about upping my prescription."

"I could ask Mr. Edwards for more hours. Or get a second job."

"Absolutely not. You work hard enough as it is, with your job and soccer and school. And besides, it's our job to take care of you, not the other way around."

"But I want to help."

"You are helping. By being happy. By helping with your sister."

"Yeah, but . . ."

"No buts." Dad smiled. "We're going to be okay."

"Okay," I said.

Dad let out a long breath.

"Come on, enough heavy stuff. Tell me something interesting that happened while I was gone."

"Well," I said. "I got kneed in the balls last week."

Dad winced, and his hand twitched, like he wanted to cover himself.

"I'm okay, though. Don't worry."

Dad shook his head.

But then he chuckled a little.

And then he started laughing.

It felt good to make Dad laugh.

"Can you grab two more boxes of Tencha?" Alexis hollered. "And one of Masala Chai?"

I set the Tencha by the door, then went to the black tea shelf. It was in total disarray: Ceylons and Darjeelings and Earl Greys all stuffed haphazardly onto shelves without their labels pointing outward.

I shoved a couple boxes of Ceylon to the side and found the Masala Chai hidden toward the back.

"Got it," I called back.

I straightened out the shelves as best I could and took the boxes to the front.

"Restock? Good." Kerry nodded toward the empty shelf space and then turned back to her customer, a twenty-something white guy with long blond hair, a full blond beard, cargo shorts, and one of those colorful sweater-hoodies that looked like it was made out of alpaca wool or something.

Truth be told, the guy looked like he should have been out on a mountaintop, herding alpacas too.

I slipped past Alpaca Man, getting an unfortunate whiff of his musk as I did (at least I hoped it was him and not me), dodged around Alexis, who was carrying a gaiwan service to a table in the corner, and made it to the shelves.

Rose City Teas had never been so packed. But it was an unusually warm Saturday, and we were launching our new Nitro Earl

Grey, served float-style over vanilla ice cream from this artisanal ice creamery down the block.

I wiped the sweat off my forehead with the crook of my arm and started unboxing, using a little retractable box knife to slice the tape and flatten the empty boxes.

Each box of sixteen tins had four smaller cardboard boxes inside, with four tins each.

I didn't understand the point and purpose of double-boxing.

"Do you have any English Breakfast?" a voice asked behind me.

"Oh." I stuck the knife back in my pocket and turned around to face a woman about Mom's age, with her purse slung over her shoulder and her arms crossed. "We don't have any traditional English Breakfast. But we have an Assam that's similar, and—"

"Can you check in the back?"

I blinked.

We didn't have any English Breakfast in the back, because we didn't actually make any English Breakfast.

Mr. Edwards once told me that English Breakfast was "terribly pedestrian."

I never knew exactly what he meant by that, until now.

"Sorry. I mean we don't make it at all. But I can help you find something similar. We've got lots of great options."

I pulled down a couple different Assams and one Keemun.

"These are all single-estate black teas. These two are from India, and this one is from China."

I had the woman smell each tea (just the dry leaves) while I described the flavor profiles.

I felt kind of like Mr. Edwards, using words like *malty* and *smoky* and *umami* as we talked. The woman's eyes lit up when she smelled the Second Flush Assam.

"This smells great!" she said.

"Want to try a cup? I can steep you one."

"All right."

I led her to the tea bar and got a cup steeping. As the leaves unfurled, she told me about how she and her wife had just moved to Portland and were looking for a new tea store.

I was telling her about some of our other teas when Mr. Edwards hollered at me.

"Darius, aren't you supposed to be stocking?" Mr. Edwards asked. His sleeves were rolled up, revealing the winding vine tattoo on his left forearm, and his cheeks were flushed.

"Sorry, I was—"

"I need more nitro. Like now."

"Sorry." I turned back to the lady, my ears burning. "Sorry. Enjoy your tea."

"I will. Thanks."

I tried not to blush.

I loved it when I could help someone find the perfect tea.

I squeezed past Kerry toward the stock room, where we kept the wooden palette of nitrogen tanks. They were about three feet tall, with no handles: awkward, but not that heavy. I weaved it back out to the tea bar, where Mr. Edwards had me set it down.

"Thanks." He knelt under the bar and disconnected the empty tank. "Here. You know where the empties go?"

"Yeah."

But before I could grab it, there was a tinkling crash of porcelain from one of the corner tables.

Mr. Edwards made this sound that was part sigh, part laugh.

"Can you . . ."

"Yeah."

I had been back and forth from the store to the stock room so many times, I was surprised I hadn't worn a groove into the floor. I grabbed the broom and dustpan off the wall and snagged a couple towels off the shelf.

"I can clean that up for you," I said to the pair of older men, who had managed to knock two gaiwans off their table. Shards of white porcelain and long green leaves of oolong lay in a forlorn puddle of wasted tea on the floor.

One of the men nodded at me but didn't make eye contact. I swept up as best I could and knelt down to get it all into the dustpan, but as I did, I heard something.

A terrible something.

A ripping sound.

I scooped up the last few pieces of gaiwan and sopped up as much as I could with the towels, but there was so much.

"I'll be back with a mop. Sorry."

"Could we get some more of your Da Hong Pao?"

"Um. Sure."

I tugged my shirt down behind me with one hand and hurried into the back.

Something terrible had happened to my pants.

I hid behind the door and felt my pockets to find the problem.

The edge of the box knife I'd been using was still sticking

out, just enough to poke a hole into my jeans. A hole that had stretched and expanded, bit by bit, every time I bent over or squatted, until my jeans had finally experienced a non-passive failure.

I glanced toward the door and then reached my hand inside my pants just to make sure nothing felt bloody.

What was I going to do?

I heard a commotion outside, in the store, so I grabbed a roll of packing tape off the shelf, ripped off a couple pieces, and patched my pants together as best I could.

I hoped no one would notice.

I grabbed the mop and more towels and went back out.

"There you are," Landon snapped when I emerged, waddling slightly so I wouldn't make the rip worse. "What took you so long?"

"Uh."

Landon's cheeks were red, and his brows were creased.

"Someone almost tripped over your spill!" Landon's voice was sharp as a box knife. Everyone turned to look at us: Kerry at the register, and Alexis at the tea bar, and the customers in line.

I'd never heard Landon use that voice before.

I felt like I'd been kneed in the balls again.

My eyes prickled as I mopped up the rest of the tea. I wiped my face against my shoulder and sniffed.

I had to get back on my hands and knees to get the last of it up, an operation that was destined to further damage the structural integrity of my jeans. The packing tape tugged on my leg hairs, and when I stood back up, I felt cool air against my inner thigh.

Great.

"Sorry about that," I said to the table above me. I cleared my throat and squeezed my legs together to hide the damage to my jeans. They were already sipping on new cups of Big Red Robe.

"It's fine," they said without even looking at me.

I nodded at the floor.

"Enjoy your tea."

STRUCTURAL INTEGRITY

I wanted to cry.

I mean, I was crying. A little bit. But I wanted to cry more.

I locked myself in the bathroom so no one would see me.

I'd had bad days at work before. My old job, at Tea Haven, had Corporate-Mandated Clearance Sales once a quarter, which had been way worse.

But I guess I thought Rose City would be different.

I thought it was going to be about serving people the finest teas, and helping them discover new favorites. Not profit margins and import taxes.

I had this feeling for a second.

Like I didn't like working at Rose City.

But that was ridiculous.

I sniffed, kicked off my shoes, and slid out of my damaged jeans.

They were utterly destroyed. The rip had lengthened along the inseam, up to the crotch seam and down about twelve inches. Frayed edges waved in the air like tiny blue anemones.

I closed the toilet lid and sat on it in my underwear (a pair of green square-cut trunks with a shiny black waistband) and pulled my phone out of my jeans pocket to check the time.

I had another hour on my shift.

What was I supposed to do?

Someone knocked on the bathroom door.

"Darius?"

It was Landon.

"You okay?"

"Yeah," I said.

It was quiet for a moment. And then Landon said, in a softer voice, "You mad at me?"

"No."

I wasn't mad.

Just hurt.

And embarrassed.

"I'm sorry I yelled at you. I didn't want my dad to get upset." He tapped the door. "Are you gonna come out of there?"

"I can't."

"Why?"

I cleared my throat.

"Darius?"

"I've got a hole in my jeans."

"I'm sure we can fix it."

"I don't think so."

"Just let me in?"

"I'm in my underwear."

"It's okay."

I sighed.

And then I got off the toilet seat and hid behind the door as I unlocked it and swung it inward.

Landon squeezed through the gap and then closed the door behind me. He looked down at the shredded jeans in my hands.

And then his eyes kept going, down toward my underwear.

My leg hairs stood on end.

Landon's eyes snapped back up to mine.

"I don't think we can fix them," he said.

"What am I going to do?"

He almost glanced toward my underwear again. Like maybe he didn't realize he was doing it.

"Alexis might have some safety pins or something. And I think we have an apron somewhere. You could cover up with that."

My lip quivered.

"Don't be embarrassed."

"I'm not," I said.

"You are." He stepped closer to me, so close he pressed my hands—still holding my jeans—back against me. "But you don't need to be. It's just me."

He leaned up to kiss me, but I scooched back.

Landon's face fell. "You are mad at me." He rocked back onto his heels. "I said I was sorry."

"I . . ."

"It's like I can't ever do anything right for you."

"That's not true."

"Then what?"

"I mean. Yeah. What you did hurt." I hated how my voice wobbled. "I was already cleaning up and you just yelled at me in front of everybody. Instead of helping me out or . . . like, doing it yourself. And I've been trying to keep up with everyone needing ten things at once, and I barely got any sleep for worrying about my dad, and it's been a really tough day. Okay?"

I took a deep breath and looked up at the ceiling.

Landon looked at his feet.

The silence between us hung fragile and tender.

"You're right," he whispered at last. "I'm sorry."

He used his thumbs to wipe away the tears at the corners of my eyes.

"Why are you worried about your dad?"

"He's having a depressive episode."

"He is?"

I nodded.

"He'll be okay."

"Are you, though? Okay, I mean."

I shrugged.

"I guess."

Landon studied me for a second. He reached up and brushed my hair off my forehead.

"You stay here for a little while. All right? Just . . . take a break. And I'll bring you something to wear. Okay?"

"Okay."

"I really am sorry, Darius."

He stood on his toes to kiss me on the cheek, and then rested his palm against it.

"It's okay."

He unlocked the door, but then he turned around, his cheeks turning pink.

"Just so you know." He glanced down again. "I really like your underwear."

My own face went to Red Alert.

And for a second, I wondered what Landon looked like in his underwear.

He gave me a quick, shy grin, and then he closed the door behind him.

Landon came back with an apron and some safety pins, and we pinned my jeans back together as best we could.

He didn't say anything else about my underwear, but he kept glancing at me as we worked.

Somehow, being with Landon in my underwear, I felt even more naked than I had with Chip in the locker room.

"Thanks," I said when my jeans were as repaired as they could be.

"No problem." Landon leaned in and kissed my shoulder, something he'd never done before. It was just a quick peck, but it felt like a lot more than that. "Seems like a shame to get all dressed again, though."

"Stop," I said, but my skin broke out in goose bumps.

I had this idea. This image of us making out in the bathroom.

But then the image turned to someone knocking on the door, interrupting us, and getting in trouble (or at least suffering a Level Twelve Embarrassment).

I slid my jeans back on, tied the black apron around my waist, and stuffed my feet back into my still-tied shoes.

I didn't want to risk bending over: The safety pins could only do so much to reinforce the structural integrity of my jeans.

"I talked to Alexis. She said she'll switch with you at the tea bar for the rest of your shift."

I hooked my fingers into Landon's belt loops and leaned down to kiss him on the shoulder.

It was a good spot to kiss, I decided.

"You're the best."

Landon beamed at me.

"I try."

When five o'clock finally hit, Mr. Edwards came over and relieved me.

"Good job today, Darius," he said as he knelt under the counter to hook up another tank of nitro. "There's something for you by your bag."

"Oh. Thanks."

Sure enough, in the cubby with my messenger bag lay a long windowed envelope.

The window just showed a white page, but the envelope wasn't sealed, so I opened it up.

"Oh," I said.

It was my first paycheck from Rose City Teas, a little over two hundred dollars after taxes. Not as much as I used to make at Tea Haven, but still. It was money that could help with soccer clothes. Or more underwear, since Landon seemed to like what I was wearing. Or a new pair of jeans.

But I thought about the broken dishwasher at home too.

And Laleh's depleted college fund. And the school supplies she would need in the gifted program.

I thought about the circles under Mom's eyes, and how Dad wasn't bothering to shave anymore.

And I felt really selfish for some reason.

"What's that?" Landon said.

"My first paycheck."

He grinned.

"You can set up direct deposit if you like. But Dad likes to give the first check on paper. Says it feels more momentous that way."

"Cool," I said.

And it was cool.

But I had this lump in my stomach.

I knew I was supposed to be happy, but all I felt was tired.

And I had this thought.

Like I wasn't supposed to feel this way.

"Hey." Landon's fingers grazed my palm. I used my thumb to trap his hand, and he curled his fingers around mine. "What's wrong?"

"Nothing," I said.

Everything was wrong.

I just didn't know how to say it.

"I guess it's just kind of weird. I wanted to intern here for forever. But I never thought it could be a job."

"You work harder than anyone here. You deserve it."

"Maybe."

I was doing what I wanted to do.

So why wasn't I happy?

EVIL BEAN
CONGLOMERATE

Dad extended his stay through Monday so he could catch our soccer game against Willow Bluffs High School. It was an early game, so I hung out in the library until it was time to hop the bus to Willow Bluffs' field. The coffee shop in the library had terrible tea—in fact, it came from Tea Haven, which had been bought out by some sort of Evil Bean Conglomerate in the months since I had left—but they had free hot water, and like I said, I kept a few sachets of Rose City tea with me for such emergencies.

Chip sat next to me, and I gave him a sachet of Ceylon too. We sipped our tea and compared notes on our American Lit reading: *Catcher in the Rye,* which was slightly more interesting than *A Separate Peace,* but disappointingly lacking in queer coding. Well, mostly Chip talked, and I listened, because I didn't really get *Catcher in the Rye.* I wish we could have read fantasy or science fiction. Or at least something more recent.

"It's not that bad," Chip said. "At least he's not shoving his friend out of a tree."

"There is that."

Chip's arm lay on the table pressed against mine. I shifted over to give him more space.

"How's your Algebra II coming?"

"What's the square root of terrible?"

"Ouch. Come on, show me what you got."

"You don't have to do that."

"I want to help."

I studied my folded hands.

Chip put his left hand on top of them. Like that was a thing it was okay for guys to do.

"I'm serious," he said. "Let me help. Please?"

"Okay." I freed my hands and pulled out my laptop to show him our latest problem set.

With five minutes left in the second half of our game against the Willow Bluffs High School Trojans—seriously, their fight song was "Roll on, roll on, Trojans," the sort of innuendo that constituted psychological warfare against teenaged guys—we had kept the score tied, 1–1.

The Willow Bluffs High School Trojans fought hard.

Coach Bentley pulled out Christian after he took a strike to the xiphoid process making this excellent save where he leaped across the width of the whole goal. He stopped the ball but he couldn't catch his breath. She sent in Diego after that.

Diego was good, but he was no Christian. Not yet. And that meant Cooper and Bruno and I had to work twice as hard to fend off the Trojans' number 7, who had the fastest feet I'd ever seen.

The Trojans kept pushing us deeper and deeper into our side. I snagged the ball and passed it up to Chip, who only got two steps before he had to pass it back to Jonny Without an H to keep it from being stolen.

From the stands, Dad kept shouting "Defense! Defense!" like we weren't already doing that. But he cheered every time we got the ball moving forward again. He'd managed to bring Grandma and Oma with him too, though they were far more reserved: A few polite claps were the most enthusiastic response the Chapel Hill Chargers managed to elicit. I thought Oma might have whistled, once, when we scored our goal in the first half, but that was it.

Jonny Without an H managed to get the ball forward to Jaden, which took the pressure off us long enough for me to wipe my face with the collar of my jersey. I ran my hands through my hair and shook the sweat off in the grass. I'd gotten my haircut touched up over the weekend, and my fade was crisp and smooth again.

Across the field, Nick and Jaden exchanged the ball, zigzagging around the Trojans' defenders. At the last second, Jaden passed up to Chip, who went for the goal.

He would have made it too, if their goalie hadn't been like six foot seven, with ridiculous noodle arms that could catch things at the most impossible angles.

He lobbed the ball back toward us. Chip shook his head and changed direction, headed back toward midfield.

The Trojans passed back and forth, back and forth. They had Bruno and Cooper marked as number 7 sprinted toward me, angling for our goal.

"You got this, Darius!" Dad hollered.

Stephen Kellner, Soccer Dad, was a force to be reckoned with.

Number 7 tried to fake me left, then right. I stayed with him, looking for an opening.

But then he kicked the ball right between my feet and darted past me while I spun around to give chase.

That is, I tried to spin around.

Instead, I slipped and fell onto the grass, face-first.

For a second it was like I had fallen onto oil instead of grass. My cleats couldn't catch any traction. I finally got my feet under me again, but it was too late. Diego had been marking number 12, counting on me to deal with number 7, and couldn't course-correct in time.

Number 7 struck.

The whistle blew.

Trojans goal.

It was our first loss.

All because I let number 7 get past me.

It felt like it should've been raining as we lined up to shake hands with the Trojans.

Maybe even a bit of thunder in the distance or something.

But the sun was out, and I squinted at it to keep myself from crying.

As we went down the line, number 7 gave me a fist bump. "Tricky," he said.

"Thanks."

Not tricky enough, though.

I let him get past me.

I wished Sohrab were around.

With Sohrab I was invincible.

As we trudged toward the lockers—some of the guys, like Jaden and Gabe, with their hands behind their heads in Surrender Cobra—Chip rested his hand on my shoulder.

"You okay?"

"Yeah."

Chip gave me a little squeeze.

"Don't—"

But he didn't finish, because Trent Bolger was whistling and waving at him from the stands, still dressed in his Chapel Hill High School varsity football jersey. He must've come straight from practice.

I couldn't believe Trent Bolger, of all people, would drive across town after practice to watch Chip's soccer game.

Chip patted me on the back and jogged over toward Trent.

I followed behind, a little slower, angled to meet Dad where he stood with Grandma and Oma.

"Good game, son," Dad said.

"Thanks," I said. "I wish you could've seen us win."

"You were great out there. You played your hardest."

Next to him, Oma said, "I bet you won't fall for that trick again."

"I guess not."

"That number 7 was something," Grandma said. "Is he already committed somewhere?"

"Oh. Um. I don't know his name."

"I'll go ask the coach." Grandma patted my arm as she passed me. "You'll do better next time."

Oma turned to Dad. "My knees are acting up. Meet you at the car?"

"Sure."

Once my grandmothers were both out of earshot, Dad let out this low breath.

"They don't mean it like that," Dad said.

"Like what?"

"Like . . ." Dad swallowed. "I just don't want you to think they're disappointed in you."

"Oh."

I mean, I did think that.

How could I not?

Disappointed was the default setting for Oma and Grandma. Just like love was the default setting for Mamou and Babou.

My eyes started burning again. I looked up toward the sun so Dad wouldn't notice.

Next to us, Trent said something that made Chip laugh like a donkey.

Cyprian Cusumano had a hilarious laugh.

I glanced their way at exactly the wrong time, because Trent caught my eye. He did that thing where you stick your chin out to acknowledge someone.

Trent Bolger was the kind of guy you see in movies, where there's always one guy who's kind of mean to everyone, but they put up with him because he's good-looking or something. But Trent wasn't even good-looking. His nostrils were too big for his nose, and he had a terrible haircut: an undercut with a little oval of longer hair on top, combed to the side for the most part but left to do whatever in the back.

It did nothing for his very aggressive forehead.

"Darius?"

"Hm?"

Dad chuckled. "Go be with your friends."

"Okay." I stepped in for one of those diagonal shoulder hugs, to try and keep my sweat and grass stains off him.

Dad kissed my forehead. "I'm so proud of you." He held on to my neck and looked into my eyes.

And then he said, "I love you, son."

"I love you too, Dad."

He let out this tiny sigh.

"See you at home?"

"Yeah."

I headed for the lockers. Chip was still talking to Trent, but as I walked past, Trent said, "Right between the legs, huh? Guess you're used to that."

Chip gave Trent a little shove. "Hey, man."

Trent shrugged. "Later, D-Cheese."

I stared at them both for a second.

Chip looked down at his feet.

"Whatever."

THE SPORTSBALL-INDUSTRIAL COMPLEX

It was pretty much the quietest bus ride ever. Even the rumble of the engine seemed muted by the fog that had descended over the team after our first loss.

I let that goal past me.

My fault.

I slumped down in my seat and pulled out my phone to text Landon about the game.

No answer, though. He was probably in rehearsal.

I hugged myself and stared out the window. The afternoon sun had turned into a golden dusk, more beautiful than it had any right to be.

I wiped my eyes with my cuffs.

"Hey." Chip sat across the aisle from me. "Darius?"

"What."

It still stung, how Chip had just stood there and let Trent make fun of me.

But that was what Chip Cusumano always did.

"Scooch over."

I wanted to tell him no.

I wanted to tell him to go find someone else to bother. Someone who wasn't D-Bag, D's Nuts, D-Breath, D-Cheese.

I wanted to be alone.

But Chip hopped across the aisle, and I scooted closer to the window to let him onto my seat. Our thighs rested against each other, but he didn't seem to mind.

"You okay?"

"I'm fine."

"You crying?"

"No."

"It's not your fault."

I sniffed and wiped my eyes again.

I didn't say anything.

Neither did Chip. He just sat there next to me, like he didn't mind the silence.

Finally I said, "I let that guy past me."

"So did I. So did everyone. So did Diego."

"Diego was on their number 12."

Chip sighed.

"We're a team. We win and lose together."

"But I let everyone down."

"No you didn't. I promise." Chip rested his hand on my knee and shook it back and forth. "Hey. You didn't."

"Then why do I feel like I did?"

"Because you care. Because you're too hard on yourself." He squeezed my knee. "Because you're Darius."

I stared at Chip's hand. It was kind of square shaped, and his fingers were shorter than his palm.

It was a nice hand. I could feel its warmth through my joggers.

It made me sweat a little bit.

"It just feels like I've been doing everything wrong lately."

"That sucks."

He gave me another squeeze and met my eyes.

My chest felt tight. My ears burned.

"Um."

I looked down at my knee. Chip still had his hand there.

I took a deep breath.

"Yeah."

Jaden, Gabe, and I were all quiet as we got dressed for Conditioning the next day. I think Gabe was even more upset about the game than I was. Coach Bentley let slip that there'd been a recruiter from UC Berkley there.

I'm sure, if nothing else, they'd left with a favorable impression of Robbie Amundsen, the Trojans' indomitable number 7.

Grandma had made sure to find out his name.

And then made sure to tell me when I got home.

And then asked me for help googling to see if he was already committed anywhere.

(Arizona State University, of all places.)

When we got to the weight room, Coach Winfield was standing in the corner, talking to Trent, who held his left foot behind him in a calf stretch. Both of them glanced over at us as we came in.

"Get stretched out," Coach Winfield said. "You're doing a five-mile run."

I did a couple basic stretches—lateral lunges, inchworms, stuff like that—and then lay facedown on the ground. I arched my right leg over my left, twisted my hips, and lowered my foot to the floor.

It hurt so good.

"Kellner, what're you doing on the floor?" Coach Winfield asked.

"Getting ready for his next date," Trent muttered.

It was loud enough for everyone to hear, but quiet enough for Coach Winfield to ignore.

"What's that, Bolger?"

"Just teasing, Coach. He ate ass at yesterday's game."

"What?"

"Grass. He ate grass. When he tripped."

"Hmm." Coach Winfield narrowed his eyes but let it go.

He always let football players get away with stuff like that.

The Sportsball-Industrial Complex at work once more.

"Hey. Darius blocked twelve shots yesterday," Gabe said. "When's the last time you got up off the bench?"

"All right, cool it." Coach Winfield let football players get away with all kinds of stuff, but he never let soccer players talk back.

He loomed over me as I switched sides, arching my left leg over my right. "Kellner?"

I let out a slow breath. "Hip extensors. Coach Bentley told us to do it before running."

"Hm."

He didn't say anything after that, just wandered off to check on a trio of sophomores from the cross-country team, who had probably run ten or fifteen miles before school even began.

I was pretty sure Coach Winfield was a little frightened of Coach Bentley, because if we said she'd told us specifically to do something, he always said the same thing: "Hm."

And then he always let it go.

"You've got thirty seconds, gentlemen. Let's go."

Jaden offered me a hand. I hooked our thumbs and let him pull me up.

"Don't listen to him," he said, nodding toward Trent.

"I won't." Trent Bolger was like a warp core without antimatter: powerless. He kept trying the same old tactics to make me miserable, but I had grown up. I wasn't so easy to bully anymore.

I even had friends.

The very foundations of Trent's worldview seemed to depend upon me always being a Target.

Coach Winfield whistled. "Let's go, gentlemen!"

I stuck with Jaden and Gabe as we ran down the halls, out the side doors, and toward the track. Five miles meant twenty laps. The cross-country guys looked longingly toward the road, but we weren't allowed to leave school grounds during class.

"What is it with Trent, anyway?" Jaden asked as we dodged around a line of goose poop stretched diagonally across the track.

"I don't know," I said. "He's been like that pretty much since first grade."

"You ever want to just, like, kick him in the balls?"

"No. Maybe. I don't know." I sighed.

And then I said, "Having been through that myself, I don't think I'd wish that on anyone. Not even Trent."

Gabe spun around so he was jogging backward, looking at us.

"Yeah but, is it just me or is he way worse lately?"

"I don't know." I glanced behind us where Trent was running by himself, ahead of a couple seniors who had only signed up for the class because they'd nearly made it to graduation and needed one more physical education credit.

"I think he's kind of mad that Chip tried out for soccer. That he's on our team now. He and Trent were always on the same team before that."

"Yeah, but they still hang out all the time," Jaden said.

"I guess."

I wondered how much of their hanging out turned into baby-sitting these days.

Was Trent angry about that too? Or did he like babysitting Evie? Holding her in his lap and chasing her around the house and listening to her giggle?

"I don't know if Trent has any friends. Other than Chip, I mean. Maybe he's mad he has to share."

I didn't point out that Trent was sharing Chip with me in particular. That we studied together. And I'd even been to his house. And sometimes, we sat together on the bus, and talked about nothing, and Chip rested his hand on my knee.

I couldn't point any of that out.

I still wasn't sure what to make of it.

"Well," Gabe said, "I know I'm supposed to have school spirit or something, but I hope he gets creamed at the homecoming game."

I grinned.

"That would require him getting off the bench."

That night, Landon cooked another one of his famous dinners for us: asparagus risotto with Italian sausage. After, we lay on my bed facing each other, with one of my arms under Landon's head and the other draped over his hip.

Landon had his own hands folded together in front of him. I loved how, when the light caught them just right, his gray eyes had little streaks of blue in them.

Landon Edwards had beautiful eyes.

"What?" he asked.

"Just thinking."

"About what?"

"How beautiful you are."

He beamed at me, and leaned in to kiss me on the nose.

"You're beautiful too."

I shook my head, but he gently grabbed my chin to stop me.

"You are."

"Thanks."

"I wish you weren't so down on yourself all the time."

I looked down at Landon's hands so I wouldn't have to meet his eyes.

"I can't help it sometimes."

That's what being depressed does. It's like a supermassive black hole between your sense of self and your actual self, and all you can see is the way you look through the gravitational lensing of your own inadequacies.

"Hey. Don't."

"Sorry."

"I wish you wouldn't say sorry all the time." Landon rested his hand on my cheek. "I wish I could reach in and scoop all that depression out of your brain. So you could be happy."

I wrapped my fingers around his. "I am happy," I said. "I'm just depressed too."

My depression was part of me. Just like being gay was.

A part, but not the whole.

Landon bit his lip. "That doesn't make sense."

"I'm just . . ."

I thought about Dad, and his depressive episode.

And I thought about Sohrab, who was worried maybe he was depressed too.

And I thought about how sometimes, telling people I was depressed felt like its own kind of coming out.

"Being depressed doesn't mean I'm not happy. It's like, happy is one color. And depressed is another color. And you can paint happy, and then paint a little depression around the edges."

Landon traced his index finger down the bridge of my nose. I shivered a little.

"If you say so."

"I do."

He traced his thumb along my bottom lip, and then down to my chin.

"Sorry I missed your game."

"We lost anyway," I said.

"Hey."

"It's okay."

Landon's thumb moved down to my collarbone, feather-light strokes that gave me goose bumps.

"Homecoming is coming up. Isn't it?"

I swallowed hard. My heart thumped.

"Yeah," I squeaked.

I cleared my throat.

"So."

"So?"

"Have you thought about . . . maybe . . . going together?"

"Um."

I'd never thought about that before.

How did you ask another guy to homecoming?

How did anyone ever ask anyone to homecoming?

"Wow," Landon said. He started to roll away from me.

"Wait," I said. "It's just, I've never gone to a dance before."

"Never?"

"Not a school one. I've been to plenty of Persian dances before. But those are different."

Landon chuckled.

"I guess . . . I never really thought about it before."

"And now?"

My face felt like a fusion reactor.

"Do you want to go to homecoming with me?"

I said bye to Landon and then curled up on the couch with my new American Lit reading: *The Chocolate War*, which was even more of a let-down than *The Catcher in the Rye*.

We had to do an essay on its "themes," which as far as I could tell were "people are awful and bullies always win."

I yawned, marked my place, and went to make a bowl of matcha. I had fifty more pages to get through, and I knew I'd never make it without something to keep me awake and focused.

"Will you be able to sleep after all that matcha?" Oma asked as I sieved the emerald powder.

"I'll fall asleep without it."

"Is there any water left?"

"Yeah."

Oma made a pot of Genmaicha while I whisked my matcha. I used the M-method, just like Mr. Edwards taught me, moving the chasen—the bamboo whisk—in the shape of an M to get the optimal froth, though I threw in an occasional sweep around the circumference of the bowl to grab any particles I might have missed.

Oma and Grandma had set up on the couch, each with her own iPad, playing one of those puzzle games where you match colored dots on a grid to make them vanish. I took my book and folded myself into the armchair with my legs splayed out.

If I'd been back in Yazd, with Mamou and Babou, maybe we would have talked about my day. And drank tea, and eaten dessert, and shared old family stories.

But instead, we sat in silence, except for the music of Oma's game.

I found my place and started reading again, but I'd only gone a paragraph before Grandma asked, without looking up from her iPad, "What were you and Landon talking about?"

"Huh?"

"In your room."

I blushed.

I knew we hadn't done anything, but that didn't make me feel any less guilty.

Why did I feel guilty?

"Just talked. About homecoming."

"That's coming up?" Oma asked.

"Yeah." I looked down at my book. "We're gonna go together."

"Really? Your school's okay with it?"

"Oh. Yeah."

Grandma got this wistful look in her eyes. "Just like that?"

"What?"

She locked her iPad and looked at Oma for a long moment. And then she said, "You know, when we were growing up, two guys never could have gone to a dance together. And we were lucky we were married long before Oma ever came out."

Oma patted Grandma's hand.

"There were times I thought we might not get to stay married, once I started transitioning. But now . . ." She pursed her lips for a second. "You and Landon can just walk down the street holding hands like it's no big deal."

"Um."

"What your grandmother means," Grandma said, "is that things are so much easier for you now. You don't have to fight for acceptance as much as we did."

I blinked.

Some days it felt like I'd done nothing but fight to be accepted. For being depressed. For being Iranian. For being gay.

I couldn't tell them that, though.

Not when they were finally opening up to me a little bit.

"But you know, you're always going to have it easier than us," Grandma said. "As a cis man. You'll always have it easier in life."

"Oh."

I sank back into my chair, my ears aflame.

I didn't know what was happening.

It felt like my grandmothers were mad at me.

"Sorry," I said.

Oma studied me for a second. "You don't have to be. You've got your own problems. It's not like it's exactly easy now. We're just a couple of tired old queers."

I shook my head.

Grandma chuckled. "We are. Spend enough of your life fighting and you'll be tired too."

"I wish you didn't have to fight."

Oma shrugged. "It is what it is."

I'd never talked to Oma and Grandma like this. Not ever.

I didn't want them to stop.

"Um."

I picked up my matcha and took a sip. And another.

And then I said, "Maybe we can go to Pride together next summer."

Grandma sighed. "I don't know."

"Oh."

"We've done our marching. You were so little you probably don't remember, but we used to be up here every month marching for one thing or another. For years. Don't Ask, Don't Tell. DOMA. Prop 8." Oma shrugged. "After a while you run out of steam." I didn't even know Grandma and Oma had gone to protests before.

I wanted to know every protest they'd ever been to. What their signs said. What they chanted.

But before I could ask, Grandma opened up her iPad and started playing again. And after a second, Oma did too. Conversation over.

I didn't get my grandmothers.

I used to think there was a wall between me and Mom's side of the family: a sort of force field that time and distance had created between us.

There was no wall between me and Grandma and Oma. Just a door. But no matter how many times I opened that door, they always closed it again.

I wanted to know them.

I wanted to know how being queer had shaped their lives.

I wanted them to give me advice, and teach me our history, and yes, go to marches.

But instead I finished off my matcha and found my spot in my book.

And the door between us creaked shut again.

A PLASMA CONDUIT

Thursday morning I called Sohrab.

"Hi, Darioush," he said. "I can't talk long."

"Is this a bad time?"

"It's okay, just busy."

"Oh."

Sohrab wiped his arm over his forehead. I couldn't tell if he was sweating or not, but he was breathing hard.

"What're you doing?"

"Helping Maman with some things."

"Oh. How're you doing? How's school? Have you played football lately?"

"I'm fine. School is—"

Sohrab's picture froze while he was scratching his nose.

"Sohrab?"

I waited about thirty seconds, but when he still didn't unfreeze, I hung up and tried again.

This time it took a couple rings.

"Darioush?"

"Hey. I think we got cut off."

"Yeah, sorry. Listen, I have to go. But we'll talk soon, okay?"

"Oh." I swallowed.

I got this feeling, right behind my sternum. This bubble of sadness that slowly floated upward toward my throat.

Sohrab had never rushed off a call like this.

Had I done something wrong?

I didn't know what was happening.

So I just said "Okay."

"Take care. Bye."

We won our game against Hillsboro West that afternoon, 3–0. It felt kind of harsh to shut them out so badly, but after our loss against the Willow Bluffs High School Trojans, it did a lot to boost morale.

By the time I got home, everyone had already eaten. Mom had brought carryout from the Thai place near her office.

"I got your favorite." She held up a foam clamshell.

"Sweet and sour?"

"Extra beef."

"Thanks."

I scooped the stir fry—it had beef and bell peppers and onions and pineapple—onto a dome of rice and stuck it in the microwave.

"How was your game?"

"We won."

"That's great!"

"Yeah."

The microwave beeped, so I grabbed a pair of chopsticks and took my plate to the table.

Mom went to the stove, where the kettle was steaming, with a smaller pot set on top Persian-style. "Tea?"

"Yes please."

Mom poured two cups, using the special glasses she only

served Persian tea in, and kissed the crown of my head before she sat down.

"Mmmm." The tea was perfectly scented with cardamom. And something else: "Cinnamon?"

"I like how you do it."

I always put a pinch of cinnamon in my Persian tea.

I never knew Mom liked that.

"Thanks."

Mom sipped her tea and watched me wolf down my food. I normally had a snack before a game, but I was so nervous I hadn't been able to get anything down other than some purple Gatorade.

"We heard back from Laleh's school."

"Really?"

"She starts the gifted program on Wednesday."

"Wow. You already told her?"

"Thought some fried rice might help her nerves."

My sister loved fried rice.

"Oma said you asked Landon to homecoming?"

I coughed.

"Oh. Yeah. I meant to tell you."

"It's fine," Mom said, but there was this thing in her voice.

Like maybe it wasn't fine.

"Do you need to go shopping? I can take you."

"I need a suit. Mine doesn't fit anymore."

Mom chewed her lip.

"Don't worry. I can pay. And there's this consignment shop Landon knows."

Mom sighed. She reached up and twisted a lock of my hair around her finger.

"We can pay too. It's your first dance. It's a big deal."

"It's not that big a deal, Mom."

"It is to me. And your dad." She smiled, but it didn't quite reach her eyes. "We're going to help. All right?"

"All right."

Laleh was curled up on her bed, in a cocoon of pillows and stuffed animals, when I went to check on her.

"Hey, Laleh. What're you reading?"

She held up a worn copy of *The Phantom Tollbooth*.

"That's one of my favorites."

"I borrowed it," she said. "Is that okay?"

"Of course. Can I sit?"

She moved her knees over, and I sat on her bed.

"Mom told me the news."

"Yeah."

"Is this what you want?"

Laleh looked down at her hands. "I don't know."

"That's okay." I wrapped my arm around Laleh and kissed the top of her head. "Are your classmates any better? Or Miss Hawn?"

"No," Laleh grumbled.

"I'm sorry. I wish I knew how to fix it."

"It's okay."

"It's not okay, though. I want you to know that. It's not okay when your classmates do it to you. And it's not okay when Soulless Minions of Orthodoxy do it to me. Just because they do it doesn't mean it's okay."

"What's a Soulless Minion of Orthodoxy?"

"Oh. That's what I call bullies."

Laleh scrunched up her nose.

"Sorry. But you know what makes it easier, when I get picked on?"

"What?"

"I know when I go to soccer practice, there's no one like that. That I'm with people who care about me. And it makes it easier to go through the day, knowing at the end I get to go somewhere like that. Where I don't have to worry."

Laleh looked down at her hands again.

I closed them in mine. They fit so perfectly I wanted to cry.

"Will you try it out? Just for a little while?"

"Okay."

"No, wait." Chip pointed to my mistake. "i^3 is $-i$."

"Crap."

I scratched out my mistake and started over.

I had a test in Algebra II on Monday, and Chip had agreed to help me study, as long as we did it at his place so he could babysit Evie.

She sat on his lap, absolutely entranced by the orange plastic bowl of Cheerios in front of her. Her tiny fingers grasped a few at a time, let some fall like drops of water, and then stuffed whatever remained into her mouth.

Every once in a while, Chip would lean down and kiss her head.

I worked through my equation again, but I kept glancing at Chip and his niece.

Somewhere along the way, Cyprian Cusumano had changed from Trent Bolger's sidekick, to a guy on my soccer team, to a real friend. A friend who looked cute sitting at the table with his little niece on his lap.

I snapped my eyes back to my paper and kept working.

"Wait," I said, after a few more minutes of scribbling. "So this whole thing just adds up to zero?"

Chip leaned over to look. His lips moved silently as he read over my work.

"Yup. That's—"

But before he could finish, Evie smacked the rim of her bowl and sent Cheerios flying everywhere.

"Evie! Sorry about that." He set her on the floor, and she squealed and ran into the living room, her little legs pumping up and down like her quads were burned out from a superset of heavy back squats.

"It's okay."

I shook the Cheerios off my laptop onto my scratch paper and got on the floor to help Chip scoop up the ones that had fallen.

"Thanks." He glanced up at me and giggled.

"What?"

He reached into my hair and pulled out a Cheerio. I shivered as his fingers grazed my scalp.

"Oh. Thanks."

Chip grinned that funny grin of his.

He didn't say anything, just looked at me.

I swallowed.

My whole body was warm, like I'd been dropped into a plasma conduit.

"Um," I said.

And then I tried to stand, but I hit the top of my head on the table.

"Ow."

Chip busted out laughing at that.

"Sorry. Sorry. It's not funny."

"Yeah. Well. If I get a brain injury, maybe I can get out of taking this test."

"Hey." Chip furrowed his eyebrows. "You got this. Really."

From the living room, Evie let out a squeal of joy. Or maybe mischief.

There was the sound of something plastic hitting the floor.

Chip exhaled out the side of his mouth.

"Gimme a second," he said.

Once he'd gotten Evie under control—which required bribing her with some watered-down apple juice in a sippy cup—he sat back down and leaned over to look at the rest of the practice problems.

"You're getting the hang of it. But here."

He showed me where I'd missed a step and then sat back as I worked.

"Ah, wait. You've got to factor it first." He scooted his chair closer to me, so our knees were touching. Evie took the opportunity to wiggle her way from his lap to mine.

"Evie . . ." Chip began.

"It's okay. I don't mind."

Evie rested her head against the crook of my elbow as she drank her juice and I fought with imaginary numbers.

I didn't really get the point and purpose of imaginary numbers.

"Okay. Better." Chip looked over everything and nodded. "I think you've got it."

I sighed. "Now I've got to do it on the test."

"Don't worry. You'll do great."

"Maybe."

The thing about Chip was, he just got things. And he didn't know what it was like to not get things.

To try and try and still not succeed.

Evie squirmed in my lap.

"You want down?" I asked.

She nodded. I held her as I scooted away from the table, then set her down. She tossed her juice onto the floor and ran off again.

Chip shook his head and scooped the sippy cup off the floor. He looked at me and did this kind of half smile.

I blinked and then looked down at my hands.

"I guess I better get home."

"No rush." He patted my knee. "Hey. What're you doing for homecoming?"

"I. Uh." My cheeks started to warm. "I asked Landon to go with me."

"Cool."

"How about you?"

"I think I missed my window." He shrugged. "Should've spoken up sooner."

"Oh. Sorry."

"Yeah. Kind of sucks when you like someone but they don't like you back."

"As a gay guy I definitely have no idea what that feels like. Definitely never crushed on any straight guys ever."

Chip snorted.

"Trent doesn't have a date either, so we're just getting a big group together. Why don't you and Landon join us?"

"Oh," I said. "I think we're good."

Chip's eyebrows furrowed. "What?"

"What what?"

"You made a face."

"No I didn't."

"You did!"

To be fair, the statistical likelihood of me making a face at the mention of Trent Bolger was definitely non-zero.

"You're doing it again!"

"Doing what?"

"That face!" Chip poked me in the little crease between my eyebrows.

I leaned back.

"Don't."

"Sorry. But what is it?"

I sighed.

And then I said, "Why do you keep trying to get me to hang out with him? You know he hates me."

"He doesn't hate you."

"Well, he's never been nice. Why are you friends with a guy like that anyway?"

As soon as I said it I wished I could take it back.

You couldn't just say things like that to someone. Try to control who someone was friends with.

But then I said, "I get you have to deal with him because of Evie and stuff, but . . ."

Chip shook his head. "It's not like that. I mean, we've been friends ever since preschool. You remember?"

"I remember you and Trent calling me Doofius."

Chip lowered his eyes.

"Sorry."

"Whatever. We were kids. But now, you're . . ."

"What?"

"You're nice." I swallowed. "I mean, the last couple months, you've been nice to me. Ever since I got back from Iran. And Trent is still . . . kind of mean."

"You just don't know him very well. That's all. It's his sense of humor. He's just teasing."

"It doesn't feel like teasing," I said. "It never has."

Chip blinked at me.

I looked down at my hands again. My cuticles were looking rough, probably because I'd taken to chewing them every time I thought about the square root of negative one.

"I didn't mean it that way," Chip said. His voice was quiet and small. "I'm sorry if I hurt you."

"Thanks."

"I did hurt you, didn't I?"

I shrugged. "Sometimes."

Chip let out a slow breath.

"Well."

"Yeah."

We sat like that, in a Level Twelve Painful Silence.

I'd made it weird between us.

But then Evie ran back into the room with a pair of safety scissors she'd found somewhere.

Chip sprang out of his seat. "Evie! That's not a toy." He chased after her.

And the moment had passed.

VERTICALLY GIFTED PEOPLE

Wednesday morning I popped a pair of cherry Toaster Strudels into the toaster oven to surprise Laleh for her first day at the district's Innovation Center.

(We didn't have a regular toaster at home, just the toaster oven. Persians tend to toast big pieces of flatbread, so regular toasters are insufficient.)

Grandma was at the kitchen table, drinking coffee and doing her latest sudoku.

"That's what you're having for breakfast?"

"It's for Laleh," I said. "For her first day."

Grandma chuckled. "That's hardly a treat. Here."

Before I knew what was happening, Grandma had grabbed the flour out of the pantry, a bowl from beneath the counter, and a couple eggs.

"Pancakes are a real treat," she said.

The toaster oven dinged.

I would have left the strudels in there—the sight of Melanie Kellner making pancakes had me transfixed, like a meteor shower—but when I started smelling burned pastry, I had to turn away and get the strudels out.

We heard Laleh stomping down the stairs before she emerged into the kitchen, still in her pajamas.

"Hey, Laleh," I said.

"Morning," Grandma said. "There's pancakes."

Laleh perked up at that. Grandma set her plate on the table, along with a bottle of maple syrup.

I watched Laleh eat her pancakes, and Grandma work on her sudoku with a little smile on her face.

What just happened?

It was like, for a brief moment, the moon had shifted in its orbit, and this happy Melanie Kellner had eclipsed the Melanie Kellner I thought I knew.

But then, just like an eclipse, it was over.

I didn't understand.

I got my stuff together and kissed Laleh and Grandma goodbye.

"Have a good day, Laleh."

She looked up from her plate and gave me a toothy smile.

"Thanks."

I ran into Chip at the bike rack.

"Hey," he said, but he didn't grin his usual grin.

Things had been weird between us ever since Sunday.

I wished I could take back what I said.

Well. Not really. I was telling the truth.

But I never realized the truth would be so dangerous.

"Hey," I said.

"Did Ms. Albertson post your grade yet?"

"Last night."

I almost smiled.

Almost.

"I got a B!"

That got a grin out of Chip.

"That's great."

"Thanks again. For helping me."

"Sure." Chip kept grinning at me, but after a minute it slipped away.

And then things were weird again.

"See you at practice?"

I swallowed.

"Yeah."

When I got home from practice, I felt like I had stepped onto a holodeck.

The scene before me was too surreal for normal existence.

Laleh, Grandma, and Oma were sitting around the kitchen table with bowls of warm water in front of them. A pile of towels lay between them with nail files and clippers on top, and next to that, a little basket of fingernail polish.

"We're doing manicures!" Laleh announced when I came in. She held her pruny hands up to show me.

"That's great."

I leaned down to kiss her head, then Grandma and Oma on the cheeks.

"How was school?"

"Good. Miss Shah is so cool. You know her family is from India?"

"That's great."

"She said my name right and everything."

My sister was practically effervescent.

"Are you hungry?" Oma asked. "We can clear out."

"No, it's okay."

Laleh looked up at me. "Want to do manicures too?"

"Um," I said.

Grandma and Oma looked at me.

I looked down at my hands, and my shredded cuticles. I'd never had a manicure before.

"That sounds really nice."

Oma pulled out a chair for me. "Have a seat. I'll get you a bowl." She added a few drops of tea tree oil, the most deceptively named oil I'd ever heard of, since it didn't actually come from *camelia sinensis*.

I soaked my hands while Laleh told us all about her day: the reading they did, and Bloom's Taxonomy, and "doing algebras."

I smiled at that.

I hoped algebras would be easier for Laleh than they were for me.

Oma took my right hand and started pushing my cuticles up.

"You've got to stop chewing on them," she said.

"Sorry."

"You get nervous. Like Stephen."

I nodded.

"You like this?"

"Yeah. It's nice."

"When I was your age, guys could never do this."

"Some guys still won't."

Grandma snorted and said, "The patriarchy at work." And then she went back to painting Laleh's middle finger a violent and excellent shade of pink.

When my nails were shaped, Oma said, "You want to paint yours like Laleh?"

"Not really," I said.

But then I said, "Do you have a blue?"

Oma's eyes lit up.

And Grandma said "Here," and handed over a bottle of this really pretty turquoise.

"Have you ever painted your nails before?"

When they were dried, my nails were this perfect color. It made me think of Yazd. Of the turquoise minarets of the Jameh Mosque shining out in the sun.

Of sitting with Sohrab on the roof of this bathroom in the park where we used to play soccer/Iranian football.

Of drinking tea in companionable silence with Mamou and Babou.

Grandma insisted on doing the dishes, so Laleh and I sat in the living room and helped Oma with a puzzle.

"Hello?" Mom called from the kitchen.

I hadn't even heard the garage door open.

"Oh. Hi."

Mom was laden with Target bags. I set them on the counter and grabbed the rest from her trunk.

When everything was unloaded, I hugged Mom and let her kiss my forehead.

"Wait."

She grabbed my hands and turned them over.

My ears burned.

"Do you like it?" I whispered. "Oma did it. We all did our nails this afternoon."

"It's nice," she said.

But her voice was pinched when she said it, and there was this look in her eyes.

I got this ugly feeling. One I couldn't shake.

I wondered if Mom was embarrassed by me.

"It reminded me of Yazd," I said.

Mom rested her palm against my cheek.

"Mom! Mom!" Laleh ran in. "Look!" She showed off her pink nails, which transitioned from fuchsia on her thumbs to bubble-gum on her pinkies.

"They're beautiful, Laleh," she said. "How was school?"

Laleh told Mom all about her day while I made a pot of jasmine tea.

But by the time it was ready, the puzzle had been cleared off, and Oma and Grandma were playing on their iPads again.

Laleh was curled up reading her book, and Mom had gone upstairs.

It was like we had been living in this static bubble of joy, but it had undergone a subspace field collapse, and now everything was covered in a melancholy residue.

Our perfect moment had evaporated.

I didn't know how to get it back.

I had a hard time sleeping that night.

When I was in eighth grade, in the middle of Yet Another Prescription Change, there were nights I lay awake, staring at the ceiling, feeling like I was being smothered.

I felt like that again. Like the weight of a dark matter nebula rested on my chest, and every sad thought kept echoing in my mind, poised on the event horizon of the singularity of my life.

I wanted to cry. Or howl.

But it was late, and the whole house was asleep.

So I turned my pillow over to find a cool spot and tried to sleep.

Around two in the morning, someone knocked on my door.

I reached for my trunks and slipped them on under the covers.

"Come in?"

The door creaked open. Mom stood silhouetted in the hall light.

"Mom?"

She just stood there.

"Is everything okay?"

"No," she said. "I just heard from your Dayi Soheil."

My heart thudded.

"Babou passed away."

ACROSS TIME AND SPACE

There was no going back to sleep after that.

I put on some clothes and went downstairs to put the kettle on.

When we visited Iran, Babou showed me how Iranians make tea. And then he drank it while clenching a sugar cube between his teeth.

I was crushing cardamom pods when I couldn't hold in the tears any longer.

The thing is, I knew Babou was dying. We had known that for months.

But it didn't hurt any less, losing him bit by bit, because it still felt like we had just lost him all at once.

There was no more Ardeshir Bahrami.

There was a hole in the center of our family.

Oma and Grandma trudged down the stairs, Oma in her robe and Grandma in her pajamas.

"I'm so sorry, Darius," Grandma said. She took both my hands, and then pulled me in for a brief hug. "Don't cry."

"Where's Mom?"

Oma pulled a paper towel off the roll and handed it to me. "With your sister."

I nodded and blew my nose.

Grandma said, "Shouldn't you try to go back to bed?"

"I can't sleep." I hiccupped. "I should go check on them."

I poured three cups of tea and put them on the little wooden tray Mom had brought back with her from Iran. It matched the one Mamou had in Yazd, the one she would use to bring tea and snacks to Babou when he was resting.

I held in a sob.

Upstairs, Laleh's door was cracked.

"Mom?"

"Come in."

I elbowed the door open. Mom was sitting on Laleh's bed, holding a sobbing Laleh and rocking her back and forth.

She looked up at the tray of tea.

"I didn't know what else to do," I croaked.

Mom nodded and scooted over to make room for me. I set the tray down on Laleh's nightstand and sat on Laleh's bed. I wrapped my arms around Mom and Laleh both. Mom rested her head against my shoulder.

I'd been taller than Mom for a couple years, but for the first time, it really struck me how she would never hold me again the way she was holding Laleh. And one day, Laleh would be too big for her to hold too. And she would grow older.

Time would flow inexorably forward.

And someday, she would be gone too.

I held my mom as tight as I could.

And I cried harder than I had ever cried before.

Oma and Grandma came in to check on us, and to take away the tray of cold, untouched tea. They brought a fresh box of Kleenex and an extra trash bag, and kissed Laleh on the forehead, and whispered in Mom's ear, and patted my shoulder. But mostly, they left us to our grief.

Once we'd cried ourselves out—Laleh actually cried herself back to sleep—Mom kissed us each about a hundred times. She sniffed and whispered, "I need to call Mamou."

I stood as quietly as I could and helped Mom tuck Laleh back in. She brushed Laleh's hair off her forehead and kissed her one last time, and then we closed the door behind us.

Mom got the call started on her computer while I wheeled over a chair to sit next to her.

We waited.

And waited.

And just when I thought Mom was going to hang up and try later—

"Hello?"

Mamou's pixelated face appeared on the screen. Her voice sounded robotic and compressed, like her bandwidth was throttled, which it probably was.

Mom started crying again, but she sniffed and wiped her eyes. "Hi, Maman. Chetori?"

Mom and Mamou started talking in Farsi.

Normally I could halfway follow their conversations, but with Mamou sounding like she was at the other end of a broken subspace relay, and my own sniffling, I missed some stuff.

Eventually there was a pause, and Mamou said, "Hi, Darioush-jan. How are you doing?"

"Hi, Mamou," I said. I tried to smile for her, but my face probably just looked constipated. "I'm okay. How are you?"

"I am holding on," she said.

Mamou blinked at me and wiped her eyes, and I did the same.

I wanted to tell her how sorry I was.

I wanted to tell her how much I missed her.

I wanted to tell her about the hole in my heart.

But I was helpless against her grief, and Mom's grief, and my own.

I hated how powerless I was.

"I love you, Mamou," I said. "I wish I was there."

And I meant it so much.

But it didn't feel like nearly enough.

Maybe nothing would ever be enough.

Maybe not.

Mom went back to bed after we said bye to Mamou.

I lay in bed and stared at the ceiling. And then, when I couldn't take the silence anymore, I called Sohrab.

Sometimes you just need to talk to your best friend.

But the call rang and rang. His icon pulsed on the screen.

Eventually, a little error message popped up.

I don't know why, but the little *blip* noise is what got to me.

My grandfather was gone.

I curled back up in my bed and wound my blankets around myself like a burrito and cried into my pillow until I finally fell asleep.

At some point, Mom must've called into school for me, because when she knocked on my door around noon, all she asked was if I needed anything.

"I'm okay," I said.

And then I said, "We have a game tonight."

"I talked to your coach. She knows you'll be gone."

"Okay."

Eventually, I got that feeling in my legs, like they were full of springs, and I knew I had to get out of bed.

I went with Oma to the grocery store that afternoon. When we got back, I sat in the living room with Laleh while she read.

I tried calling Sohrab again—no answer—and then wrote him an email.

We called Dad, and I talked to him for a while.

"I'm so sorry," he kept saying, like it was his fault Babou was gone. "I'll be home soon. It'll be okay. I love you."

That evening, Oma made grilled cheese and tomato soup.

Linda Kellner's solution to all of life's problems was grilled cheese and tomato soup.

It's not like either the sandwiches or the soup were particularly good. Oma used regular American cheese slices and white bread for the sandwiches. And the soup came from a can, made with water instead of milk since, according to Oma, milk gave Grandma gas.

But I thought maybe cooking for us was Oma's way of showing she loved us, since she almost never said it out loud.

"Can I help any?" Landon asked.

He'd come over after school, with a little bouquet of flowers for Mom and a card for me.

"I'm fine," Oma said. "You relax."

Landon shifted in his seat.

I think the sight of Oma cooking with American cheese was deeply disturbing to him.

"Why don't you make some tea?" Oma suggested.

"Okay."

So Landon put the kettle on while I pulled down some Second Flush Darjeeling Mr. Edwards had us sample a couple weeks ago. It was maltier than the first flush from the same estate, and brisker, but it was still pretty good.

While the tea steeped, Oma cut the sandwiches into quarters diagonally—the only acceptable way to cut grilled cheese sandwiches—and started ladling soup into bowls. Landon set the table and I went to get Laleh from her room.

"Laleh?"

She was curled up against her pillow, a new book open on her lap.

"What're you reading?"

Laleh held up the book so I could read the cover: *The Fifth Season.*

"Is it good?"

"Better than *Dune,*" she said.

"Cool. You want some dinner?"

We ate in silence, all of us dunking our sandwich triangles in the velvety processed soup product.

It actually did make me feel a little better.

After, as Landon was getting ready to leave, he said, "Are you going to be okay?"

"Yeah," I said.

And then I said, "It's not like it came as a surprise."

And then I said, "Is it awful that I'm kind of glad it's over?"

I felt terrible as soon as I said it.

What kind of grandson says something like that?

Landon took my hand. "It's not."

I sniffled.

"It's okay."

He pulled closer to try to kiss me, but I shook my head. "I'm sorry. I—"

Landon bit his lip. "No. It's okay."

The doorbell rang.

"That's probably Dad," he said.

But when I opened the door, it wasn't Mr. Edwards standing there.

It was Chip.

"Oh. Hey," I said.

"Hey." He ran his hand through his hair. It was messy and smushed from his helmet. He looked past my shoulder and nodded at Landon.

"How's it going?"

I shrugged.

"Yeah." He twisted his lips back and forth. "The guys all signed this for you." He pulled a card out of his messenger bag. "We missed you."

"Thanks."

I don't know why, but the card made me want to cry again, and I hadn't even opened it.

I never thought I'd have the kind of friends who'd get me cards when my grandfather died.

"How'd we do?"

"We won."

"Good."

"Yeah." Chip shifted back and forth on his feet. "Your nails look nice."

I looked down at my hands.

"It's a good color on you."

"Thanks," I said. "Um."

"I'd better get home. But. Well. If you need anything?"

"Yeah," I said. "Thanks, Chip."

"See you," Landon said from behind me. He stepped onto the stoop and wove our hands together.

Chip looked from Landon to me and back. "Yeah. See you."

We watched him bike away.

Landon held up my hand to study my nails.

"It really is a pretty color on you, you know."

I smiled.

It felt like breaking the rules.

"Thanks."

AN OVERABUNDANCE
OF FOOD

We held Babou's memorial at the Portland Persian Cultural Center.

The PPCC (an acronym that always seemed hilarious to me as a child) was a converted mattress store, with a big tiled common room in front and offices in the back for meetings and small gatherings. There was a tiny bookstore, which mostly just had cookbooks and Farsi language learners and pamphlets for local activities.

And then there was the kitchen, which had required the most extensive remodeling.

Iranians are notoriously exacting when it comes to kitchens. Mom used to talk about remodeling ours, at home, but she hadn't mentioned it for a while. Not when our savings were drained, and the dishwasher was still broken.

Mom showed her ID to the security officer at the door, who beeped us in.

It made me feel weird, that the Portland Persian Cultural Center had to have a security guard.

Apparently there had been lots of windows broken, and even some harassment incidents, before I was born. And after too, but Mom always said the worst was right after 9/11.

For as long as I could remember, the PPCC had security officers at the doors and little cameras tucked into the corners of the ceiling. But those hadn't been around when Mom first found the place, and invited Dad to a Hafez reading for their third date.

Dad was supposed to be here, but his flight got delayed out of LAX, and he didn't know when he'd make it home.

"Can you take these?" Mom passed me a huge cardboard box full of tiny vases with jasmine blossoms in them.

I missed the smell of jasmine in Babou's garden.

"Yeah."

I took the box in one hand and offered Laleh my other. She rested her fingers in my palm, and I led her to the kitchen, which was also the staging area for decor.

The nice thing about the Portland Persian Cultural Center was, it was already an explosion of all things Iranian: Photographs of Iran lined the walls, many of them faded pre-revolution images of Tehran and Tabriz and Shiraz. There were even some of Yazd. Paintings of Nassereddin Shah—the least controversial figure in Iranian portraiture—hung in a few spots. (Not that he was without controversy, but still. He predated the Islamic revolution and even the Pahlavi dynasty that had preceded it.)

Tinny speakers in the ceiling played the Iranian equivalent of elevator music.

"You thirsty, Laleh?"

"Yeah."

I poured her a cup of water and went back to help Oma and Grandma carry in the aluminum trays of rice and kabob from Kabob House, this Iranian restaurant in Beaverton.

No gathering of Iranians would be complete without an overabundance of food.

Everyone wore nice dresses—Mom's was black, but not mournful—while I was in gray dress pants and a dark blue button-up. Underneath I had on my jersey from the Iranian national soccer team, Team Melli.

Sohrab had gotten it for me, when I visited Iran. It made me feel closer to Iran, and Babou, and playing Rook, and sitting in silence drinking tea.

I grabbed a paper towel and wiped my eyes.

I kept crying at weird times.

I had never lost someone I loved before.

I didn't know how to deal with it.

"Darius? Hey."

There was one other Iranian at Chapel Hill High School: Javaneh Esfahani.

She was a senior, and now that we didn't eat lunch together, I barely ever saw her. She was in AP classes during the day, and busy with Associated Student Body after school.

Javaneh wore a sleek black dress with a red blouse over it and a dark red headscarf. She had on new glasses too, cat-eye ones with green highlights on the frames.

"Oh. Hey."

"You look like you could use a hug."

"I guess so."

Javaneh snorted and pulled me in.

I couldn't remember ever hugging her before. She felt warm and comfortable, like your blankets when you first wake up in those late fall days before you turn the heat on, and you can't imagine ever getting out of bed because you know the floors are going to be cold.

"How're you doing?"

"Okay. Trying to keep it together for my mom."

She nodded. "When my grandmother passed away, my dad had a really hard time too."

"That sucks."

"Yeah. I still miss her sometimes."

I sniffed. Javaneh pulled a couple Kleenexes out of her huge black purse.

She was still in high school, but she already had the voluminous purse of a True Persian Woman, the kind that opened into an alternate dimension.

"Thanks."

"Sure." She looked behind me. "I think someone is here for you."

"Oh?" I turned to find Landon standing in the doorway. He was dressed all the way up, in a dark suit with a white shirt and gray tie.

He looked impeccable.

"Hi."

"Hi," he said, and wrapped me in a hug. I melted into him.

We didn't kiss, though. I think maybe he was trying to figure out what the rules were, surrounded by a bunch of Iranian strangers.

Maybe he was.

Maybe I was too.

When we pulled apart, I said, "Javaneh, this is my boyfriend. Landon."

Javaneh beamed and offered her hand.

"Javaneh Esfahani. I go to school with Darius."

Landon's shoulders relaxed as he took her hand. "Nice to meet you."

"Same." Javaneh glanced toward the big room, and her eyes bugged out for a second. "Oh, no. My parents are trying to help."

Landon blinked. "Is that bad?"

"My parents are, like, Olympic-level taarofers."

"Oh no," I agreed.

Landon looked between us. Despite my best attempts to explain taarof—the complex set of Social Cues that governed all interpersonal relations between Iranians—he had yet to grasp it fully.

"Wish me luck." Javaneh squeezed my arm and hurried out to stop her parents from taking over the entire memorial.

Landon held my hands and looked me up and down.

"You got rid of your nails," he said.

Grandma helped me take off the polish. Turquoise nails felt too happy for a memorial.

Too gay.

I would never get to tell Babou I was gay.

I hated my own cowardice.

"Didn't seem like the right occasion."

"You still look nice." He played with a few locks of hair that had fallen over my forehead. "Are you doing okay? Really?"

"I'm okay."

Landon fussed with my shoulder seams.

And I had this feeling, like I was annoyed with him for some reason.

Dr. Howell said it was normal to feel things—ugly things—when I was processing grief.

I tried not to let it show.

"You ready to head out there?"

I took a deep breath.

"Yeah."

QUINTESSENTIAL
PERSIAN PROFESSION

The memorial service was simple: Once everyone arrived (about an hour after we asked people to show up because, as a people group, Iranians are predisposed to tardiness), Mom said a prayer, first in English, then in Farsi, then in halting Dari. She talked about Ardeshir Bahrami's life growing up in Yazd: how he was born into the Zoroastrian community, went to school, opened a shop, weathered the revolution, raised three kids and eight grandchildren (with a great-grandchild on the way). How he was kind, thoughtful, generous. How he was a demon at Rook. How he loved his garden.

"The only thing my father loved more than his garden was his wife, Fariba. And the only thing he loved more than Fariba was her cooking."

Everyone had been somber up to that point, and some people were even crying. But when Mom said that, the whole room's mood changed. First there was a little chuckle here and there, and then some uncomfortable giggles, and then finally some actual laughter.

At the table right behind us, Javaneh's dad let out a full belly laugh. He—like most of the men in the room—was dressed in a suit.

Clearly I had once again failed to accurately gauge the appropriate iteration of Persian Casual for the event.

Mom wiped her tears and smiled. "I wish my mom were

here to cook for us tonight. But instead we have Kabob House. Noosh-e joon!"

Grandma and Oma got up to help at the buffet. I got up too, and took Laleh's hand.

"Can I help?" Landon asked.

"Sure."

Laleh manned the bread station—her favorite—while Landon scooped rice onto people's plates, and I portioned out the tah dig, which Kabob House made with thinly sliced potatoes on the bottom of the pot.

The line moved slowly, as everyone took time to talk to each other, sometimes in Farsi and sometimes in English and sometimes both, arguing and taarofing and catching up with friends they hadn't seen since the last time everyone came to the PPCC.

Landon gave me this bewildered smile when two older Iranian ladies, who I recognized vaguely but whose names I didn't know, stopped in front of us, arguing in Farsi. Their voices rose, shrill and sharp over the din, until they suddenly cackled. They turned to me.

"Darioush!"

"Hi."

"Look at you. You've lost weight."

"Um."

My ears burned.

"Who is this? Your friend from school?"

"My boyfriend," I said. "Landon."

The woman on my left, who wore her brown hair in an elaborate bun, turned to her friend and asked something in Farsi.

Her friend, who was taller, with long black hair and ornate

230

gold hoop earrings, said something back. She eyed me, and then Landon, then said something else to her friend. "Just tah dig for me, Darioush," she said.

I gave her a wedge with a nice chunk of potato. "This okay?"

"Perfect."

Her friend kept looking from me to Landon and back.

"No rice for me, thank you," she said.

And then she said, "Nice to meet you," and moved along.

"What just happened?" Landon whispered to me. "What were they talking about?"

I didn't catch enough to understand.

I was pretty sure I didn't want to understand.

"Not sure."

Javaneh's dad, a doctor, held his plate out for Landon to spoon him a wedge of rice. He had a mustache that reminded me of Babou's, though his was black and trimmed instead of gray and bushy. "Oh, just a little," he said, when Landon offered him a big scoop.

"Sorry," Landon said, and started to put back half the rice.

Panic flashed across Dr. Esfahani's face.

"Please have more. There's lots," I said.

"If you insist."

Landon glanced at me, baffled, and then gave Dr. Esfahani his rice.

Like I said, Landon still hadn't mastered the art of taarof, which required you to politely decline food even if you actually wanted it, and to force people to take food they said they didn't want.

"Darioush. Javaneh said you're on the soccer team this year."

"Yeah."

"How's it going?"

"Good. We're six and one."

And Landon said, "He's the best defender on the team."

I blushed and shook my head.

"Of course he is! Persians are excellent at soccer. It's genetic."

As a doctor—a quintessential Persian profession if ever there was one—Javaneh's dad was always claiming things were genetic.

Dr. Esfahani accepted a big piece of tah dig without argument—he was clearly still shaken up by his near-miss with the rice—and moved down the line toward the kabob.

I served Javaneh's mom, who was also a doctor—a PhD, who taught physics at Portland State—and then Javaneh's two brothers, who were still in middle school.

When our first tray of tah dig ran out, I took it and a couple other empties to the back. Mom was in the kitchen too, refilling huge thermoses of tea from the hot water spigot on the coffee maker.

"Oh, Darius. Can I talk to you for a second?"

"Yeah, sure. Are you doing okay?"

Mom nodded. She'd made it through the day so far without smudging her mascara.

I had already cried four times myself.

"What's up?"

Mom pursed her lips for a second.

"You know, a lot of our guests are more . . . traditional Iranians."

"I know." I held up my hands, nails out.

Mom's eyes fell.

"I'm sorry."

"It's okay."

Mom looked at me like she wanted to say something else, but Oma stuck her head in. "We're almost out of kabobs."

"I'll get some." I turned back to Mom. "Have people been saying things about Oma and Grandma?"

"No. You know Iranians. They'll just mutter to each other."

"Okay."

Mom grabbed my arm.

She looked at me for a moment.

"Make sure Landon gets enough to eat. It was sweet of him to come."

Once the line had died down, I helped Landon make a plate. It was his first true chelo kabob experience, so I showed him how to make the most of it: layering his plate with bread to soak up the juices, explaining the different philosophies for rice (butter or no butter, mixed with chopped-up grilled tomato or not), introducing him to sumac as a seasoning.

"I think you gave me too much," Landon said when he beheld the heaping pile of rice and meat and vegetables I had squeezed onto his paper plate.

"That's Persian tradition too."

He snorted and smiled.

"Thank you for being here. Really."

"Of course." He set his plate down and brushed my hands with his. "I'm glad to do it."

I made a plate for myself and then we sat next to Laleh, who was already shoveling up her rice with a serving spoon wider than her mouth.

After dinner, while everyone drank tea and ate zoolbia—essentially a syrup-soaked, starchy Persian funnel cake—Mom and Laleh and I told stories about Babou.

"The first time I met Babou he was on the roof of his house," I said. "He wanted to water his fig trees."

"He loved his fig trees!" Mom shouted. "I think he loved them more than he loved his children!"

That made everyone laugh, especially because there was a non-zero probability that it was true.

"He was all dressed up too, in dress pants and his nice shoes."

Mom nodded and laughed, but her eyes were sparkling. I wasn't sure if it was from laughing too hard, or because it was finally getting to her.

Maybe it was both.

"He kept shouting at Sohrab to help him. Sohrab's his neighbor. My best friend. Anyway, Sohrab was trying to untangle the hose, and I was there watching the whole thing, and Babou was like, 'I'll be down in a minute, I don't care you just flew across the globe to meet me, I need to finish watering my figs.'"

"You didn't tell me that part!" Mom shouted.

After that, Laleh told everyone—through occasional hiccups and tears—about watching Iranian soap operas with Babou, who knew every character and every plot line going back twenty years.

There was a lull after that, and I refreshed Landon's tea for him.

"Thanks," he said. I squeezed his hand under the table, and he looked at me kind of funny.

"Hey Mom," I said. "Have you told everyone about Babou and the aftabeh?"

Mom's eyes got huge as the crowd around us tittered.

"Who told you about that?"

"Zandayi Simin."

"I am going to kill Simin-khanum!" Mom said. She sighed, and then started talking in Farsi.

Behind me, Grandma asked, "What's an aftabeh?"

"It's kind of like a watering can. You use it sort of like a bidet."

Oma snorted, and Grandma covered her mouth, but then I couldn't say anything else over everyone cracking up.

E ventually the last guests trickled out. Landon helped Mom
fold up the tables and stack the chairs while Laleh picked up
paper cups and plates for the trash. In the kitchen, I helped Oma
and Grandma manage the mountain of leftovers.

"You doing okay?" Grandma asked.

"I guess."

I held open a gallon-sized ziplock bag for Oma to load with
kabobs.

"You're awfully quiet," Oma said. "Something bothering
you?"

"I never told Babou I was gay."

Oma took the bag from me and zipped it closed. She looked
at Grandma and then back to me.

"Do you think . . ." I started to say, but Oma cut me off.

"You know, I knew your parents had trans friends in college.
But it was still hard coming out to them."

"Why? Did they take it bad?"

Oma shook her head. "No. And they were so busy with you
I don't think they processed it all that much. You were just a
baby."

I nodded.

"I remember your mom, she kept asking what she was supposed to do with all her photos. From their wedding, from when
you were born. But then she got used to it. She and Stephen
both did. I think they adjusted quicker than Melanie."

Grandma cleared her throat, and Oma shook her head and started shoveling rice into another plastic bag.

I had never heard my grandmothers talk about Oma's coming out.

I wanted them to keep talking.

"What do you mean?"

Grandma gave me this long look. She glanced at Oma, who had emerged from the refrigerator with two bags of sabzi.

"Just that people can surprise you," Oma said. She set down the sabzi and rested a hand on Grandma's shoulder. "And sometimes you have to let them, and trust that things will work out."

Mom popped her head in. "I just heard from Stephen. His plane's finally landed."

"We'll finish up here. You go get him," Grandma said.

"Thanks. See you at home?"

"Sure."

Mom kissed me. "I'll take your sister. She's exhausted."

"Okay. Love you."

"Love you."

After we finished up, Landon and I filled the trunk of Oma's Camry with the leftovers.

"You wanna come over?" I asked.

"Can't tonight."

"Oh."

"Will you be okay?"

"Yeah."

Landon squeezed my hand. "I think maybe you need to be with your family anyway."

Oma turned on her NPR but left it on low. It was kind of soothing: this low, melancholy voice I couldn't quite make out, whispering in my ear.

Landon looked at me and gave me this sad smile.

And then he rested his hand on my leg, kind of on my inner thigh.

I stared at it: the way his fingers rested against the smooth gray fabric of my dress pants. His pinky traced the inseam back and forth, back and forth.

My ears burned.

I had this ugly feeling in me again.

I wanted to tell Landon to stop, but I couldn't.

He had been so patient with me today, and maybe I should've been more patient with him in return.

But I didn't want to get an erection in my grandmother's car.

So I took my hand and wrapped it around his. I pulled it off my leg and wove our fingers together.

He gave me this look.

Like he was annoyed with me, maybe.

Or disappointed.

And I got another ugly feeling. Like I wanted him to just leave me alone.

That's normal.

Right?

Even with finishing up at the PPCC—and dropping Landon off—we still made it home first.

I put the kettle on, set to 165 degrees so I could make some Dragonwell, and got changed out of my Persian Casual clothes.

I still felt kind of weird and tingly where Landon's hand had been on my inner thigh, perilously close to my penis.

The garage door rumbled beneath my feet. I shook my head and pulled on some clean underwear and a pair of joggers.

I had to wait a minute before going downstairs.

Mom was at the door, holding it open for Dad. She murmured something to him, and he laughed and whispered something into her ear, and then he saw me.

"There he is," he said, and pulled me into a Level Twelve Hug.

I couldn't remember the last time Dad hugged me so tight or for so long. His beard rubbed against my cheeks. It had gone past the scratchy phase and into the coarse phase, where it wasn't super soft but it wasn't bothersome anymore.

I had never seen my father with a real beard before. It was darker than his sandy blond hair, almost a light brown, and it was patchy around the corners of his mouth.

I felt something wet against the side of my cheeks too, but I didn't say anything about that.

I didn't know how.

So I said, "I'm glad you're home," and squeezed him back as hard as I could, until he finally seemed to have enough. He patted my back, then rested his hand on the nape of my neck and pulled me in to kiss my forehead.

"I'm sorry I'm late."

"It's okay. I'm glad you're home."

I let Mom and Dad through, and Laleh followed, bringing Dad up to speed on everything he'd missed—including, according to her, "Miss Hawn doing Mike Progressions."

Dad looked from Mom to me.

"Microaggressions," I whispered, and slipped out to grab Dad's suitcase.

I popped the trunk and fought the big suitcase, which kept catching on the rubber lip of the trunk. Usually Dad packed his suitcase perfectly flat, but this time it was lumpy and awkward, like he'd balled up everything and tossed it in, rather than folding or rolling his clothes into neat rows.

I set the unwieldy suitcase on its wheels and pulled out his smaller one, then grabbed his leather Kellner & Newton messenger bag from the passenger-side footwell.

"You hungry?" Mom asked. "We have some kabob left."

"Some" kabob was an understatement.

We had enough leftovers to feed the entire Chapel Hill High School varsity men's soccer team.

"Here. Sit." Mom forced Dad into his seat at the table. Laleh clambered into the seat next to him and kept up her tales about school.

The kettle was ready, so I filled the teapot and hauled the suitcase upstairs.

Mom followed me.

"Thank you, sweetie," she said.

"No problem."

"You can leave it there. I'll sort out the laundry."

"Okay."

I laid the suitcase in the corner by the closet. Mom unzipped it and started pulling out clothes.

Sure enough, they were all jumbled up, and mixed in with Dad's shoes, which weren't even in the drawstring cloth pouches he normally used.

Mom let out a sigh so quiet I might have imagined it.

I thought about her living through Stephen Kellner's depressive episodes before.

I thought about her living through mine.

I thought about how she had to grieve her father on top of all of that.

"Um," I said. "Do you want some tea?"

"Yes please."

"Okay."

While Dad ate his kabob, Grandma and Oma came downstairs. They had changed out of their Persian Casual clothes too, into comfy sweatpants, though Oma still had her hair up.

"Don't get up," Grandma said, but Dad did anyway. He gave them each a kiss on the cheek.

"You need a shave," Oma said.

Dad just shrugged and went back to his dinner.

Everyone was quiet for a second, the kind of quiet you could snap like a twig.

I said, "How was California?"

"Busy," Dad said.

"When do you have to go back?"

He sighed. "Monday."

"At least it's warm there," Grandma said.

Oma nodded but didn't add anything. She was studying Dad with pursed lips.

The silence came back.

That's the thing about silences. Sometimes they keep coming back.

"Anyone else want tea?"

"Sure." Oma glanced at Grandma and then back at Dad. "You sure you're doing okay, Stephen?"

"I'm sure."

"All right."

Grandma rested her hand on Dad's shoulder. "You look tired."

"Really. I'm fine, Mom." Dad smiled, but it didn't reach his eyes.

What was happening?

There was some shrouded tension lurking in the kitchen, but I couldn't figure out why, so I did what I always did and poured some tea.

"What's this?"

"Dragonwell." I handed Dad the mesh strainer of steeped leaves so he could smell. "Pan-roasted green tea. From China."

Dad gave the leaves a long sniff. "It smells good."

"Yeah."

"Does it have much caffeine?"

"Not really."

"Hmm. Better make something stronger next, so we can stay awake for *Star Trek*."

"Really?"

Dad smiled, this time for real. He had dark bags under his eyes, and his hair was a mess, but for the first time since he'd been home, he looked like my dad again.

"Really."

THE VISITOR

For as long as I could remember, Dad always had a rule: one episode a night, unless it's a two-parter, and then we get to watch both parts. (Three-parters still get split up into three separate nights, for some inexplicable reason Dad refuses to disclose.)

But when we finished "The Way of the Warrior, Parts I & II"—where Worf from *The Next Generation* joins the crew of *Deep Space Nine*—Dad didn't turn the TV off, or even stop the next episode from cuing up.

"We've got to make up for lost time." Dad's voice was hoarse, and he cleared his throat as he scooted closer to me. He wrapped his arm around my shoulder. "I've missed this."

I cleared my own throat. "Me too."

We were quiet for a second. Not the brittle silence from the kitchen, but a comfortable sort of silence. Dad breathed, and I breathed, and I sank into the couch under the weight of his arm.

"Hey, Dad?"

"Yeah?"

"Are you really doing okay?"

Dad hit pause (the teaser for "The Visitor" had just started) and looked at me. "Why do you ask?"

"It's just, last time you were home, you said you were depressed."

Dad's mouth twisted to the side.

"And you seem . . ."

"What?"

Rumpled was the first word that came to mind.

But I couldn't say that.

I couldn't.

"Tired," I said instead.

And then I said, "Sad."

And then, because I didn't know when to shut up, I said, "Lonely."

Dad sighed. He stared at the screen and ran the back of his index finger under his lip, tracing the gaps in his beard.

I wanted Dad to say something. To answer me.

But instead, he wrapped his arm around me again, grabbed the remote, and hit play.

"The Visitor" is one of the best episodes of *Star Trek: Deep Space Nine*. It's about Captain Sisko's son, Jake, trying to bring his dad home after he gets lost in time.

It was just my luck, watching an episode like that, when my own grandfather was lost to me forever.

When I was afraid I was losing my dad to depression.

The last time Dad's depression got really bad, we lost each other for almost seven years.

I didn't think I could take it if he drifted away from me again.

Next to me, Dad was crying. Not just a single tear, like he usually had, but full-on crying. He sniffed and wiped his eyes and then he made this sound, like a groan or a whimper, and he pulled me so close to him I thought he was going to crush me.

I wrapped my arm around him too, and we held each other for a long time.

"Dad?" I asked, once it seemed like he had calmed down enough to talk.

"Sorry." Dad wiped his eyes with the backs of his hands. "That just really got to me."

"It's okay. Really."

I wanted Dad to know it was okay for him to cry in front of me.

When the episode was over, and the ending credits played, I handed him a couple Kleenex and used one to blow my nose.

Dad leaned back and sighed.

"One more?" he asked.

"Um."

It was already past midnight.

"Please?"

Dad had this thing in his voice.

It broke my heart to hear it.

"Sure."

So we watched another episode ("Hippocratic Oath," which is kind of a forgettable one, to be honest), and I leaned my head against Dad's shoulder when I started getting sleepy. Dad rested his hand on my head and played with my hair.

I couldn't remember Dad ever doing that.

Mom did it all the time. But Dad never did.

He kept combing it back and playing with the three little whorls in the crown of my head.

"Hey," he said, not much louder than a whisper. "Does it ever make you feel worse, being around me when I'm depressed?"

"No," I said. "Not really."

Dad's fingers paused on my head.

"You sure? It doesn't make you more depressed?"

"I'm sure. Why?"

Dad's fingers started up again. He was quiet for a long time.

I stifled a yawn.

"Sometimes being around your grandparents . . . I don't know. It makes me feel like I'm thirteen again, lying in bed and thinking depressed thoughts. And feeling their depression too, like a cloud over the house."

"I didn't know Grandma and Oma had it too."

"Well, they don't like to talk about it. And they've never been to see anyone for it, so they've never been officially diagnosed. I always thought they might be bipolar."

"Oh." I stifled another yawn. "Did they make it hard for you to get help?"

Dad rested his chin on my head. "Sometimes. They wanted me to manage it on my own."

"I'm sorry."

"Don't be."

My eyelids got heavy. I kept blinking, but I knew I had to stay awake.

"Is that why we never see them?"

"No. Maybe." Dad sighed. His breath tickled my hair. "I don't know."

"Oh."

"Them being here, I thought . . . well, I want you and your sister to have a better relationship with them than I did."

To be honest, I wasn't sure Dad's plan was working.

But I couldn't say that to him.

I yawned.

Dad chuckled.

"Okay." He kissed my head again. "You need to get to bed."

"I'm awake," I said, though my eyes were closed.

"All right."

I let Dad hold me. And I held on to him too.

"Don't worry about me," he whispered. "I'm going to be okay."

"You promise?"

"I promise."

ELECTROMAGNETIC
RADIATION

"Darius, can you take the trash out?" Polli asked.

"Yeah."

Most of our trash actually went into the compost—we gave it to a farm-to-table restaurant down the street to use in their garden—but I had to sort it first, because sometimes people threw outside trash in our cans: plastic wrappers, empty glass bottles, used Red Bull cans.

I didn't understand the point and purpose of Red Bull.

Once I'd gotten everything sorted and dumped into the big compost bin, I ran to the bathroom to wash my hands and make sure I hadn't spilled anything on myself.

"Excuse me?" a twenty-something in a beanie with huge gauges in their ears said as soon as I stepped out front.

"Hey. Can I help you?"

"I'm looking for a gift for my partner."

"Oh. Do you know what they like to drink?"

"She doesn't like caffeine," they said.

So I led them over to our herbal selection. I talked about rooibos and fruit-based and butterfly-pea flower, letting them smell sample tins as we went.

From the counter, Kerry hollered at me. "Darius, we need more nitro!"

The back of my neck burned.

"Um. Sorry. Will you be okay? I have to . . ."

"Sure," Beanie Person said.

"You can ask up front if you need more help."

"Thanks."

"We're about to do a tasting," Mr. Edwards said when I got back with the nitro tanks. "Just got a new batch of Darjeelings in."

"Awesome."

I started to follow him, but I heard a shout and a clang and the sloshing of liquid. A table had just spilled a full carafe of iced hibiscus, which was dark purple and sticky from agave nectar and hard to get off the floor if it set too long.

Polli waved me down. "Darius?"

"I'll take care of it." I turned to Mr. Edwards. "Be right there."

I mopped the spill up, and then helped break down some boxes for recycling. I was headed to the tasting room again when Kerry said, "Darius. I need some Uva. And New Vithanakande."

"Tins?"

"Packs."

"Okay."

"It'll be a second," she said to this tall, beardy person with a trucker hat waiting at the register.

To be honest, they were the last person in the quadrant I would have expected to be looking for fine teas from Sri Lanka.

"Thanks," Kerry said when I handed off the packs.

"Sure. I'm gonna catch this tasting if it's okay."

"Have fun."

Mr. Edwards and Landon had already steeped four different cups of Darjeeling, and were dipping their spoons into the third when I knocked on the tasting room door.

"Just in time," Mr. Edwards said. "Grab a spoon."

I sat next to Landon and dipped my spoon into the first tea.

"Mm," I said. "It's good."

"First or second flush?" Mr. Edwards asked.

"Um."

I smelled the tea, studied the liquor, took another sip. It was lighter and smoother.

"First?"

"Good. What else?"

"Floral?"

"Hm." His lips pursed for a second. "More spicy than floral, I think. Cardamom."

"Oh."

It didn't taste like cardamom to me at all, and I drank cardamom all the time.

I tried number two. "Um. Tropical?"

"Yes, guava and passionfruit. Be more specific when you taste."

That burning in my chest came back: this weird, kind of fluttery feeling, like I had a pulsar lodged behind my sternum, spinning and flinging electromagnetic radiation outward in rapid intervals.

I wished I could just drink the tea and enjoy it.

Next to me, Landon's pen scratched against his notebook.

Mr. Edwards cleared his throat. "How about this third one?"

"Kind of nutty? Like almonds?"

"Better. And number four?"

I felt like I was back in Algebra II. And there was no Chip to help me study either.

I sniffed and sipped and thought.

"Fruity."

"Grapefruit," Landon added.

"Right. You've got to work on that palate, Darius."

The pulsar spun faster.

And I had that ridiculous feeling again, stronger than ever.

Like I didn't like working here anymore.

Like sooner or later, tea was just going to be another test for me to fail.

"All right. Better get cleaned up. Good work."

"You mind taking care of it?" Landon asked. "I've gotta do some stocking."

I cleared my throat. "Sure."

I emptied the cups and put them in the dishwasher, wiped off the table, and told myself everything was okay.

Really.

I was going to go home after work, but Landon invited me over.

Landon almost never invited me over. For some reason, we usually hung out at my house.

So when he asked me to come over, I knew I had to say yes.

Landon and his dad lived in a condo downtown, just a couple streetcar stops away from Rose City. It was in a remodeled art-deco office building, on the eighth floor. Landon punched in the code to the front door and led me up in the elevator. He grabbed a paper notice wedged into the door frame and let us in.

Every time I saw Landon's home, I was kind of amazed. Their living room had these big windows that looked out over downtown—you could even see Rose City Teas, if you were tall enough, like me—and everything was white and chrome and sleek.

Landon led me to the angular black couch. "You want anything?"

"I'm good."

He sat down and rested his head against my shoulder.

"You okay? You were awfully quiet today."

"I don't know. I just . . ." I played with the hem of my shirt. "I don't know."

Landon snaked his arm behind me to hold my waist. "Talk to me."

I didn't know how to tell him how tired I was of never having the right answer at tastings.

How I just wanted to drink tea and share it with people.

How I wasn't happy at Rose City.

I didn't know how to say any of that out loud.

So instead I said, "I'm just worried about my dad, I guess."

"He still depressed?"

"Yeah. Plus I'm still sad about my grandfather."

"I get that."

"Babou loved tea. Now, every time I make a pot, drink a cup, it's like . . . it hits me. I don't have a grandfather anymore."

"I'm sorry."

I took his free hand in mine and twined our fingers together. "It's okay."

Landon kissed my shoulder.

I sighed.

He smiled at me, and then leaned in closer to press his lips against mine, warm and soft and lingering.

It was gentle and nice. His hand moved from my waist to the back of my neck, fingers playing along my hairline before moving up my head and twisting into my curls.

I shivered.

Landon leaned back. His lips were red and a little chapped in the corner. His tongue darted out at the spot.

"Is this okay?" he asked.

"Yeah," I said, because when we were kissing, I didn't have to talk. I didn't have to think.

I didn't feel that pulsar in me anymore.

Landon scooted closer until he was almost in my lap and kissed me again. He tapped his tongue against my teeth, and I opened up a little bit to meet it. But then he did this thing where he hollowed out his cheeks and sucked my tongue into his mouth.

My breath hitched. It was the weirdest thing I'd ever felt.

Weird and excellent.

I finally had to break the kiss and catch my breath. Landon's cheeks were flushed. His eyes shone.

"Someone's excited," he whispered, and poked at the weird pooch my jeans made in the front.

"That's a joner," I whispered back, and Landon giggled.

I mean, I was hard, but it was trapped against my left thigh.

Landon used his thumb to trace my lips. I kissed the little pad of it, but then he stuck it into my mouth and rubbed it against the inside of my cheek.

It was the kind of thing you would see in porn.

(If I'm being honest, it was the kind of thing I had, in fact, seen in porn.)

"What are you doing?"

"Nothing."

"I don't think I like that."

Landon blanched. "Sorry."

"It's okay." I kissed his shoulder.

He rested his hand on my thigh (my right one, thankfully) and rubbed it back and forth. He leaned in for another kiss, and he did that tongue-sucking thing again.

My skin tingled all over.

This time it was Landon who broke the kiss.

I was pretty sure he was excited too.

"My dad won't be home until late," he said. "What should we do?"

"You could play for me. You never let me hear you play bassoon."

Landon stared at me.

"Or we could just stay like this. Cuddle for a while."

Landon kissed me and rested his head against my chest again. "I like cuddling with you."

I took his hand off my thigh and brought it up to my lips. I kissed his knuckles, one after another.

Landon shifted a bit, his hair tickling my chin, as I wrapped my arms around him and laid us across his couch.

I took a long, deep breath.

And then Landon snorted and muttered "joner" under his breath, and we both started cracking up.

THE SECOND STEEPINGS

That night, after Dad and I watched "Indiscretion," a kind of trippy episode of *Deep Space Nine*, I tried Sohrab. Again. But the little green CALL icon kept flashing, and the *doot-deet-doot, deet-doot-deet* music echoed in my bedroom. And Sohrab didn't answer.

I didn't know what to do.

Sohrab was the one who always helped me figure out what to do.

I hung up and tried again. And a third time. Let it ring until it timed out.

Nothing.

I chewed on my lip for a little while, and then tried Mamou instead.

I hated how selfish I was, calling my grandmother because I couldn't get ahold of my best friend.

How was I supposed to talk to Mamou now that Babou was gone?

She picked up almost instantly. There was a second of weird, ringing feedback, and the screen flashed black and then white as we connected.

"Hi, Darioush-jan."

"Hi, Mamou." I almost cried, I loved my grandmother's voice so much. "How are you?"

She sighed. "I am doing okay, maman. You know, it's hard."

"Yeah."

"I miss you. I wish you could come visit again."

"Me too."

At that I think I did start crying. Just a little.

"Is Dayi Jamsheed around? Or Sohrab?"

I hated the thought of Mamou being alone in that house.

And, I thought maybe Sohrab was there.

"No. Just me. Zandayi Simin is coming later to make ab goosht. You know ab goosht?"

"Yeah."

Ab goosht more or less translates to "meat water." But it's actually a stew, made from meat braised until it falls off the bone, and eaten with crusty bread.

"You know, it was Babou's favorite."

I sniffed.

"How are you doing, Darioush-jan? How's school? How's soccer? How's your job? How's your dad? Your mom?"

"Um. They're okay. Everyone's doing okay." I couldn't tell her about how Mom was tired. Or how Dad was depressed. Or how I was beginning to hate going into work.

I had to pretend like everything was okay here, because I knew that it wasn't over there.

"Hey, Mamou?"

"Yes?"

"You haven't seen Sohrab lately, have you?"

Mamou looked off to the side.

"It's just, I haven't heard from him in a while."

And I needed him.

I hated how selfish I was.

But I needed my best friend.

"You know, he is very busy right now. With school. And his mom."

"Oh."

"I will tell him you called. Okay?"

"Yeah. Okay."

"It was nice talking to you, Darioush-jan." Mamou's voice was different. Higher.

I didn't know what was happening.

What was it that Mamou wouldn't say out loud?

"I love you, Mamou."

"I love you too, Darioush-jan. Bye."

I wished Dad could've stayed longer.

I wished he could've told me what to do about Rose City. About everything.

But instead, I got a minute to say goodbye before he drove to the airport Monday morning.

"Dad?"

"Yeah?"

"Come back soon."

"As soon as I can."

He held my face between his hands. The circles under his eyes had darkened again.

I would've done anything to erase those circles.

"Love you."

"You okay?" Chip asked me as we walked out of the locker room Monday afternoon.

"Yeah. Why?"

"You keep playing with your tassels. You do that when you're nervous."

I dropped my tassel.

I didn't know it was the kind of thing people had noticed.

I didn't know Chip was the kind of guy who would notice it.

"You want to hang out or something? Evie really likes it when you come over."

"Can't."

"Oh."

Chip ran a hand through his hair.

"I've gotta go to work."

"Oh. I thought maybe you were still mad at me."

"I'm not. Just . . ."

"Just what?"

"I don't know."

Chip leaned against the bike rack and looked at me.

He didn't say anything.

And for some reason, I said, "I just don't want to go to work today."

"How come?"

"I don't know."

"You still like it there?"

"Yes," I said automatically. "Maybe. I don't know."

"It sounds like you do know."

I shook my head.

And then I said, "I've wanted to work there forever."

Chip said, "You know why I tried out for soccer this year instead of football?"

I reached for my tassel but stopped myself.

"'Cause I hated football. I'd been playing since I was a kid and every year I liked it a little less. Last year I dreaded going to practice every day. And Trent was the only friend I had on the team. The only thing that got me through the season."

"Oh."

"It was hard quitting. Coach Winfield is still mad at me. Mom's kind of mad we spent all that money on pads and helmets and stuff. Sorin used to play too, you know?"

Chip swallowed. His Adam's apple bobbed up and down.

He had a really pronounced Adam's apple.

"I guess what I'm trying to say is, if something's not making you happy, doesn't it make sense to let it go?"

My chest felt warm again. That pulsar feeling was back.

Could I really let go of Rose City?

Just like that?

I cleared my throat. "I have to have a job, though. My parents are both working overtime and they're still worried about money."

"There are other jobs."

"But I'm not good at anything else."

Chip gave me this look then. Like it hurt him when I said that.

I don't know why I felt so ashamed.

"Sorry. Um. I better go. Don't want to be late."

"Oh. Yeah. Hey, you got your tickets for homecoming?"

"Got them today."

"Cool," Chip said, but there was this thing in his voice.

I didn't know what it was.

He unlocked his bike.

I unlocked mine.

"See you tomorrow?"

"Yeah."

He helmeted up.

"And Chip?"

"Yeah?"

"Thanks."

As the bus rumbled toward downtown, I gnawed on my protein bar—a peanut butter one Coach Bentley recommended—and turned over what Chip had said in my head.

I felt that pulsar inside me flare back to full intensity as I tucked my stuff into my cubby.

"Hey," Kerry said. "Can you take over the register?"

"Sure."

It was a slow day—Mondays were usually slow—but a steady trickle of customers made their way through the store. I rang up growlers of Nitro Earl Grey, and tins of Darjeeling, and big fifty-count bags of Genmaicha sachets.

In the tasting room, Mr. Edwards and Landon were steeping some Bai Mu Dan to try.

I wondered if maybe Chip was right about everything.

I thought maybe he was.

That pulsar inside me flared out.

And I knew what I had to do.

Eventually, Mr. Edwards came out of the tasting room and headed to his office.

"Can you cover me for a few minutes?" I asked Kerry. "I need to talk to Mr. Edwards."

"Sure."

I rubbed the back of my head and knocked on Mr. Edwards's door.

"Darius," he said. "Come in."

"Thanks."

"Everything all right?"

My throat clenched up. I swallowed.

"Um. I wanted to talk to you about something."

"Sure."

"Um," I said.

And then I said, "I've been thinking a lot about some stuff lately."

And then I said, "I'm really sorry. But I think I want to quit."

"Oh."

Mr. Edwards sat back in his chair and looked at me.

"Did something happen?"

I shook my head.

"No. It's just. I don't think I'm cut out for this."

"I don't think I've ever met anyone so perfect for this job."

"I'm not, though," I said. I felt myself tearing up and fought it. "I get all the tastings wrong. I get overwhelmed with stocking and inventory and everything. I just . . . I love tea. But I don't think I want to sell it." I tried to keep going, but my throat had pinched shut.

Mr. Edwards let out this chuckle.

It wasn't a mean one.

It was more like he was remembering something.

"You know I play guitar?"

I nodded. Landon had shown me his dad's guitar collection.

"I'm pretty good at it, you know. I always hoped Landon would pick it up, but he liked bassoon better."

"Oh."

"Anyway. I was in a band for a while. The Second Steepings."

I giggled at that.

"Hey, give me a break. We were pretty good. We put out an album. Did shows. Made some money. But you know what?"

"What?"

"After a while it stopped making me happy. I loved playing guitar, but I didn't love being in a band." He leaned forward and patted my knee. "It's okay to keep something you love just for you."

"Really?" I squeaked.

"Really. It's okay."

And I got this feeling. Like I could breathe again.

"Thank you."

"Of course. I'm sure going to miss you, though."

"I'll still come in and get my tea here. I love this place."

Mr. Edwards beamed.

He had his son's smile.

"I'm really glad. I wanted this store to be a place for people who love tea." And then his smile faltered a little bit. "Do you want to tell Landon or should I?"

I chewed my lip. "I will."

"Was it something I did?" Landon asked.

"No."

"Something someone else did?"

"No. I promise." I pulled my bag out of my cubby. "It's me. I can't do this anymore."

"Why?"

"It's hard to explain."

Landon studied his feet. I reached for his hand, rubbed my thumb over the top of it in little circles.

Finally he asked, "Are you mad at me?"

"Of course not."

"Okay."

I kissed him on the nose. He giggled.

"Hey."

"Hey what?"

"I got our tickets for homecoming today."

Landon's whole face softened. "You did?"

"Yeah."

"What're you going to wear? Should we match?"

"Mom's taking me shopping this weekend."

"What's your favorite color?"

"Oh." I don't know why it struck me so much, Landon asking me my favorite color. "Blue."

"Easy enough."

"Easier than orange, at least." That was Landon's favorite.

He smirked. "That would definitely get us noticed. But I've got a gray suit that still fits."

Landon Edwards looked perfect in gray.

It brought out his beautiful eyes.

"What about . . . after?" he asked.

"After?"

"Yeah. We could go somewhere."

"Um."

"I know it's cliché, but. Well." His smirk slowly faded, and a blush crept up from his jawline to his cheeks. "Sometimes couples will, you know. Get together. After a dance."

His face was nearly glowing.

"Oh," I said.

My stomach did a little flip.

I didn't know what to say.

And I got this really ugly feeling.

Like Landon only wanted sex from me.

I knew that wasn't fair. I knew he really cared about me. But I couldn't help it.

That's normal.

Right?

"Think about it," Landon said, and kissed me on the shoulder. "Okay?"

"Okay."

IN THE GOLDEN LIGHT

"Are you nervous about homecoming?" Mom asked as she pulled her car into a parking spot.

"Hmm?"

She turned off the car and looked at me. "Are people giving you a hard time at school?"

"Oh. No."

I couldn't tell Mom that I was worried Landon thought we were going to do stuff afterward.

Sex stuff.

I never wanted to talk about gay sex with Shirin Kellner.

"Hm," Mom said, but I unbuckled my seat belt and opened the door before she could say more.

The Dragon & Phoenix Consignment Shop + Boutique (a name that sounded more suited to oolong than gently used fashion) was this huge store at the corner of a strip mall in Beaverton. The inside was practically glowing from the eclectic collection of ceiling lamps, and the scent of incense tickled my sinuses.

"Do you know what you're looking for?"

"Not really."

I showed her the picture Landon sent of his suit: a gray one with thin, slick lapels.

"Nice," Mom said.

"Yeah."

"Okay. Let's see what they have."

Mom wandered around, pulling nearly every suit off the rack

to examine it, while I went straight for the big and tall section. I traced my fingers along the rows of hangers. Most of the suits were black, or brown, or too tall, or not big enough.

And then, as I turned a corner, I saw it.

The perfect suit.

Bright blue, not quite pastel but nearly. And it was shiny, like there was something metallic in the threads.

It was like nothing I had ever worn in my life.

"Oh," Mom said. "What've you got there?"

I held it up. "I like it."

"You do?" There was this thing in her voice. "You sure it's okay for homecoming?"

"Yeah." It was bright, and colorful, but I knew it would be okay.

Mom grabbed the wrist to look at the price.

"You sure you want to spend this much?"

"Yeah." It would eat up most of my final paycheck, but still. "I can wear it again."

Mom held the sleeve up to the light and watched it shine. "Can you, though?"

"Why?" I asked. "Is it too gay?"

Mom blinked at me.

"No." She blinked again and let the sleeve fall. "No."

I wondered what Shirin Kellner considered "too gay."

I wondered why I thought that.

It was an ugly thought.

"You'll look very handsome in it," she said. "Come on. Let's try it on and see if you need it altered."

※ ※ ※

"Hey," Chip said as we walked to our bikes after practice Wednesday. "What're you doing now?"

"Headed home."

"Oh?"

"Yeah. Landon's busy. Plus I quit my job."

"Really?"

"Yeah. You were right. I need to find something that makes me happy. Hopefully soon."

"Oh. Cool." Chip ran a hand through his hair. "You wanna come over and study, then? My mom's making empanadas."

"Oh. Thanks. But I can't. I'm watching Laleh."

Chip let his hand fall. "Oh."

I felt kind of bad, letting him down.

Especially since he hadn't even mentioned Trent.

"Want to come to mine instead?"

He grinned.

"Yeah."

We biked to my house as the crisp fall sun finally peeked out from behind the heavy clouds. The wet streets shone, and Chip laughed as he rode through a puddle.

I don't know why, but it made me laugh too.

Cyprian Cusumano looked really beautiful in the golden light.

I did my best not to notice.

Laleh already had the kettle on the stove when we got home. She scooped some tea into the teapot.

"Hey, Laleh," I said. "You remember Chip?"

"Hey," said Chip.

Laleh glanced at Chip and blushed.

"Hi," she murmured. Then she turned back to the counter. "Want to help me smash some hel?"

Chip looked at me.

"Cardamom. For the tea."

"Oh. Sure."

Laleh's blush was spreading from her cheeks to her ears. But she arranged five cardamom pods on a paper towel and folded it over. "It's easier if you use the bottom of the pot."

"What do I do?"

"Smash them until they pop open. But you can do it as much as you want."

Chip grinned, and Laleh gave him a gap-toothed smile.

"Hey." I knelt and looked at Laleh's smile. "Did you finally lose that tooth?"

"Yeah. At lunch." She stuck her tongue through the gap where her canine used to be.

On Laleh's other side, Chip rolled the bottom of the teapot over the cardamom.

"You have to hit them hard," Laleh said. "Here."

Chip handed her the pot. She banged it five times against the counter, *whack whack whack whack whack!* I winced at the sound.

I usually just pinched them open myself. But Laleh loved smashing hel.

Chip looked at me, his eyes wide.

I chuckled. "Want me to pour the hot water?"

"Sure," Laleh said.

※ ※ ※

When our tea was made, we all sat at the table with our home-work spread in front of us.

"What're you working on?" I asked Laleh, who was frowning at her half-finished drawing.

"We're doing a space unit."

"Oh. Cool."

We never did a space unit in regular classes.

I might've actually done okay at that, with all the *Star Trek* I watched.

"I loved that," Chip said. He leaned over the table to look at her paper. "Where you make your own constellations?"

Laleh nodded.

Sure enough, the paper was covered with connect-the-dots figures of Laleh's devising.

"These look great," I said.

"We have to come up with a story for them."

"What are you going to do?"

"It has to be about our family."

"What about our trip to Iran?"

"I don't know," Laleh said. "What if they make fun of me?"

"For what?" Chip asked.

"For being Iranian," I said, but then I turned to Laleh. "I bet Miss Shah won't let them. Didn't you say some of your class-mates were Fractional Kids too?"

"I guess."

Chip said, "Would people really make fun of her?"

"I mean . . . people made fun of me."

I didn't say it out loud. That Chip and Trent had been the ones making fun of me, the way Micah and Emily and other Proto-Soulless Minions of Orthodoxy had been making fun of Laleh.

But I think Chip understood what I was saying anyway.

He got this serious look on his face and nodded.

And then he turned to Laleh and said, "Your brother's right. You should talk about Iran. So your classmates will understand you." He swallowed. "That's how you make friends."

Laleh looked from Chip to me, and then back down at her paper.

"Okay."

And then she said, "Will you help me?"

"Sure." I scooted closer.

"You too," she told Chip, though her cheeks reddened again as she said it.

He grinned. "All right."

Laleh pointed to one of the stick-figure constellations she'd made, one that might've almost had a mustache. "This one is going to be Babou."

FULL PERSIAN MOTHER

S aturday morning I tried Sohrab again.
He still didn't answer.

I thought about calling Mamou again, but I couldn't call her every time I couldn't reach Sohrab.

That wasn't cool.

So I wrote him yet another email.

When I first got back from Iran, we emailed each other all the time, until we figured out a schedule to call each other. And once we'd sorted that out, email felt so impersonal.

I couldn't see his eyes squint up when he smiled. Or hear his laughter.

Even that was a pale illusion of the real Sohrab.

I missed being in Iran with him.

I missed sitting with him on our rooftop and watching the sun kiss our khaki kingdom.

I missed the way he would throw his arm over my shoulder, like that was a thing guys could do to each other.

But email was my only option.

So I asked him how he was doing, and said I hoped he was okay, and that he'd write back soon. I told him about my soccer games (we were ten and one now) and quitting my job. I told him about Laleh and my dad and my mom. I told him about Landon and homecoming.

Did they have homecoming in Iran?

And I told him I was doing okay, depression-wise. And I

hoped he was doing okay too, because he was my best friend in the whole world and I wanted him to be happy and healthy.

I didn't tell him I was scared.

Scared that he hadn't written back or called. Scared that something bad had happened to him.

Scared that he was mad at me. That I had done something wrong.

I would have given my life for Sohrab's.

So I just wrote *Ghorbanat beram. Love, Darius*, and hit send.

Sohrab used to tell me that my place was empty.

It's an Iranian saying.

But now his place was empty.

I missed him terribly.

"Mom?"

"Yeah?"

"Have you talked to Mamou lately?"

"Yesterday. Why?"

"I haven't heard from Sohrab for a while. And when I asked Mamou about it, she got kind of weird."

Mom looked up from my hands. She was painting my nails that perfect Yazdi blue for homecoming.

"She didn't mention it," she said. "I'm sure he's okay, though."

I wasn't sure.

I couldn't shake this feeling. Like Mamou knew something and wouldn't tell me.

The silence between us was thick as toffee. Sticky too.

Mom let go of my left hand and picked up my right. She twisted it a bit to flatten out my thumb.

And then she said, without looking at me, "Landon knows about Sohrab, right?"

"Huh?" I blinked. "Yeah."

I didn't understand why Mom had brought it up.

"Does he ever get jealous?"

"Of Sohrab?"

Mom nodded.

"No. I don't think so. Why?"

"I just wondered," Mom said. "From the way you were, with Sohrab. When we were in Iran. I wondered."

My neck prickled.

"Wondered . . . what?"

"If there was something between you two."

"Um."

Mom met my eyes, but I looked down at my hands.

And then I said, "We're just friends, Mom."

"I know, but back then."

"We were just friends."

Mom sighed.

I sighed too.

"I think I really needed a friend."

"So you never . . ."

"No."

Mom looked down at my nails again.

"Maybe I had a little crush on him."

Mom nodded.

"You know it's different for guys in Iran. Right?"

"What?"

"It's more common for men to express affection for each other.

Platonic affection. It doesn't mean the same thing it does here."

I didn't know why Mom felt like she had to tell me that.

"Why are you asking all of a sudden?"

"It just makes me wonder what else I missed."

"What do you mean?"

"If I didn't know this about you. That you're . . ."

"Gay?"

Mom nodded.

"You told your dad before you told me."

"Um."

"Some days it just feels like everything about you is new."

I didn't know what to say to that.

Mom finished up my right pinky and sat back.

"All set. Just let them dry before you get dressed."

"Okay. Um. Thanks."

"Of course." She reached up and brushed my hair off my forehead.

I'd gotten my haircut touched up yesterday. It was soft and sleek and full, the fade nice and crisp.

"Have fun tonight."

Mr. Edwards dropped Landon off about an hour before dinner.

I was still getting dressed when he knocked on my door.

"Hey," I squeaked.

"Hey." He looked amazing: His suit must've been made just for him, the way it tapered around his slim waist and nice legs.

I sucked in my stomach as soon as I saw him.

His hair was parted to the side, super formal, except for this one lock that fell into his forehead. His smile was perfect.

"Wow," he said. He looked me up and down, with this soft smile. "You look beautiful."

My ears burned.

"It's not too . . . um . . ."

"It's perfect." He nodded at my tie. "Having trouble?"

"Usually my dad helps me," I admitted.

He slipped his own tie off, a deep blue one with thin orange stripes: It was a clip-on.

"Can't help you there."

"I'll get it."

He stepped closer to me and rested his hands on my chest. I let go of my tie and leaned down to kiss him.

"Hey," I said.

His hands slid down to my waist.

"You smell nice."

"Thanks." I'd borrowed some of Dad's cologne, a woodsy one—juniper and sage—that he always wore in the fall. "So do you."

He smelled like honeysuckle and citrus peel.

"Come on. Tie your tie. We don't wanna miss dinner."

"I'll make sure not to order onions this time."

"Good. I've got plans for us."

I gulped.

"Okay."

Mom went Full Persian Mother on me and Landon: It took at least twenty minutes to get through all the photographs she wanted. Shots of each of us by ourselves, so she could get our outfits from pretty much every angle; and then a whole series of us together, though she had us stand rigid with our arms by our sides for the first couple, until Landon asked if she wanted us to hold hands.

"Oh," she said. "Sure."

Grandma and Oma were in the kitchen, mostly ignoring us and playing Monopoly with Laleh, though I thought I saw Oma look in and nod once.

Finally, I said, "Mom. We're going to be late."

"Just one more," she said. "Do a fun one."

Landon said, "Got it." He pulled me in and kissed me. Right in front of my mom.

I heard the click from Mom's phone, and then she said, her voice kind of pinched, "Great." She wiped away a tear. "Great. Okay."

I kissed Mom's cheek. "Thanks, Mom."

"You're so handsome," she whispered to me. "Have fun."

"I will. Love you."

"Love you too."

Like I said, I had never been to a homecoming dance before. Or any dance at Chapel Hill High School, really.

The bleachers were pushed up against the walls of the Main Gym, and huge banners hung from the rails with images of palm trees and beaches and sunshine and all the "Fun in the Sun" imagery the homecoming committee could come up with.

I held Landon's hand as I led him around. We said hi to Gabe and Jaden and their dates: Samantha and Claire, both seniors on the varsity women's soccer team.

"Looking good," Jaden said. He fist-bumped Landon and

then turned to me. His eyes narrowed and he grabbed my hand to examine my nails. "Nice!"

My ears burned. "Thanks. You're looking sharp." He was in a burgundy suit with a bright white shirt and sneakers.

The DJ was blasting Journey's "Don't Stop Believing" over the crappy speakers built into the ceiling, the ones that were dented from basketball impacts.

It was hard to believe I wasn't in some sort of Teen Television Drama.

Guys like me didn't get to be in Teen Television Dramas.

Landon looked the part way better than I did. He was smiling and chatting with Gabe and Samantha about something, but I couldn't make it out over the music.

Chapel Hill High School's Main Gym was not designed with acoustics in mind.

Journey finished, and the DJ faded into a K-Pop single everyone was obsessed with.

"Hey." Landon took my hand. "It's a dance, right?"

"Oh. Right."

He led me out to the floor, where the music was even louder, and everyone was pressed together as close as they were allowed by the Chaperone-Mandated Minimum Distance.

I spotted Chip in the crowd, dancing with a big group of people. He looked really handsome, in a maroon suit with a white shirt underneath, and a floral-print tie.

I hated that I thought he looked handsome.

I shouldn't have thought that.

I caught a glimpse of Javaneh Esfahani in a beautiful red dress and gold headscarf, dancing with Mateo, vice president of

Chapel Hill's QSA. Mateo had dyed their hair purple and swept it up into a pompadour, and their black suit sparkled like it had glitter woven into it.

"He's cute," Landon said, nodding Mateo's way.

"They."

"Oh, sorry. I like their suit."

"Yeah. I was kind of worried about mine."

"What about it?"

I looked down at my sleeves.

"I just never wore anything like this before."

Landon chuckled and put his arms around my waist, at the Chaperone-Approved Hand Level.

"You look great."

My cheeks burned.

"Thanks."

Landon swayed me back and forth, way slower than the beat of the song. But I smiled at him, and he smiled back.

And it was nice.

Really nice.

Still, after about five dances—some faster, some slower—the press of bodies all around, and the constant thrum of DJ Premature Hearing Loss's Muzak, made me anxious.

"I need a moment," I shouted to Landon, and we slid out past Jonny Without an H's gyrating hips—certainly not Chaperone-Approved—to the drinks table. I grabbed a cup of water and passed one to Landon. He drank his but I sniffed mine first.

"I kind of thought it would be spiked."

He chuckled. "I think that only happens in movies."

"Oh."

I brought my cup to my lips, right as someone bumped me from behind. I spilled it all down my front.

"Crap." I looked around for napkins or something. "Um. Be right back."

Landon thumbed the water off my chin. "You need help?"

"I'll be okay. Just give me a second."

The locker rooms were shut, so I had to make my way to the South Hall bathrooms. Chapel Hill High School didn't have paper towel dispensers, only air dryers, so I went into the third stall to grab some toilet paper.

I dried off the front of my jacket as best I could, and then my pants where I'd gotten a big wet spot right around my zipper. If I'd been wearing black it wouldn't have shown up that much, but on my light blue suit the dark spots were noticeable.

Noticeable, and deeply suspicious.

I rubbed at the spots, but the flimsy single-ply toilet paper in use at Chapel Hill High School just broke apart into little white pearls of debris.

What was the point and purpose of single-ply toilet paper?

"Hey. No jerking off at school, Dairy Queen."

I spun around and banged my shin on the toilet bowl, which was great.

Trent Bolger was at the sinks, washing his hands and looking at me in the mirror.

I always pictured Trent Bolger as the kind of guy who never washed his hands after going to the bathroom.

"Leave me alone, Trent."

I brushed the little white crumbs off my pants and went to wash my hands at the farthest sink from Trent's.

I hadn't done anything, but I still had to wash my hands when I'd been in a bathroom.

It was a thing.

Trent stuck his hands under the dryer. "Having fun with your boy?"

It was an innocuous question, but nothing about Trent Bolger was ever innocuous.

"Yes." The only other hand dryer was right next to Trent, and I didn't want the water to get onto my cuffs.

He gave me this sidelong look, and then he said, "Did you paint your nails?"

"Yeah."

He snorted—an alarming experience, given the size of his nostrils. "I don't know what Chip sees in you."

"What's that supposed to mean?"

"Don't act like you can't tell. He's got such a boner for you."

I swallowed.

"Chip is my friend. Sorry if you're jealous or whatever."

Trent rolled his eyes. "Hardly. Chip and me, we've been friends forever. And we're family now. I'll still be here, long after he gets over you."

He pushed past me, slamming my shoulder on his way out.

"Later, D-Cheese."

THE FORESKINNED FIDDLE

I waited in the bathroom for a few minutes, playing on my phone and turning what Trent had said over in my mind.

Trent Bolger was a bully, no matter what anyone said. No matter how many times he avoided punishment because he was on Chapel Hill High School's varsity football team.

And Cyprian Cusumano was my friend. Even if I still didn't understand why, exactly.

But what did Trent mean, that Chip had a boner for me? He was jealous of us being friends, and jealous that Chip was outgrowing him, and he would say anything to make trouble.

There was no way Chip liked me as more than a friend.

For as long as I'd known him, Chip had only ever dated girls. If he liked guys too, he would have said something.

Even if he didn't like me, he would've said something.

Right?

I slipped my phone into my pocket. Landon was waiting, and I refused to let Trent Bolger ruin my night.

"You okay?" Landon asked as he led me back to the dance floor.

"Yeah."

"Your face is red."

"It's hot in here."

Landon's hands rested on my hips as we swayed along to the music—DJ Loud Noises had picked a nice slow song, one I'd heard Dad sing to Mom when he thought no one else could hear.

I waited for one of the chaperones to come along, but no one did.

"This is nice," Landon said. He stepped in closer to me, so close our bodies were nearly touching. I could smell his cologne and a little bit of his sweat too.

The song switched to a faster one, with thrumming bass and some innuendo-laden lyrics. Landon stepped closer, and even though I was okay with breaking the Chaperone-Mandated Minimum Distance, I wasn't sure I was comfortable with him grinding against me on the dance floor. Not when everyone could see us.

Landon did this thing where he rolled his hips against me. I arched my back to pull away a tiny bit.

"What?" he asked.

"I just don't want to get in trouble," I shouted over the music.

He rolled his eyes.

"You're no fun."

All around us, everyone else was dancing and smiling and even stealing a few kisses here and there.

But Coach Winfield was prowling the fringes of the dance floor, frowning at anyone who got too close to their dance partner.

Landon followed my gaze and kind of shrugged. He backed away, just a little bit, but kept dancing. I did my best to keep up, swiveling my hips to the beat. I wasn't the best dancer, but I wasn't the worst. Years of dancing at Persian functions had at least given me a sense of rhythm, and some decent footwork.

Cyprian Cusumano, on the other hand, was an abysmal

dancer, but he didn't seem to care. I caught sight of him across the gym: He was jumping and flailing and smiling and laughing, like he didn't care who saw him. He caught my eye and waved, this goofy grin splashed across his face. I shook my head.

"What?" Landon shouted. He glanced behind him and watched Chip hopping around. "Wow."

He took my hand and spun me around. I grinned and spun him back.

And then I decided to risk it: I leaned in and gave him a super-quick kiss, barely more than a peck on the lips.

"Kellner!" Coach Winfield bellowed from behind me. "Watch it!"

"Sorry, Coach."

He stared me down for a second—despite being a few inches shorter than me—and then disappeared back into the nebula of dancing bodies.

Landon started laughing.

"How did he do that?"

"Coach Winfield has it out for me."

"Well. You'd better behave, then."

"I'll try."

When the heat from so many people packed together started getting to me, I led Landon off the floor to rehydrate. The drinks table was a mess, though, so I pulled him out to the hall. As soon as the gym doors closed behind us, the wall of noise pressing against us fell away, except for the bass hum that reverberated through the soles of my shoes.

I dabbed the sweat off my forehead with the back of my hand. "I can think again."

"I can breathe again," Landon said. "I think some of your classmates forgot their deodorant."

"That's a recurring nightmare of mine. Forgetting my own deodorant."

"Really?"

"Yeah." I shrugged. "I just don't ever want to be that guy who smells bad."

"You always smell nice."

"Thanks." I wound my fingers through his and led him down the hall toward the bathrooms where I'd run into Trent Bolger earlier. There was no wait for the water fountain.

Landon drank his fill, and then stood aside for me.

Once again, I wished Chapel Hill High School used paper towels, because that would have been great for wiping off my sweaty brow.

The hallway walls were lined with pictures of Chapel Hill High School's student athletes. Closest to the Main Gym was the varsity football team; and next to that, above the restrooms, the JV team. Landon nodded at the row of photos.

"You got a picture up somewhere?"

"Down the Art hall."

"Show me?"

I led Landon back past the gym toward the Art hall. The fluorescent lights were off, except for a few intermittent panels that were always on at night. Our dress shoes sounded like hooves clop-clop-clopping on the tiles.

As we neared the corner, the photos changed from the varsity wrestling team (where a photo of Chip in his red-and-black singlet from last year still hung on the wall), to the JV wrestling team, and finally to the varsity men's soccer team.

Go Chargers.

Here's the thing: I don't photograph well. I think it's genetic. Iranians always frown in photos.

(As a Fractional Persian, I only looked constipated, but still.)

I was wearing my jersey and had my arms crossed in front of my chest: the Standard Student Athlete Pose. We took the photo the first week of school, before I got my hair cut, so my former halo of black curls framed my face.

"Your hair was so cute."

"Yeah? Maybe I should grow it out again."

I rubbed the back of my head.

Landon reached up and put his hand over mine. "Nah. It's sexier this way." He pulled my head down to kiss me.

I kissed him back, but not too hard: We were still at school, and it just felt weird to be making out in the halls of Chapel Hill High School.

The sound of echoing footsteps made me pause, my lips hovering over Landon's. I opened my eyes and looked around, but I didn't see anyone.

I rested my forehead against Landon's. He slipped his fingertips under my waistband, right along my hip crease.

"You remember what we talked about?"

"Um."

"My dad's gone tonight." He leaned in and kissed me again. "We'd have the house to ourselves."

"Oh."

My face felt so hot, I was surprised Landon's forehead hadn't melted into mine.

"Um."

My heart raced.

"Want to come over?"

I almost wanted to.

Almost.

But what if Landon didn't like the way I looked?

What if I was too big?

What if I was too small?

What if we didn't fit together the way Landon wanted us to?

What if I didn't like it?

What if I didn't want it yet?

"Um."

Maybe that was the only thing I was capable of saying anymore.

Landon looked up into my eyes.

"What do you say?"

I swallowed. "Nervous."

"It'll be fun. I promise," he said. "I want this for us. Don't you?"

"Yes. Maybe. I don't know."

He frowned.

"What do you mean you don't know?"

"I mean it's a big step. For me."

"Well. You've got to take it sometime. Right?"

I don't know why it bothered me, the way he said it. Like I had to want sex.

There were lots of people who didn't.

To be clear, I did want sex. I really did.

And I even thought maybe it would be fun to do it with Landon.

But every time I thought about it, it felt like the end of the world. I don't know why, but it did.

I was scared.

I thought maybe I'd be ready for sex when that fear was overshadowed by the wanting. When the gravity of my desire shifted.

"I . . ."

Landon sighed. He opened his mouth but then glanced to the side.

We heard footsteps again, right around the corner. And voices.

"Dude, you struck out so hard."

"Shut up."

It was Chip and Trent.

"It was painful to watch. Like having teeth pulled," Chip said.

"Whatever."

"I'm not sure I can be seen in public with you anymore."

"Like that's new."

"What's that supposed to mean?" Chip asked.

"I mean I only see you at school, or when we're watching Evie. It's like you're ashamed of me or something."

"You're my best friend."

Someone's shoe scuffed the floor. The squeak echoed down the hall.

Landon bit his lip and glanced between me and the corner where Chip and Trent stood, just out of sight.

We were trapped.

"Then why don't you act like it?" Trent said. "You always . . ."

But whatever Chip was always doing, we didn't find out, because they picked that moment to round the corner.

Trent stared at us—our arms around each other, Landon pressing me back against a locker—while Chip's brow furrowed.

"Oh," Chip said. "Hey."

"Hey," I said.

Trent's lips curled. His eyes lingered where Landon's fingers were still hooked under my waistband.

"Um."

"Taking a break?" Chip said.

Landon nodded. "It was getting kind of stuffy in there."

"I think we're going to take off soon," Chip said. "Seems like things are kind of winding down."

"Oh."

"We're gonna go back to mine and play video games or something. A couple other guys from the team are coming. You two wanna join?"

I looked at Landon.

"I think we're gonna go back to my place." He grinned at me. "Spend a little time together."

Trent snickered.

"Time to play the foreskinned fiddle?"

Time stood still, like we were all suspended on the event horizon of some black hole about to swallow us.

And I finally understood why Trent had started calling me D-Cheese, right after Chip saw me in the locker room.

My eyes met Chip's for a split second. They were full of shame and panic.

"What the heck, dude?" he shouted.

And even though my ears were ringing, and I felt like a stellar nursery had ignited in my chest, I thought about that. How Chip said "heck" instead of actually swearing.

Trent just laughed. "What?"

Chip had this horrified look on his face. Like maybe he was the one who wanted to cry.

Landon looked at me, and then Chip, and then Trent, and then back to me. He studied my burning cheeks and bit his lip.

"Not cool." Chip shoved Trent down the hall.

"Have fun!" Trent cackled. "Rubber up!"

Chip dragged Trent away, shooting me an apologetic look as he went.

Landon stepped away from me, and I shivered, with the cold locker against my back and Landon's warmth removed from my front.

"What was that about?"

"What?" My voice croaked. I cleared my throat. "Um. What?"

"That got really weird all of a sudden. When he mentioned us having sex." He glanced down at my pants. "Playing the 'fore-skinned fiddle,' huh?"

"Trent is an asshole," I said.

And then I said, "They both are."

"I thought Chip was your friend?"

"So did I."

I pulled away from the locker and wrapped my arms around myself.

I still kind of wanted to cry.

"So are you . . ." Landon's eyes darted down again.

"What?"

"You know."

I shook my head.

"Uncut?"

"Intact," I said.

"Oh. Huh."

I hated that word: *huh.*

I wiped at my eyes, because I wanted to cry but I didn't want Landon to see me do it.

I was more or less immune to Trent humiliating me. I had adapted.

But what was I supposed to do when it was Chip who did it?

"It doesn't bother me. I've hooked up with uncut guys before."

"Hooked up?"

"Just jerking off and stuff."

I didn't want to know about Landon masturbating other guys.

"Is that all you want to do? Hook up?"

"No. That's . . ." Landon's cheeks were on fire. "Don't put words in my mouth."

My own cheeks began to burn too.

"Why are you so mad at me?"

"Why won't you be honest with me? Why does Chip know you're uncut anyway?"

"He saw me that day when I got hurt."

I wiped at my eyes again.

This felt like a knee to the balls.

Worse, even.

Landon stared at me for a long moment.

And then he said, "Do you have a thing for Chip?"

"What?"

"Do you like Chip?"

"He's my friend," I said. "That's all."

I didn't have a thing for Chip.

I couldn't.

"You won't even take your shirt off around me. But he's seen your dick?"

"That's just soccer," I said. "It was an accident. But us . . . you . . . I need more time. I told you I'm not ready."

"Well, what about what I need? What about what I'm ready for? Why is it always about you?"

"It's not," I said. "I care about you. And what you want."

"I've told you sex is important to me. But you never want to talk about it. You want to go to dances and look cute together, you want me to cook for you and your family, but when it comes to doing stuff—stuff that I told you I wanted, stuff that matters to me in a relationship—you say you're 'not ready.' We've been together for four months now and you won't even take your shirt off around me. You're a coward. And you're selfish."

"I'm sorry. I don't know what else to say. I'm sorry. I'm not ready."

"But you'll go around swinging your dick in front of Chip?"

"It's a locker room. What am I supposed to do?"

"I don't even know." Landon closed his eyes. "You know what? I'm going to go."

"What?" I squeaked.

"It's clear you're not coming home with me. Are you?"

"Um."

I wanted to say yes.

I wanted to say yes to everything.

But I couldn't.

I wiped my eyes and said, "Landon . . ."

But he shook his head and said, "This is bullshit."

And then he said, "I'm leaving."

And then he walked away.

SUITABLY MELANCHOLY

I wanted to follow Landon.

I wanted to chase him into the rain, and reach out for him, and have him change his mind and turn around, and tell me he was wrong and he was sorry and everything would be okay.

But first of all, it was barely drizzling. Not nearly heavy enough for any sort of dramatic reconciliation.

Second, I was a coward.

And third, I didn't know anything I could say that would change his mind.

I hovered inside the double doors while he waited for his ride to pick him up. Once he was gone, I slipped outside into the empty parking lot and watched the car's taillights disappear into the haze, which at least felt suitably melancholy.

It was the type of situation that called for some sort of heavy piano music, or maybe a haunting cello motif, but the only soundtrack was the bass beat of "Despacito" rattling off the windowpanes of the Main Gym behind me.

I sat on the curb and wiped my eyes and felt the yawning void of self-hate open up beneath me.

The thing about having depression is, you can recognize the cycles your mind goes through, even when you can't do anything about them.

Landon kept echoing in my head: "Selfish."

And I kept seeing Chip's eyes too. How he couldn't quite look at me.

I trusted him.

I knew his history with Trent. Knew he had never, ever stood up to him. Knew he was as much accomplice as witness, since Trent worked best with an audience.

And I trusted him anyway.

This is what I deserved.

I sniffed and pulled my phone out. The droplets left tiny rainbow flecks on the screen.

What was I supposed to tell Mom?

Were Landon and I broken up or was it just a fight?

Ditching me at a dance felt like a breakup.

"Darius?"

I glanced behind me and then looked down at my phone again. Mom was sending Oma to get me.

Chip lowered himself to sit next to me. His knees splayed to the side and bumped against mine.

"Well, that was super awkward," he said, and did this sort of nervous chuckle.

"What do you want, Chip?"

He frowned and looked at his hands.

"Just wanted to apologize for what Trent said."

What Trent said.

Chip only ever apologized for Trent.

I didn't say anything.

"Are you okay?"

"I'm fine."

"Where's Landon?"

I shook my head.

"What happened?"

"You and Trent happened!" I shouted, but then I lowered my voice. "He was already frustrated with me, but then you and Trent making jokes about me, it was just . . ."

"I didn't joke about you," Chip said.

"But you told Trent about that day in the locker room."

Chip sighed.

"Yeah."

"Why would you do that?" I choked out. "I thought we were friends."

"Because I like you, okay?" Chip gulped. "I like you, and I was telling Trent about it because I couldn't get you out of my head. We were alone and you were so beautiful. You are. You're beautiful and funny and thoughtful and kind. You're the nicest person I know. And I couldn't stand hurting you. I couldn't stand being so close to you."

Chip put his hand on my knee and tried to squeeze it, but I took his hand and lifted it off me.

"Don't touch me," I said.

"But—"

I couldn't believe Chip.

If he liked me, why didn't he treat me better?

The pulsar inside me destabilized and exploded.

"This isn't some . . . some TV show, where you can torment me for years and then kiss me and be like 'Guess what? I was gay for you all along!' It doesn't work like that."

"I'm queer. I've always liked guys too," Chip whispered. "And I never tried to kiss you. I wasn't tormenting you."

"You've stood there, every time Trent said or did something to me. Every racist joke. Every homophobic nickname. You never stopped him."

"Trent's not homophobic. He knows I'm queer."

"You can have queer friends and still be homophobic, Chip."

He sniffled.

I couldn't tell if he was crying or if it was just the rain.

"Is that why you told me to quit my job?"

"What?"

"You wanted me to quit because I worked with Landon?"

"No! I wouldn't . . . You seemed so sad. I just wanted you to be happy. I promise."

"Why should I listen to anything you say? You're just as bad as Trent is."

"I'm sorry. I didn't know. I'll make him leave you alone. I promise."

Cyprian Cusumano didn't get it.

It wasn't just about how Trent treated me.

It was about how he treated me too.

I recognized the glow of Oma's headlights curving around the parking lot. She pulled up and honked.

I sighed and stood.

"Darius?" Chip said. "I'm sorry. I didn't mean to hurt you. I'm sorry."

Chip was always saying sorry. But he never acted like it. He never changed.

I wiped my own face and cleared my throat.

"Yeah, well."

I didn't know what else to say.

Maybe there was nothing else to say.

MENTAL HEALTH DAY

Monday morning, Mom knocked on my door.

I rolled over in bed and groaned.

I'd turned my alarm off when it woke me for my run, and I'd fallen back asleep, despite the noise of everyone else waking up.

Well. First I tried Sohrab.

Again.

And he didn't answer.

Again.

That's when I went back to bed.

Mom knocked again.

"Darius?"

"Yeah?"

Mom cracked the door and peeked in at me.

"You okay?"

I sighed.

"Can I take a mental health day?"

I hadn't taken a mental health day since fall of ninth grade, when I was going through a medication change and having anxiety attacks every morning when it was time to get dressed.

Dad was a big believer in mental health days.

Mom came in and sat on the bed. She brushed my hair away from my eyes and rested her hand on my forehead, as if she could diagnose my mental state like a fever.

"Are you sure it won't just be harder tomorrow?"

That was the thing about mental health days. Sometimes,

you needed them, and they got you back on your feet. But sometimes, when you said you wanted a mental health day, what you really meant was you were avoiding something, and the more you put it off, the bigger it got.

"Maybe," I admitted.

I hadn't told Mom much about the dance.

Just that I had gotten into a fight with Landon.

And another one with Chip.

"Well, if you need to stay home, you can. You have some time to decide. I'll check on you before I leave for work."

"Thanks, Mom."

She kissed my forehead.

"Love you."

I guess Mom's talk worked, because I dragged myself out of bed and got ready.

I spent the day avoiding Chip. We had an evening game, and I needed to study—I had a test in German on Friday—but I knew I couldn't go to Mindspace.

There was a public library a few blocks away. I found a table in this little nook, not far from the Kids Korner, which was full of little kids enjoying story time.

There was this cute toddler in pink overalls. I wiggled my fingers at them. The polish on my left index finger had chipped. I needed to learn how to take better care of my nails.

The kid returned a little flappy-handed wave and then ran off.

It made me think of Evie, and how she had been so comfortable around me.

Was she that way with Uncle Trent too?

And then I thought of Chip, and how I had been so comfortable around him.

I should never have let my guard down.

That's what stung more than anything else.

I knew the kind of guy Chip was, but I imagined him the way I wanted him to be.

I was so disappointed in myself.

Like always, Coach Bentley summoned us to circle up before the game. I sandwiched myself between Diego and Bruno, far away from Chip, who was over by Gabe and Jaden like usual. Jaden gave me a look, but I pretended not to notice.

I also pretended not to notice Chip trying to catch my eye.

And I definitely did not notice that his hair, usually pristine even after a long school day, was a complete and utter mess. Or the way the corners of his mouth drooped, almost into a frown, instead of his usual pre-game grin.

As we went around, I couldn't come up with anything to say. I totally blanked.

Bruno said, "At homecoming, Christian gave me some gum when I was nervous about my breath not smelling fresh. Thanks, Christian. Heather thanks you too."

Everyone chuckled at that, but I just felt a kind of twist in my gut.

"Uh." It was my turn. "I'm blanking. Sorry. Um."

I felt the weight of everyone's eyes on me.

"I had kind of a crappy weekend. But I'm glad for tonight's game, and the chance to go do something. So, thanks for tonight, everyone."

Some of the guys nodded, but others looked at me kind of curiously, or turned to their neighbors like they wanted to gossip. But Coach Bentley said, "Glad we can be here for you, Darius," and the whispers stopped.

Diego thanked me, of all people, for lending him a pair of socks last week, which I had completely forgotten about. "Sure thing."

And on we went.

When we got to Chip, he said, "Darius told me something I didn't want to hear. But I know I needed to. So, thanks."

I looked up at that, but Chip had his eyes squeezed shut, like he was afraid of what was going to happen.

So I looked down at my feet and said, "I'm glad I could help."

My heart thudded against my sternum, and my ears felt full.

It felt like the whole team was watching us.

But after a second, Jaden spoke up, and the circle continued.

THE MINUTIAE OF
MIDFIELDING STRATEGY

Wednesday afternoon, after practice and another carefully executed avoidance of Chip—courtesy of Jaden, who had noticed things were kind of weird and made a point of dragging Chip into a conversation about the minutiae of midfielding strategy—I took the bus to Rose City with a swarm of stellar remnants in my stomach.

I had to do something.

I still couldn't reach Sohrab, and Dad was still depressed, and things with Chip were weird.

But Landon was there, and we needed to talk.

Besides, Mom needed some Earl Grey (regular, not nitro) and I was running low on Moroccan Mint since Grandma and Oma were drinking so much.

When the bus stopped, I grabbed my bike and walked it toward Rose City. It had been a long time since I used the customer entrance.

Alexis was at the register and waved when I walked in. I waved back and headed to the shelves.

It was weird, pulling tea off the shelves instead of stocking it.

"Running low?" Alexis asked when I took it to the counter.

"Yeah." I glanced toward the tasting room. "Um. Is Landon around?"

Alexis nodded. "I think they're almost done."

"Cool."

I stood against the wall and sucked on my tassels.

"We'll probably do two cases. Maybe three," Mr. Edwards said over his shoulder. He turned and saw me. "Oh. Darius."

"Hi."

"Good to see you," he said.

"You too."

He gave me this sad, closed-lip smile.

"He's inside."

"Thanks."

I knocked on the door frame.

"Hey."

Landon turned around, and nearly dropped the gaiwan he was holding.

His cheeks colored as he set it in the sink.

"Hey."

We looked at each other for a long time.

When the silence between us became unbearable, I stepped inside and closed the door.

Landon's shoulders slumped. "I kind of messed up, huh."

"I don't know. Maybe we both did."

"I'm sorry I left you at the dance."

"Not as sorry as my grandmother was when she had to get out of the house at ten p.m."

Landon grimaced.

"I'm sorry I kept pressuring you. I didn't mean to. I just wanted us to be close. Physically."

"I know. I'm sorry too. I wasn't good at being honest with you about what I wanted."

"I never meant to hurt you. It's just . . ." He sighed. "I love you. I should have said it sooner. And sometimes it feels like you don't love me back."

"I . . ."

Did I love Landon?

I wasn't sure I knew what that meant.

It didn't feel like it did with my family. Where I knew that no matter what, they were part of my life forever, in my veins and in my heart.

And it didn't feel like Sohrab either, who felt like the kind of person I could count on for anything. Who knew me inside and out. Who accepted all my flaws and still made me wish I could be better.

"I don't know," I whispered.

Landon let out a low breath and sank into a chair.

Now I knew what it was like, when you're the one who hit a guy in the balls.

"I'm sorry."

Landon shook his head and wiped at his eyes.

My own were weirdly dry.

"I didn't mean to hurt you. I never wanted to hurt you."

Landon sniffed.

"Well. I better finish up."

"Yeah. Sorry."

I let myself out of the tasting room and slipped out of the store. Unlocked my bike and headed for the bus stop.

I wondered why I wasn't more upset. If it was because I was depressed. Or because of my medication. Or because deep down I was still mad at how Landon had treated me.

No one had ever made me feel as small as he had that day. Not even Trent Bolger.

But no one had ever made me feel beautiful before either. Not until Landon. No one ever held my hand or kissed me or smiled the way he smiled when he saw me. No one ever came and made soup for my sick sister, or held me tight until our breaths synced up and I could just lie there, with my mind turned off, enjoying the way it felt to have a warm body curled up next to me, happy and content.

I made it all the way to the back of the bus before I started crying.

HOLDING HIM UP

Here's the thing: This wasn't the first bus ride I'd spent crying. That kind of thing happened when you lived with depression. Some days you just had to cry.

It was good to cry. It excreted stress hormones.

And here's another thing: Everyone leaves you alone if you're crying on a bus. Most humans are averse to other people's stress hormones, as if they were a communicable disease.

I don't think I had ever hurt anyone in my life the way I hurt Landon.

I hated myself for that.

And I hated myself for not regretting it.

There was probably something wrong with me.

There were a lot of things wrong with me.

When I opened the garage door, Dad's car was in its spot.

I had never been so happy to see Dad's Audi in my entire life.

I kicked off my Sambas without untying them and ran through the door.

"Dad?"

But the kitchen was empty. Laleh was in the living room, curled up against the side of the couch, with a huge book in her lap.

"Hey, Laleh. I saw Dad's car in the garage."

"He's upstairs," she whispered.

I knelt down and whispered back, "Why are we whispering?"

Laleh didn't look up at me. Her lip turned down and quivered a bit.

"I don't know."

It wasn't like Laleh not to say what was bothering her.

Not to me, anyway.

"I'll go check on him. Okay?"

"Okay."

I padded up the stairs. Mom and Dad's door was shut.

I knocked. "Hello?"

After a moment, Mom opened the door wide enough for her face. "Darius?"

"Hey. Is Dad here?"

"He's in the shower."

As soon as she said that, the water turned on.

"Oh. Okay."

"He'll be down soon."

"Is everything okay?"

"Everything is okay," she said, but I wasn't sure if she was talking to me or to herself.

"I got the tea you wanted. Should I make a pot?"

Making tea seemed to be the only thing I was good for in a crisis.

"Sure."

After about ten minutes, I finally heard the shuffling of footsteps on the stairs.

Stephen Kellner never shuffled.

I nearly knocked my chair over as I ran into the living room.

"Hey, son." Dad pulled me into a hug as soon as I was within range.

I wrapped my arms around him and rested my head on his shoulder.

There was this thing, though. His shoulder felt bonier. Like he'd lost some weight or something.

For as long as I could remember, Stephen Kellner had been the same weight and size.

I kind of hated that about him. My own weight seemed to be in a state of constant flux, always on the heavy side.

Dad's beard had grown out even more. It was properly brown, much darker than his head hair, which looked dark gold now that it was long and shaggy enough to brush the tips of his ears.

Whenever I hugged my dad before, I always felt like he was holding me up.

But this time, I was holding him up.

"Dad?" My question was muffled against his shirt.

He brought his hand up to rub the back of my neck and kind of rock me back and forth.

"I'm glad you're home."

"Me too."

I studied Dad as he drank his tea. Really studied him. The dark circles under his eyes. The slump in his shoulders.

"It's getting worse. Isn't it?" I asked.

He sighed and nodded.

"It's just hard. Being away from you and your sister and your mom."

"You don't have to keep doing that," I said. "You can come home."

"I can't. We need the money, son."

"I'm sending out applications. And I've got money in my savings. Let me help."

"No. It's our job—me and your mom—to take care of you and Laleh. Not the other way around."

"But . . ."

"We'll get through this."

"But we're not getting through it. You look like hell. And I need you." My voice cracked. "Please."

Dad looked down at his teacup. He rolled it back and forth between his hands.

"I need you too. You and your sister and your mom." He let out this shaky breath and cleared his throat. "You're my whole world."

"Then you can stop. Really. We'll be okay."

Dad sniffed.

"Remember what you told me, when we were in Iran? That you can lose people to depression lots of ways?"

"I remember."

"Well, I don't want to lose you."

"You won't. I promise."

"Okay."

He slurped his tea and took a deep breath.

"I missed this."

"Yeah."

We sat together. The silence between us wasn't exactly awkward, but it wasn't particularly comfortable either.

"Landon broke up with me," I said.

And then I said, "Or I broke up with him."

"Oh, son." He reached out and rested his hand on the back of my neck. "I'm so sorry."

"Yeah. Me too."

"Do you want to talk about it?"

"Not right now," I said. "Can we just sit like this?"

"Of course. Or . . ."

"Or what?"

"We could go put on some *Star Trek*."

"Yeah."

PENILE HUMILIATIONS

After *Star Trek*, we ate dinner and then Dad turned in early. I finished up my homework and got ready for bed.

I was feeling so weird and sad, I didn't even go number three before tucking myself in.

I was almost asleep when my computer rang.

There were only two people who ever called me.

I leaped out of bed, pulled my underwear and a shirt on, and went to my desk.

Sure enough, Sohrab's avatar—a picture of the two of us, the same one I had framed on the wall next to my bed—was bouncing up and down.

I dropped into my chair and hit accept.

There was that weird moment of feedback, and my screen went white for a second. And then there he was, squinty smile and all.

"Hello, Darioush!"

"Hey Sohrab," I said.

I almost wanted to cry.

Almost.

I was so happy to see him, I thought my cheeks might lock into their smile and I would have to live the rest of my life with lockjaw.

I would have been okay with that.

"I didn't know where you were."

"I know. I'm sorry. I couldn't tell you before we left."

"Left? For where?"

Sohrab leaned back, and for the first time I noticed he wasn't in his room. The walls were white and blank.

"Where are you? Are you okay?"

"I'm in Hakkâri, Darioush. Turkey."

"What?"

"Maman and I left. We are going to try and get asylum."

"Asylum?"

My head spun.

"You're becoming refugees?"

"Yeah. Lots of Bahá'ís do it."

"Oh my god," I said.

My best friend was a refugee.

"I was so worried about you. I thought something bad had happened."

Did this count as something bad happening?

What did this mean for Sohrab? For his mom?

"Last time we talked you told me you thought you might be depressed. And then you were just gone. And no one would tell me anything. I thought . . ."

Sohrab's face fell.

"I wouldn't do that, Darioush."

"Sometimes people can't help it."

He let out a deep breath.

"I'm okay, Darioush. I promise. I'm sorry. We had to keep it quiet."

"Why?"

"It's dangerous. And complicated. You remember my khaleh got asylum?"

"The one in Toronto?"

He nodded.

"Is that where you're going? Toronto?"

"I don't know. Maybe."

I felt this little burst of happiness.

Sohrab, in Toronto?

Compared to Iran, that was practically next door.

"Don't cry, Darioush."

"I was scared. I'm sorry."

"No, I'm sorry. I wish I didn't have to keep it secret. But Maman and I are okay. We're going to be fine."

I nodded and sniffed.

"I missed you," he said.

"I missed you too."

"And I heard . . . about Babou."

I nodded.

"I'm sorry, Darioush."

"I'm sorry too. I know you loved him."

In a way, Babou had been like Sohrab's grandfather too. Maybe even more than he had been mine.

I wished I were there with him.

I wished I could hug him and cry with him and let him tell me all the little things I never got to know about Babou. Things he got to see, growing up next door to Ardeshir Bahrami.

But at least I could see him on the screen.

We had a lot of catching up to do.

I told Sohrab about quitting Rose City.

I told him about homecoming and Landon.

I told him about Chip.

"I'm sorry, Darioush," he said when I was finished. "Are you going to be okay?"

"I guess."

He looked at me.

"Did you, though?"

"Did I what?"

"Did you love Landon?"

I leaned back in my chair. It was a used office chair Dad brought home from work when they switched to standing desks. But it was also slightly broken, and if I leaned back too far it would tip over.

I grabbed the edge of my desk and sat back up.

"I don't think so," I finally said.

And then I said, "He was the first guy that ever liked me."

I swallowed away the lump in my throat.

"What if no one else ever likes me the way he did?"

"Darioush."

"Yeah?"

"You're a good guy. And lots of guys are going to like you. I know."

I shook my head.

"What about Chip? He likes you."

"Ugh."

Sohrab laughed at that.

"Darioush."

"What?"

"He is your friend. Are you going to stay mad at him forever?"

"Yes. Maybe. I don't know."

"You remember our first fight?"

I nodded.

It was because Sohrab had teased me after seeing me naked in the showers after we played soccer.

He said my penis looked like it was wearing a turban.

Was my entire life going to be one long string of penile humiliations?

Maybe it would.

Maybe that is what it means to have a penis.

"Why are we still friends?"

I shrugged. "You said you were sorry."

"And you forgave me."

"Yeah."

"Friends forgive each other. Did Chip say he was sorry?"

He did.

A lot.

I just wasn't sure that was enough.

"But you didn't just say you were sorry. You didn't do that again."

"We had other fights."

"Yeah," I said. "But we never had the same fight twice."

"And Chip is doing the same thing?"

"Yeah. He's still friends with Trent. No matter what Trent does to me."

"Hm. Then maybe he's never going to change. But you know what?"

"What?"

"I never met anyone with as big a heart as you, Darioush. I know you'll figure it out."

My face burned.

"Thanks."

Sohrab's cheeks looked a little pink too. He cleared his throat.

"How is your soccer going?"

I told Sohrab about our wins, and our loss, and how weird and wonderful it felt to be on a team.

I told him about Grandma and Oma.

I told him about Laleh, and her project to turn Mamou and Babou into constellations.

I told him about Mom, who was never home anymore. And Dad, who was finally home, who was doing badly but was finally going to let me help.

And for the first time in a long time, it felt like maybe things were going to be okay.

Mom knocked on my door as Sohrab and I were saying our goodbyes. She was dressed in her robe and holding a cup of coffee.

"Hi, Sohrab-jan," she called. "Chetori toh?"

Sohrab talked to her in Farsi for a minute, and she answered, but then she said, "Okay, Sohrab-jan, khodahafes. Talk soon."

"Khodahafes," Sohrab said back. "Bye, Darioush. Talk soon. I promise. Ghorbanat beram."

"Ghorbanat beram. Always."

I hung up the call and leaned back, hooking my knees under the lip of my desk to stop myself from tipping over.

Mom leaned against my doorframe and looked at me.

"You're smiling."

"He's okay," I said. "I was so scared."

"I know, sweetie."

"Did you know?"

She shook her head.

"But I thought they might leave. Mahvash used to talk about it sometimes."

"What happens now?"

"I don't know. If everything goes well, they'll settle somewhere new. Maybe Toronto." She smiled. "Maybe even here."

"Really?"

"If we're lucky."

I let myself imagine it: Sohrab, here. Coming over for dinner.

Hanging out and playing soccer. Showing him all my favorite places in Portland. Drinking lots of tea.

Finding a spot where the world falls away, and we can talk, and tell each other all the things you can only admit to your best friend.

Mom stepped closer to me and ran her hand through my hair. "Darius?"

"Yeah?"

"I didn't mean to overhear, but . . . I heard you telling Sohrab about Landon."

"Oh."

"Are you okay?"

"I guess. I mean, I will be."

Mom looked at me for a long time. Like she was trying to understand something about me she'd never had to understand before. She sat down on my bed and patted the spot next to her.

I pulled my shirt down to try and cover my underwear—a pair of bright orange trunks—and sat next to her.

"What happened?"

"We talked. And . . . well, we wanted different things."

"Your dad said the two of you were thinking about . . . sex."

My chest constricted. "He was. I wasn't ready to."

Mom's hands went back to my hair.

"You could have told me, you know. When your dad was out of town. If you needed advice, you could have talked to me."

"I know."

"Is it because of something I said?"

"No."

"You used to talk to me about everything."

"I still do."

"But not this."

I looked down at my hands. Mom's hand, which had been twisting my curls around, paused.

"What is it?"

I squeezed my eyes closed.

"You always had this look on your face. Every time we kissed."

"No I didn't."

This is why I didn't say anything before.

Because I knew Mom would get upset.

"Did I? Really?"

Mom folded her hands in her lap.

"I'm sorry."

"It's okay."

"No it's not." She took a deep breath. "I'm not mad you're gay. I promise."

"Okay."

"You know, since the day you were born, your dad and I have been dreaming of a happy future for you. And every day you've grown up and changed and we've had to adjust that dream a little bit. For the longest time I felt like I knew which way you were going. But now . . ." Mom blinked away tears. "Everything changed after Iran."

Not everything.

I was gay when I went, even if I hadn't figured it out yet, and I was just as gay when I came back.

But Mom said, "When we got back, you and your dad were so much closer. And I was happy, because I hated seeing how distant you used to be." Mom held her hand over her heart. "But it hurt that while he was finding you, I was losing you."

I never thought about that. How Mom felt, when suddenly Dad and I became a team.

And then Mom and I weren't anymore.

I felt terrible.

"I'm sorry."

"Don't be. I'm being selfish."

"No you're not. I didn't mean to make you feel like that."

"I just miss you. The way we used to be." Mom reached for my nightstand, where I kept one of those tall cubic Kleenex boxes.

"Here." I grabbed it and passed it over.

Mom sniffed and blew her nose.

I grabbed my own Kleenex and wiped my eyes.

"I'm sorry," I said again.

"I don't want you to be. You're growing up. That's what happens."

I didn't want it to happen.

I didn't want growing up to mean Mom and I would drift apart.

"But I don't want to lose you either."

"You never will. Never. I promise." Mom sighed. "I love you, Darius. Every single part of you. I never meant for you to think I didn't."

"I know," I said.

I should've known that all along.

I was so ashamed of myself, for even thinking it.

"I was just scared."

"Scared? Why?"

I looked down at my hands and rubbed the pads of my index fingers over my turquoise thumbs.

"I don't know," I said.

How do you explain the fear that someone you love might stop loving you all of a sudden?

But Mom said, "Is that why you haven't told Mamou?"

Maybe Mom did understand after all.

Maybe she did.

"I just don't want her to be disappointed in me."

Mom held my face between her hands. "Oh, Darius. You could never disappoint her. You are the sweetest boy in the world. You know that?"

I shook my head. "I'm not."

"You are."

"I'm really not, though."

"Why would you say that?"

"Because I'm not sweet. I'm selfish."

I told her about Trent, and about Chip.

About Chip saying he liked me.

And about Chip saying he was sorry for everything, and me not forgiving him.

"Sohrab says friends forgive each other. But how can I do that when Chip's best friend has made it his personal mission to make my life miserable? I mean, Chip used to help him. And now he says he likes me?"

I shook my head.

"What am I supposed to do?"

Mom looked at me for a long time.

"You're so young."

She said it like it still surprised her. Like it was a wonderful thing, to be young and angry at the closest thing you had to a friend this side of the Prime Meridian.

"When you're young and full of feelings, sometimes they come out in the wrong way."

"So I should just forgive him?"

"I'm not saying that. I'm just saying, it's something you do when you're young. And hopefully you grow out of it. Does Chip still tease you?"

"No."

"Does he treat you badly?"

"No. He's fine." I thought about all the times Chip helped me study. About asking me over to his house. About trusting me with Evie.

"Chip treats me fine. He's nice to me. But he's still friends with Trent."

"You can't control who people are friends with," Mom said. "Especially if they're family now."

"I don't want to. That would be a crappy thing to do to someone. But I just . . . I don't know how I can ever trust him."

"Did you tell him that?"

"I don't know," I said. "I don't know how."

"You deserve people in your life who make you happy, Darius. No matter what. Just remember that. Okay?"

"I'll try."

"I'm not going to tell you to forgive Chip. But he seemed like a good friend. I hate for you to give up on him if you're not sure."

"So what do I do?"

"Only you can decide."

A NEW FUTURE

In the morning, Mom called a family meeting.

In its entire history—spanning back to its Teutonic roots in pre-unification Germany on Dad's side, and its legacy in the bedrock of Yazd on Mom's—the Kellner-Bahrami family had never called a family meeting before.

We were breaking new ground.

Mom got up early to make a big frittata. I cut my run short so I could help her segment some oranges and slice a few apples. I made a big pot of Persian tea, and Mom set out a plate of Tagalongs she'd gotten from the annual office Girl Scout Cookies sale.

As we ate, Dad announced that he was going to take one more trip to Los Angeles, just for two days, to pass the project off. And he was going to step aside from his Arkansas job.

I told everyone about Landon and me.

"But I liked Landon!" Laleh said.

"Me too," I said. "But . . . well, sometimes things don't work out."

"Who's going to be your boyfriend, then?"

"No one, I guess. I'm going to finish off the soccer season. Hopefully by then I'll have a new job. And I'll be able to work more hours, to help out."

"Just for a little while," Dad said. "And then you're going to save for your future. Whether that's college or something else. Okay?"

"Okay."

Laleh told everyone about her constellations project. She'd gotten a gold star on it—the highest ranking Miss Shah awarded—and made a new friend too.

"Avan's grandpa is from India," she explained. "That's almost like Iran's neighbor. He visits there every summer."

I was glad Laleh was making friends.

I loved my sister's smile.

Grandma and Oma announced they were going to head back home.

"We've been in your hair long enough," Grandma said.

And Mom said, "We've loved having you," which was a high-level taarof if there ever was one.

There was a strange energy, a vibration humming through the entire Kellner house.

A new future was being born.

I helped Grandma with her and Oma's laundry, folding pants and sweatshirts and matching socks, while she dealt with their "unmentionables."

Seriously.

She said, "I'll take care of our unmentionables," like that was a thing people really called their underwear and bras.

Maybe Grandma called them "brassieres."

I grinned.

"Glad to see us go?" Grandma asked.

"No. Just thinking something funny."

She studied me, her eyebrow arched.

"I think it's for the best, you know. I think your dad is better off when he doesn't see us so much."

"Why do you say that?"

Grandma did this weird flip-fold thing that got her under-wear into a tiny triangle. "He won't say it, but I think being around us depresses him."

"I don't think that's true," I said, even though I was pretty sure it was.

"You don't have to lie, Darius." Grandma grimaced. "I think it was hard for him, going through Oma's transition. Having to rearrange his whole life."

"I think sometimes he's just depressed because that's how the disease works. It doesn't need a reason. Least of all Oma's transition. Isn't she happier now?"

"So much happier."

"Then that's good. For Dad too."

"Hm."

Grandma dropped her last unmentionable into the laundry basket and started to lift it.

"I can get that."

She swatted me away and lifted it. But then she looked at me and put it back down.

"It wasn't easy, you know. Going through it all. I think it was harder on me than on your dad."

"Why?"

"Your dad and I both had to let go of our picture of who Oma was, and make a whole new one. But I also had to make a new picture of myself. I'd spent my life thinking I was a straight woman. But I was still in love with Oma. So what did that make me? A lesbian? Bisexual? Queer?"

"Oh."

"But you know what? Even though it was hard, we're closer now than ever. When you go through something like that, you come out stronger." She lifted her basket again. "I'm sorry about Landon. Breakups are hard."

It still surprised me to hear her say that. Like sometimes I forgot it had happened. Like I could go hours without remembering the hole in my heart where Landon's smile used to live.

"Yeah."

"But you're going to be okay. You know that, don't you?"

"Maybe."

Grandma took my shoulders in her hands.

"You are." She smiled at me. An actual smile.

"I'm glad we got to be here, with you."

"Me too."

"Let us know about Pride. Maybe we can go together. If the weather is nice."

"Really?"

"We'll see."

It was the softest of maybes.

But it felt like something more. Like maybe Grandma had left the door between us open a crack.

It felt like love.

I helped load the luggage into Oma's Camry while she and Grandma said their goodbyes.

It was weird, saying goodbye like it was a big thing, when they lived a few hours away. When we would see them again over winter break.

Oma surprised me by gathering me into a hug. A real one.

"You've grown up," she said.

"I have?"

"Take care of your dad for us. Okay?"

"Okay," I said. "I love you, Oma."

"I love you too, Darius."

GRAVITON DENSITY

Our first playoff was against Riker High School, about an hour south of Portland.

Even though I knew it wasn't named after Commander William T. Riker, I hoped the *Star Trek* reference was a good sign for our chances of victory.

The tension between me and Chip had resulted in a gravitational shift in the team: not in how we played, but in who talked to who, who stood where in Circle, who jogged next to each other during warm-ups.

Chip had started jogging alone, keeping his head down, and though he still played as hard as ever, he didn't have that grin of his anymore.

I did that.

I took away Chip's smile.

I wondered if I was hurting him or me more, not trying to mend our friendship. But the longer it went, the harder it became to even bring up the subject. There was a shield between us, building in graviton density with each passing day.

I had taken to jogging next to James during warm-ups. It turned out that, in addition to being into technical theater, he was also into Dungeons & Dragons and *Star Wars*.

I wasn't really a fan of *Star Wars*. I didn't not-like it, but it didn't do anything for me. Not really.

Still, it was nice talking with another nerd. James was a cool guy, though he had the absolute worst luck in dating, which he told me all about when he wasn't debating means of faster-than-light travel, and whether hyperdrive or warp drive was faster.

(Given that the theoretical limit of warp drive was infinite velocity—something that was only achieved once, in this weird episode of *Voyager* where Captain Janeway and Lieutenant Paris ended up mutating into weird salamander things after breaking the transwarp threshold—I didn't see how hyperdrive could possibly be faster.)

"Hey," James said as we stretched our calves before the game. "Can I ask you something kind of personal?"

"Yeah. I guess."

"You and your boyfriend were together for like three months, right?"

"Four."

"Did you two ever . . . uh . . ."

James had really pale skin, so when he blushed, it was super obvious.

My own face reddened in sympathy.

"Dude."

"It's just, I don't know . . . when's the right time?"

I shrugged.

"Don't ask me. We never did anything other than kissing."

"Really?"

"Yeah." I swallowed the frog trying to hop its way out of my esophagus. "Landon wanted to. But I wasn't ready."

"Oh."

"Sorry I can't help."

"No!" He smiled, and his shoulders unclenched. "That actually helps a lot. Me and Katie, we haven't done anything yet either. Except kissing. I was just worried, I guess."

"Why?"

"I don't know. It just seemed like we were supposed to want it."

I nodded. "As long as you talk about it. You have to communicate."

James clapped me on the shoulder. "Thanks, man. How come we were never friends before this year?"

We had known each other since middle school.

"I don't know. I wasn't good at making friends, I guess."

"That's on me too." He glanced at his watch, which he wore on his left wrist even though he was left-handed. "Crap, gotta take a PGP."

I snorted.

"Good luck."

"Don't need it," he said, and patted his stomach.

PGP was code for Pre-Game Poop. A lot of guys did that. I wasn't sure if it was because of running during warm-ups, or nerves, or too much food, or what. I had never experienced the phenomenon.

I retied my shoelaces and nearly bumped into Chip when I stood.

"Oh. Sorry."

"It's cool," Chip said. "James going for a PGP?"

"Yeah."

Chip chuckled.

For a second, it was like we were friends again.

I missed that ease.

I missed being friends with Chip.

"Well." He swallowed.

"Yeah."

It turns out, having your opponents named after a *Star Trek* character wasn't as much of a good luck charm as I had hoped.

Their offense was devastating, but we managed to hold them off and keep them from scoring. Gabe and James didn't have any luck getting through, and we ended up in another shoot-out.

By that point, Christian and Diego were both exhausted. We all were. So were the Riker Wombats (a Level Ten Mascot Choice, to be sure).

They won the coin toss and shot first. Christian saved the first four but, to the wild cheers of the home crowd, the fifth one scored.

We hadn't made any goals, and Chip was our last chance.

He didn't grin as he approached the ball. His jaw was set. Sweat drenched his jersey, highlighting the valley his spine made between his back muscles.

He took a deep breath and made his move: a tricky inside shot to the goalie's left. It would've gone in too, if it hadn't just barely glanced off the goalpost.

Our team didn't make a sound—we were all still holding our breath, even as the whistle sounded—but the Riker stands exploded.

We lost.

※ ※ ※

I think we were all too tired to be sad. We shook hands, bumped fists, congratulated the other team. We trudged back to the stands in silence, some guys with their arms across each other's shoulders, others in Surrender Cobra.

Chip was staring at his toes, sort of kicking the ground with each step. His shoulders were slumped.

I hated seeing him like that.

I wasn't sure why I did it—really, I wasn't—but I hung back and, when he came close, I put my arm over his shoulder.

It was the kind of thing Sohrab did to me, when I was upset. Or when I was happy, for that matter.

Sohrab just did that kind of thing whenever. Like it was a thing guys could do.

And I supposed, if Chip really did like me, maybe it was weird and unfair to do that to him.

To touch him like that.

But in that moment, I really did want to be his friend.

"Hey," I said.

"Hey," he mumbled.

"Tough game."

"Yeah."

But he didn't say anything else, and after a moment I got to feeling really weird.

Also, we were both super sweaty, and hot, and that made me feel a lot of things that I wasn't ready to feel.

So I let Chip go and angled toward the stands, where Mom, Dad, and Laleh were waiting for me.

"You were awesome out there," Dad said.

"We still lost, though."

"Doesn't matter. You played your hardest."

"Thanks."

"Gold star," Laleh said.

I knelt down.

"Really? A gold star? Me?"

"Yeah."

"Thanks, Laleh."

Mom rested her hand on my shoulder.

"We're so proud of you."

"I guess."

I ran a hand through my hair, which accidentally sprayed my family with sweat.

Laleh squealed.

"Sorry! Sorry. I better go clean off."

"We'll see you at home," Mom said. Despite my sweatiness, she pulled me down to kiss my messy forehead. Dad did too. He held on to my neck and said, "Really, Darius. We're so proud of you."

"Thanks, Dad."

I held his eyes, and he smiled and nodded at me.

He wasn't back to normal yet, but he was getting better. The bags under his eyes had shrunk, small gray crescents instead of giant blue saucers.

"Love you," I said.

"Love you, son," he said back.

At the corner of the stands, Chip was talking to Trent, who was bouncing Evie on his lap.

I knew he was her uncle, but it was still deeply disturbing to see firsthand.

Next to them, a woman with light brown skin and dark wavy hair pulled Chip in for a hug.

Was that Chip's mom?

Suddenly Evie's complexion made sense.

I always thought Chip's mom was white. I always thought Chip was white too. I didn't realize he was Fractional like me.

I don't know why finding that out made me so happy.

(I knew why that made me happy.)

Chip waved me over.

"Darius," he said, "this is my mom. Sofia."

"Hi," I said. "Thank you for all the Gatorades."

Sofia's laugh was like a waterfall. She grinned at me.

She had her son's grin.

"Thanks for keeping Cyprian out of trouble."

"Sure."

From Trent's lap, Evie waved at me. I waved back and avoided Trent's eyes.

"I better go get my stuff," I said. "Nice meeting you."

"Don't be a stranger. Come for empanadas sometime. We've got more Gatorades."

"Thanks."

I was nearly off the field when I heard someone behind me.

"Where's your boy toy, Dairy Queen?"

I shook my head and kept walking, but Trent jogged into my field of view. He must've passed Evie off.

"Hey. Which one of you is which?"

"Which what?" I said, because I couldn't make any sense of his question/insult.

I knew I should have kept my mouth closed, but it was an automatic thing, and I couldn't take it back.

"Which one's the goal and which one's the post?"

I shook my head and didn't respond.

"Which one's the plug and which one's the socket?"

My face burned as Trent followed me, offering suggestion after ridiculous suggestion.

My neck prickled, and the sweat felt cold against my skin. Trent kept getting louder and louder until—

"Hey!" I paused and looked back. Chip had his arm out, blocking Trent from following me. "What the heck, dude?"

There it was again: heck. Like that was a word guys used.

"What?"

"Why are you always such a jerk to him? What did he ever do to you?"

"Nothing. I'm just teasing."

"No you're not. You're being awful. And it's gotten worse since I told you I liked him."

Chip glanced back at me for a second.

I was frozen.

But then he turned around and said, "You're supposed to be my best friend. Why don't you act like you're worth it?"

Trent's mouth opened and closed. He looked from Chip, to me, and then to Gabe and Jaden, who had slowed down to wait for us and were watching the scene with their arms folded across their chests.

His face reddened.

I never noticed how much he looked like an angry baby with his face all red.

His overlarge nostrils flared.

"Whatever." He tried to push past Chip's arm, but Chip didn't budge, so he turned and slouched back toward the stands.

Chip lowered his arm and let out his breath. His whole body depressurized in front of me.

Jaden and Gabe murmured to each other, but I couldn't make anything out. I just stared at Chip, who nodded to himself, and then caught me looking.

He had this look in his eyes. I don't know how to describe it.

It was like he was utterly lost.

But then he shrugged, and looked down at his feet, and walked past me toward the locker room.

What just happened?

ALL OF YOU

It was a quiet bus ride back to Chapel Hill High School, but at least it was a short one. Everyone was on their phones, or watching the traffic go by, or leaning against the windows with their eyes closed and their bags as pillows.

I sat toward the back, watching Chip as he stared out the window.

Something had happened.

Something I'd hoped for. Something I'd never actually expected.

What was I supposed to do now? What was I supposed to say?

Would I even see Chip anymore? Soccer season was over now, and soon enough wrestling would consume all his time.

Were all the guys going to ditch me now?

I didn't want to go back to being lonely Darius, whose only real friend was half a world away.

I wiped my eyes.

Coach Bentley leaned across the aisle. "You okay, Darius?"

"Yeah." I sniffed. "Just gonna miss this is all."

"Me too." She smiled. "You did great this season. And the next one will be here before you know it."

"Thanks, Coach."

I cleaned out my locker, which was mostly just spare kit, extra deodorant, and a couple crumpled papers I had forgotten about at various points during the season.

(I didn't really get the point and purpose of paperwork.)

The guys were all bro-hugging each other, the kind where you shake hands, do a one-armed hug with your hands smooshed between you, and slap the other guy's back. For some, like Gabe and Jaden and Christian, it was their last season at Chapel Hill. I saw Gabe wipe his eyes a couple times, and Jaden actually gave me a regular hug instead of a bro-hug.

"It's been awesome, man," he said. "I'm glad we got to be friends."

"Me too. I'm sad it's over."

"Over?" Jaden cocked his head to the side. "You're stuck with me now. Fractional Bros for life."

"Does that make us cousins or step-bros?"

"Don't make me do math after a game." He jostled my shoulder. "Seriously, though. Let's hang out. I'll teach you to actually play Mario Kart instead of driving off the side."

I almost laughed at that.

Almost.

"I'd like that."

On our way out, Coach Bentley had us line up, and she shook our hands and congratulated us on a season well played.

We still had our big post season party to look forward to, when we'd all dress up, and Coach would give out awards for Most Valuable Player and Most Improved and announce next year's captain.

Supposedly, the food was super good, because Coach Bentley was friends with a chef at one of the fancy restaurants downtown, one that was inside a hotel but not run by the hotel, which I guess makes a difference in the world of fancy downtown restaurants.

"Proud of you, Darius," she said as she shook my hand. "Chin up."

I blinked away my tears and nodded. "Thanks, Coach."

The sun was setting over the Student Lot, painting Chapel Hill's beige walls in fiery pink. The clouds were rolling in, the air chill with the promise of rain.

Cyprian Cusumano was sitting on the curb, with his elbows on his knees and his chin in his hand.

I flopped onto the ground next to him, tucked my cold hands into the pockets of my hoodie, and stared up at the clouds. I didn't think I could look Chip in the eye.

"You didn't have to do that."

Chip laid back and sprawled next to me.

"I think I did." His voice was low and soft. "That's the guy I want to be. And I don't think I have been, very much, before."

I angled my head a little closer to him. "How come?"

"I don't know." He drummed his legs with his fingers. "I've known Trent for as long as I can remember. When my parents were going through their divorce, he was the one who let me sleep over at his house so I didn't have to hear all the fighting. And after Evie was born, he was the one who taught me how to take care of her. To change diapers and stuff. You should see him with her. He's like a completely different guy."

Chip thumped the ground with his fist. "He was the only guy who ever saw me cry. Who let me feel like it was okay to cry in front of someone. Until you."

Trent was Chip's Sohrab.

"So now what?"

"I don't know. I don't want to lose him. But you were right. He's kind of an a-hole. And I want him to be better than that." Chip blew out a breath. "I want me to be better than that."

"I think maybe you already are."

Chip turned to face me. His eyes were misty.

"I really am sorry. I messed everything up."

"Not everything," I said.

And then I said, "I really missed being your friend."

"Me too." Chip chewed on his lower lip.

He had really nice lips.

"Does that mean we can try again?"

"Yeah."

"What about . . . what I said?"

My heart thudded. "What do you mean?"

"About . . . you. Me." Chip's ears turned pink. "I still think you're beautiful."

It was my turn to chew on my lip. Chip's eyes darted down to my mouth.

I sighed.

"Landon and I broke up. I guess you probably heard."

"Yeah. I'm sorry. It's my fault."

"Don't be. It really wasn't. But I need some time. You know?"

"Yeah. I get that."

I finally looked into Chip's eyes. They were warm and hopeful.

"But I think you're beautiful too."

Chip's grin lit up like a warp core.

"And smart. And brave."

"I'm not really."

"I think you are." I nodded to myself. "But I need you to be my friend first. Okay?"

"Okay."

"Hi, Darioush-jan!" Mamou said when I called. "I miss you!"

"I miss you too."

"How are you doing?"

"Okay. A little sad. We lost our soccer game. It was playoffs."

"I'm sorry. I know you played your hardest."

"I quit my job too."

"Your mom told me."

As if summoned, Mom appeared in my doorway. She hung back, though.

"Um," I said, and glanced to Mom and back at my screen. "I talked to Sohrab."

"I'm so happy!" Mamou's shoulders relaxed. "I'm sorry I couldn't tell you, maman."

"It's okay. I understand."

"Maybe he can come to Portland someday."

"That would be amazing." I cleared my throat. "How are you doing?"

Mamou sighed. "You know. Every day is different. Sometimes sad. Sometimes mad. Sometimes I forget."

"Me too."

"Sometimes I think of something and turn to tell him. But he's not there."

There were things I wanted to tell Babou too. It was too late for that.

But I knew I had to tell Mamou.

My sternum tightened.

"Mamou? Can I tell you something?"

"Of course, Darioush-jan."

"I . . . I'm gay."

"Eh? Gay?"

Mom stepped closer and rested her hand on my head. She played with my hair and said something in Farsi. I chewed on my lips and waited for the fallout.

"Oh!" Mamou said. "Gay. I'm glad you told me, maman. Because I love all of you."

My chest relaxed.

I wanted to run around the room and laugh.

"Do you have a boyfriend, maman?"

"No," I said. "We broke up."

"I'm sorry. You are the sweetest boy in the world. And so handsome. You will find someone."

We talked for a little while longer, but eventually our conversation petered out and we started to say goodbye.

"Okay, talk soon, Darioush. Give my love to your dad and Laleh."

"I will."

"I love you, maman. Shirin-jan, khodahafes."

"Khodahafes, maman." Mom said something else, something I didn't recognize.

When Mamou's picture blinked out, Mom said, "That was very brave. I'm so proud of you."

"Thanks, Mom."

※ ※ ※

After dinner we all crowded onto the couch: me and Dad in the middle, Mom to Dad's right and Laleh to my left, with her feet curled up underneath her.

It felt like forever since we'd been a family like this.

While *Deep Space Nine*'s opening credits played, Mom cracked some tokhmeh between her teeth.

Laleh used the two minutes of music to open her book and read a few paragraphs.

Dad squeezed my shoulder and said, "I missed this."

"Me too."

I studied my dad. He had shaved—finally—and gotten a haircut too.

He was sadder than I remembered, but he was solid, and he was home.

"You okay?" I asked.

"Doing better," he said. "Really."

He brought my head down to kiss it.

"How about you?"

I took a deep breath and studied my family in the reflection from the television.

"Yeah. I'm okay."

AUTHOR'S NOTE

Why come back to Darius?

That's the question I kept asking myself. But the answer ended up being fairly simple: because he had more to say.

Growing up is hard. Talking honestly with people—no matter how much you care about them—is hard. Admitting you've made a mistake is hard. But at the end of the day, it's our connection with others, our ability to open up our hearts, that binds us together as family, as partners, as friends, as community. And I thought that maybe Darius had something to teach me about that.

Whether it's fear of coming out, or frustration at the walls a family member has put up around their past; whether it's wonder at the way someone has changed, or frustration at another's refusal to change; whether it's a mental health crisis, or a simple desire for help; having these conversations can be difficult, but that's how we grow. If you need help finding language and information around difficult questions or topics affecting you or people you care about, there are tools available:

National Alliance on Mental Illness: nami.org

Anxiety and Depression Association of America: adaa.org

Depression and Bipolar Support Alliance: dbsalliance.org

Crisis Text Line: crisistextline.org or text HOME to 741741

National Suicide Prevention Lifeline: suicidepreventionlifeline.org or call 1-800-273-8255

The Trevor Project (LGBTQ Lifeline): thetrevorproject.org or call 1-866-488-7386

Trans Lifeline: translifeline.org or call 1-877-565-8860

Gay, Lesbian & Straight Education Network: glsen.org

StopBullying: stopbullying.gov

Teens Against Bullying: pacerteensagainstbullying.org

Love is Respect: loveisrespect.org, text "LOVEIS" to 22522, or call 1-866-331-9474

National Sexual Assault Hotline: rainn.org or call 800-656-4673

Planned Parenthood Chatline: plannedparenthood.org/teens

ACKNOWLEDGMENTS

Making a book seems like it should be a singular undertaking, but it never is. No idea is born in vacuum, and no book could be written without a support system.

My agent, Molly O'Neill, and the entire Root Literary team—Holly, Taylor, Melanie, and Alyssa—have been champions of me and my career. My film agent, Debbie Deuble-Hill, and the teams at APA and Universal have been amazing, and their faith has gratified me.

My editor, Dana Chidiac, has believed in me and in Darius's story every step of the way, and this novel would not be what it is without her.

My publicist, Kaitlin Kneafsey, is a superhero and has helped get Darius's story into the world in so many ways I'll never even know.

The entire team at Dial Books for Young Readers has been a phenomenal literary home: publisher Lauri Hornik, editorial director Nancy Mercado, managing editor Tabitha Dulla, copy-editor Regina Castillo, designers Mina Chung and Cerise Steel. Samira Iravani has once again designed a stellar cover with illustration by Adams Carvalho and art direction by Theresa Evangelista.

And, at Penguin Young Readers Group: Jen Loja, president and publisher; Jocelyn Schmidt, executive VP and associate publisher; Shanta Newlin and Elyse Marshall, publicity department heads, and their team; Bri Lockhart, Lyana Salcedo, Emily Romero, Christina Colangelo, and the marketing team; the school and library marketing team: Carmela Iaria, Venessa

Carson, Summer Ogata, Trevor Ingerson, and Rachel Wease; the Moira Rose to my David, Felicity Vallence, and the social media team, especially James Akinaka; the sales team, led by Debra Polansky; and the production team.

The team at Listening Library has once again produced a stunning audiobook, and I'm grateful for the talents of Aaron Blank, Emily Parliman, and Rebecca Waugh. Michael Levi Harris, I'm so grateful to have you narrating once again.

I'm sure my family was a little nervous (and maybe alarmed) to know I was writing more books about a family like ours, but if they were, they never showed it. Thanks to my mom, dad, and Afsoneh, and to my entire extended family for all the love.

My friends have put up with me so gracefully. Hanging out with an author can be hazardous (you never know when you're going to end up in a book) but they've always been cool about it.

My writing community: where would I be without you? There are too many people to name them all, but I'd be remiss without shouting out Lana Wood Johnson, Nae Kurth, Ronni Davis, Lucie Witt, Mark Thurber, and Julian Winters for always answering my random emails, texts, and DMs. Thank you to my twin Natalie C. Parker and my twin-in-law Tessa Gratton, for welcoming me into the Kansas writing community even though I live in Missouri, and for many excellent hours of *Star Trek* watching.

Thank you to every blogger, booktuber, bookstagrammer, podcaster, and tweeter who has read and shared Darius. Thank you to all the booksellers, librarians, and teachers who have embraced his story.

And most importantly, thank you to you, the readers. In a very real way, this book would not exist without you.